MURDERS.COM

MURDERS.COM
Margaret Duffy

Severn House Large Print
London & New York

This first large print edition published 2018
in Great Britain and the USA by
SEVERN HOUSE PUBLISHERS LTD of
Eardley House, 4 Uxbridge Street, London W8 7SY.
First world regular print edition published 2017 by
Severn House Publishers Ltd.

British Library Cataloguing in Publication Data
A CIP catalogue record for this title is available from the British Library.

ISBN-13: 9780727893994

Severn House Publishers support the Forest Stewardship Council™
[FSC™], the leading international forest certification organisation. All
our titles that are printed on FSC certified paper carry the FSC logo.

MIX
Paper from
responsible sources
FSC
www.fsc.org   FSC® C013056

Typeset by Palimpsest Book Production Ltd.,
Falkirk, Stirlingshire, Scotland.
Printed and bound in Great Britain by
T J International, Padstow, Cornwall.

One

I will probably never live down being The Woman Who Shot a Crook on the Village Green. The fact that I, too, with my husband Patrick, work for the National Crime Agency, only in my case part-time as I write crime novels tinged with romance, emerged a little later – the morning after it happened, actually – when my father-in-law, John, the rector, announced it from the pulpit during the morning service. This was to prevent venomous – and otherwise – local speculation. Of course, it added to rather than detracted from my notoriety, deepest Somerset villages having no mechanism for dealing with this kind of thing.

The criminal in question, Ray Collins, had been wanted for murder and was heavily implicated in other crimes. In short, he was on the Metropolitan Police's Most Wanted list. He had arrived at the normally peaceful Hinton Littlemore with a mission to kill my husband, Patrick. He'd been hired by a London mobster and was in the local pub. Patrick had turned up to meet me for a drink and had been unarmed. Where do you conceal a Glock 17, which he officially carries for self-defence purposes, when you're off-duty and wearing jeans and a T-shirt?

This author was armed. I had previously spotted and recognized Collins – from mugshots, not to

1

mention a police dog having once bitten off a chunk of his left ear – and dashed home for the Smith & Wesson that I have in my possession, again with official permission, from the wall safe. After a stand-off, I had shot and wounded him, appropriate warnings having been given, and he is now serving a long prison sentence.

For some reason, the episode was going through my mind this autumn morning as I tidied up after the children had gone to school. Following a job change, Patrick is now the NCA's officer within Avon and Somerset Police's Regional Organised Crime Unit. 'Embedded' is the official description, the unit part of a larger organization, Zephyr, which covers the whole of the South West. Although previously termed an 'adviser', his new role is far more than that, but he is no longer required to chase down London mobsters and other serious criminals personally. He had, in his own words, 'fought his last war'. This is a huge relief to his family as now he is unlikely, as had previously been the case, to come home for the weekend in a body bag.

I was not naive enough to imagine that his new position would be without its dangers, even though it is mainly a desk job. Neither was I convinced about the London mobsters bit. When you have served in army special services, and been head-hunted by MI5, word tends to get around that you mean business. However, right now Patrick goes to work at roughly seven in the morning and is usually home by six. Sometimes he works in Bristol, sometimes in Bath and occasionally elsewhere. Every two or three weeks he travels to London for a couple of days to the NCA's HQ for an exchange of information with colleagues there and to catch up on the underworld gossip with those who have such connections.

There had been a crisis not all that long ago. Patrick had been forced to shoot a man, Martin Grindley, a retired police assistant commissioner who had opened fire on me in revenge for my having found the woman he was holding in a house against her will. Grindley had been under the delusion that the two would spend the rest of their lives happily together and planned to murder his wife in order to achieve this. He was ill, suffering from some kind of dementia. Patrick had never even met him before. This had been one killing too many after his days as an army sniper, and he had taken quite a while to get over it.

But never to carry his Glock again? No. The original reason for its presence is that we're on the hit lists of more than one terrorist organization and several aggrieved mobsters due to his success rate over the years in either getting them behind bars and/or blowing their hirelings' heads off. The weapon is still strictly for self-defence purposes.

I worked with Patrick during his time with MI5 as well and thereafter in the Serious Organised Crime Agency, which was then absorbed into the NCA. Although I am still on the payroll and he shares the more interesting cases with me, I am now not really involved. Even so, he still refers to me as his 'oracle', as I possess a certain intuition that quite often yields results.

Apart from being an author, it was good to be spending more time with the children. We have five – three of our own, Justin, Vicky and baby Mark, and also Matthew and Katie, who are older. They were Patrick's brother Larry's children whom we adopted when he was killed. We were now, I told myself, a safer, more 'normal' family.

Why, then, on this murky autumnal morning, leaves soggily dripping and dropping from the trees, was I recollecting with something approaching nostalgia the moment I had sent a ruthless hitman who had been about to kill my husband cartwheeling into the smooth turf of the village green?

Patrick's mother, Elspeth, put her head around the door. 'Ingrid, are you going to Sainsbury's as usual this morning?'

I told her that I was.

She and John live in an annexe that was created from an old garage and stable after we bought the rectory. It was about to be sold off by the diocese and the couple rehoused in a little bungalow on an ugly new estate at the bottom of the village. Once the railway goods yard, the area had always flooded when it rained heavily and Patrick had declared that they would be banished down there over his dead body.

'Would you get me some self-raising flour and mixed dried fruit – oh, and some dried apricots?'

'Of course.'

'I'd come with you and help but someone's arriving at any time now to inspect the parish

4

hall roof. Some of the tiles have slipped and I can't leave it to Bob, who does the bookings, as, frankly, he's losing the plot and the chairman of the committee's at work. And, as I expect you know, John has a funeral this morning.' She thanked me and hurried off.

I sat down and stared at nothing. People losing the plot? Funerals? Traipsing off to supermarkets? Was this my life now?

Really?

I recalled a line from an old hymn we had sung at school: *The trivial round, the common task, will furnish all we need to ask.* It had been the brainwashing of the times when you thought about it, getting children ready to be hewers of wood and drawers of water.

My life, just like that?

This wasn't the first time recently that I had brooded along these lines. I rose, noted that it was now raining harder, the wind getting up, gathered up the last of the toys that Justin and Vicky had left lying around, went upstairs and dropped them into the basket where they're normally kept. No one else was to be seen, and then I remembered that Carrie, our nanny, had said she was taking Mark and Vicky to the village shop to buy a birthday card and would then go for a short walk with them before calling on a friend for coffee. A firm believer in fresh air for the young is Carrie, even on mornings like this.

I embrace anything, obviously within reason, that keeps them happy, healthy and sleeping well.

I'm a lousy mother and can't cope with tantrums (Justin), teething problems (Mark at the moment), teenage moods (Matthew), never mind someone constantly badgering to have a horse (Katie, who already has a pony and is still a bit too small to ride Patrick's horse, George). Vicky is an angel.

To hell with it, I thought. I would shop and then go riding on George myself.

George – described to me when I bought him for Patrick as a bay middle-weight hunter – is kept at livery, five minutes' drive away. One is virtually forced to drive there as the lanes are narrow and twisting with no footpaths, and besides, we keep his tack at home as break-ins at stables and other rural buildings are alarmingly common, a fact not helped by the dismal security arrangements at most of these establishments.

I had phoned so someone had got him in for me and removed his New Zealand rug. It must be admitted that George didn't seem too pleased to see me but is too much of a gentleman to try to nip when the girths are tightened or one mounts.

I set off into the wind and rain, going straight into a large field nearby that had been harvested of grain, just the stubble remaining. The farmer does not object to horses and riders on his property as long as they stick to the edges when crops are growing. As George seemed keen to go after a warm-up trot, I let him have his head and he set off up the gentle slope of the field at a business-like gallop, scattering a flock of jackdaws. Sometimes he bucks if he's feeling particularly jolly, but not today. Patrick used to ride him on a long rein in somewhat dreamy fashion but desisted after the pair almost parted company one morning.

George was content after this to stride along, taking in the scenery, his large ears going this way and that, and only spooked slightly when a wood pigeon burst from a wood just over the fence. The trees cover several acres, a favourite place for picnics and hide-and-seek games with our children in the summer. On the far side it borders a short section of The Monks' Way, an ancient path that once connected several of the religious houses and abbeys in the south and west of England and which is now a favourite rambling route. Motor vehicles are banned.

We trotted, splashing through the puddles – it had been raining on and off for what seemed like weeks – and then George swung through a gap in the fence and under the trees before I could stop him. I reined him back, not wishing to be scraped off under one of the low branches of the beeches and berated myself for not paying attention. Then I realized that this was probably the way Patrick often came, so perhaps the horse had only been trying to be helpful.

There was a path of sorts, thick with leaves, that wove through the wood. The wind was quite strong up here, roaring through the tops of the trees above us. We finally emerged into the open on the old road. My mount immediately wanted to turn left and head for home but I prevailed over his mild disagreement and cantered, rain and flying leaves in our faces, not at all sheltered now. OK, I mentally told him, you can go home in a minute. I will not be treated as a passenger.

Then, as soon as we had started off, I saw that fifty yards or so from me someone was lying on the path. A couple of crows had alighted nearby and were sidling hopefully and horribly nearer. They flew off at my approach.

It was a man. I dismounted and saw that he was badly injured. He looked dead, the rain diluting the blood which practically covered his face, the source of this a wound to his head in which I could glimpse bone. There was blood on his soaking wet clothing, his wrist slippery with it as I tried to find a pulse.

He was alive, just.

Removing my riding waterproof, I placed it over him and then found my phone in my pocket, hoping that it would work in the deluge. George didn't help, pushing forward when I had to relinquish my hold on the reins in order to use both hands on the mobile. I grabbed for him but he had already snuffled, dripping whiskers and all, the face of the injured man. Then, presumably having smelled the blood, he backed off and flung up his head, uttering the alarmed – and very alarming – high-pitched, loud snorts equines make when they're upset and frightened.

Having endeavoured to calm him down a bit before he dragged me over the nearest hill, I phoned for help, emphasizing that a rescue helicopter was the only way of reaching us quickly. Then I rang the livery stable, begging Padraig, the proprietor, who miraculously was in his office, to ask someone to get on a horse and come and

8

collect George before the helicopter arrived. I was trying not to think of the consequences if he was anywhere near when it did. *If* it did. My request might be ignored and they could try to reach us in an ordinary ambulance, which would get bogged down. Or I might end up with a dead or dreadfully injured horse if he bolted and ran through a barbed-wire fence or into a tree.

Shoving all this to the back of my mind, I bent down again and tried to assess my find. There was still a pulse, thin and thready. I guessed him to be around forty-five years of age, perhaps a little older. His hair, where it wasn't matted with blood, was grey and neatly cut. He was tall and fairly slim, and his hiking clothes were expensive but practical. There was no sign of a rucksack.

Belatedly, I searched for anything that would identify him in an inside pocket of his anorak, but there was nothing. Perhaps his possessions had been stolen. George then decided to overcome his fear and, before I could stop him, came forward again and gave the man another snuffle, again with full benefit of dripping whiskers.

'You'll tread on him in a minute!' my over-strung nerves made me yell, hauling him away, his hooves dangerously close. To think of germs in such a situation though seemed ridiculous.

I actually thought for a moment that the man's lips twitched in a smile, but no, my eyes were playing tricks with me. He was deeply unconscious.

After what seemed a long time but was probably only five minutes or so, I heard hoof-beats, coming very fast, full tilt, up the track towards

9

me and, seconds later, a man on a mount far too small for him came into view. Unmistakably, it was Padraig, who is in his twenties and as thin as a hayfork. He looks like a windmill in a gale when he gets on a horse but can ride anything, even the ones that try to kill you. His feet weren't all that far off the ground. This cobby pony, the only other one I had noticed inside the stables, was another of his liveries, a recent addition that belonged to a lady of nervous disposition who didn't like to go faster than a trot.

George let out a ringing neigh of welcome.

'And they swore to her he wouldn't go at all!' exclaimed Padraig, having come to a ploughing halt and jumped off his mount, which was blowing hard and mud-splattered. 'Holy Mother, are you sure he isn't dead?'

'No, and please go before . . .'

'You're all right,' said the Irishman soothingly. 'I'll take your horse home for you.'

'Ride him,' I said, having offered my profound thanks. 'Give the pony a rest.'

'He's out of breath because he's fat,' Padraig commented dryly and leapt on George. Then off he went, leading the pony back down the track, and I heard them break into a fast trot. The rescue helicopter arrived some ten minutes later when I was beginning to despair, convinced by this time that I was presiding over a corpse.

The first thing Commander David Rolt of the Metropolitan Police said on regaining consciousness was, 'Where's the horse?'

* * *

10

Rolt did not die but was in intensive care for a week. His identity was soon discovered as he had put his wallet containing his driving licence and other personal items inside a 'secret' pocket of his anorak for safety. The police unit he headed, F9, a specialist undercover branch which has its HQ within an ordinary-looking detached house at Woodford on the edge of Epping Forest, now part of Greater London, had not reported him missing due to the fact that he was on a week's leave and had said something about going walking in Somerset.

His car, a diesel Jaguar, was soon found parked in a lay-by not far from Hinton Littlemore on the byway that led up to the main road into Bath. It was taken away to be examined by a forensic team. The Monk's Way could be accessed from where he had left it by using another public foot-path-cum-bridleway, the route Padraig had taken.

I was able to answer Rolt's question when I visited him in hospital, the Royal United in Bath, some ten days later. Courtesy of secure police websites and a couple of grapevines, Patrick and I knew his identity and other details about him and his unit, but it was not my job, nor Patrick's, to investigate his assault. That fell to our friend, Detective Chief Inspector James Carrick of Bath CID. Carrick had sent along his assistant, DS Lynn Outhwaite, who, due to a shortage of staff, was Acting DI.

Apparently Rolt had been polite but not very forthcoming, making it clear that he wasn't feeling well enough to be interviewed, and anyway, he would rather talk to someone from his own unit as he had an idea who had been responsible, someone under suspicion in connection with various cases on which they were working.

'I realize he's feeling bad but that's not very helpful,' Carrick had grumbled to me during a phone conversation. 'I happen to have rather a lot of other cases I'm working on too.'

'Did Lynn ask him if he thought he'd been followed?' I'd asked.

'She did, and he said he didn't think so but admitted he was so far from home he hadn't thought about it – had switched off.'

'That's what holidays are for.'

'D'you reckon the NCA might have a toe in whatever it is *he's* working on?'

'The NCA could ask him in the shape of the female who found him,' I'd suggested.

'You could try but Lynn said the man's no pushover.'

Well, that went without saying – you don't get to Rolt's position by being a big softie. The man I'm married to isn't a pushover, either.

He was in a side ward by this time – with armed protection – and sitting in a chair by the side of the bed, his head swathed in bandages, face heavily bruised and swollen, one eye half-closed. We had been told that he was being kept in mainly for observation and further tests as, together with being struck on the head with some kind of sharp weapon, he had been badly beaten and the medical staff were concerned about possible internal injuries. In their opinion, the intention had been to kill him.

12

'And it was your horse I heard?' the man asked incredulously once I had introduced myself and told him the circumstances of finding him. 'People here are saying I imagined it, was hallucinating, dreaming. Well, I have him to thank, as well as you, of course. I get the impression from what they're saying here that I might not have lasted much longer.'

I didn't tell him about the crows which had been hoping to peck out his eyes.

'He's called George,' I said when I had seated myself. 'And he belongs to my husband, Patrick.'

'It's extremely kind of you to come.'

The man spoke quietly but there was an edge to his voice and, although he was pale where he wasn't bruised, his blue eyes were steely and scrutinizing me carefully. Yes, here was a very senior policeman.

'And you're Ingrid Langley,' Rolt continued. 'Tell me about yourself.'

I said, 'Mostly, I write novels and look after my family. The rest of the time I work for the NCA. So does Patrick.'

I had had absolutely no intention of concealing this from him.

'I think I'd prefer a little proof before I say anything more,' he rejoined.

I produced my warrant card. 'Is Piers Ashley still your assistant? His name's mentioned on the restricted website.'

'Ah.' He smiled, having examined and returned it. 'No. Piers' father died very suddenly not all that long ago and he had to leave his post to run the family estate in Sussex – a big place, several

13

farms. I think he's getting married soon. Quite a responsibility for a young man.'

'Patrick heard a rumour that you'd resigned to run your brother's stud farm.'

'It must have been a garbled rumour. I took a month's unpaid leave during a very rare, quiet time as he had to go into hospital to have a major operation. That was before Ashley went.'

'Horses then.'

'Yes, horses.'

There was a short silence, and then I said, 'DCI Carrick's disappointed that you're not being more helpful.'

'Is that why he sent you along?'

'No, it was my suggestion. Besides which, I don't take orders from Bath CID.'

'No, of course you don't. My apologies.'

'Carrick's very good at his job.'

'I'm sure he is, but although the crime took place here it didn't originate on his patch. And I *have* spoken to someone from F9.'

'But if there's any overlapping of investigations – with those of the NCA, I mean – it would be a waste of everyone's time.'

He closed his eyes for a moment. 'Sorry, but can we defer this until the headache's a bit better?'

'Of course.'

'The pills they give me for that and other aches and pains knock me out, you see.'

As I rose to go he was already reaching for the bell push that would summon a nurse.

'Feeling utterly dreadful apart, I have an idea he needed to think before saying any more,' I said

14

to Patrick that evening after dinner when the youngest children were in bed and I had related what had taken place. The two eldest, Matthew and Katie, were with their grandparents. They always have dinner with them on Fridays and, if I'm at home, I cook for the whole family on Saturday evenings, Carrie included if she's here. It's quite an undertaking.

My husband was restless, pacing around the room, and would probably go out for a walk. He hates being mostly desk-bound but is making a big effort to get used to it. It has meant he has had to adopt a slightly different mindset, use police jargon – 'cop-speak', as he calls it – and learn new acronyms, something I feel a certain compassion towards him about but am also a little amused. I hope I keep the latter well-concealed. I was also hoping he would go for a walk as his caged tiger presence was rather getting on my nerves.

'What did you make of him?' he asked.

'Formidable.'

'That's the general opinion. F9 – which, if you remember, was at one time involved with national security but is now just a police unit – is small compared to other departments and doesn't have the usual structure. Its operatives work so deeply undercover that they sometimes go to prison with the gang members they've been responsible for getting arrested. It preserves their cover, reducing the risk of being hunted down and killed. They answer to Rolt alone. He runs the entire unit and if they phone in to report or have a problem they go directly to him – or, if he's off-duty, to his stand-in, a DCI who's running everything at the moment. Rolt often lives-in at HQ if there's a big job on.'

'Married to the job, then,' I murmured.

'Word is that he has a lady friend. You mentioned Ashley; he was withdrawn from active service and promoted to be Rolt's assistant after being seriously wounded in a shooting that bizarrely was nothing to do with the job. Some kind of family feud.'

'All Rolt said in connection with his own attack was that it didn't originate on Carrick's patch.'

'My patch too now,' Patrick observed. 'But that would figure seeing as Rolt deals mainly with London mobsters. I'll make some enquiries and see if I can find a connection with anything the NCA's doing – ask Mike, for a start. Who knows, we may even get a lead.'

Commander Michael Greenway is Patrick's boss in London.

It followed that Patrick did not delay in making enquiries, even though this wasn't his case. He then went on to ask James Carrick and his wife, Joanna – who at one time had been the DCI's sergeant and, having found a nanny for their baby daughter Iona Flora, is now in initial training having applied to re-enter the police – if they would like to join us for a meal the following evening at the village pub.

The Ring o' Bells, as usual, was busy but I had booked a table, requesting one that was in a quiet corner of the restaurant. The Carricks were already there but in the public bar. The DCI endeavours,

16

on occasion, to show his face in as many of the local hostelries as he can as he says it proves that the eye of the law is vigilant. Whatever the effectiveness of this, Patrick, who sometimes goes along as back-up, maintains that it's a Very Good Idea. They're a good pair of law enforcers, Patrick tall, slim, his dark, wavy hair usually needing a cut, and Carrick slightly shorter but with broader shoulders. Any resemblance to gritty sheriffs in a Western is coincidental.

'We haven't bothered Rolt with any more questions,' Carrick said. 'It was obvious that the poor guy was suffering and, as Ingrid told me, he's spoken to his own people. Which doesn't help me a lot, of course, and I'm waiting to be told to drop the case and leave it up to them.'

'But to keep you in the picture, I do have some names,' Patrick told him when we had seated ourselves at our table. 'Three, actually.' He took a sheet of notepaper from his wallet and gave it to him.

'Are you working on these cases then?' Carrick enquired slightly sharply.

'No, but the NCA is. These are mobsters that F9 has on its radar as well.'

'Only the first of these names means anything to me,' said Carrick after a quick look. 'Kenneth Mackie. I happen to know that he has a younger brother who stayed behind in Glasgow, carrying on the family criminal tradition and right now is inside for being drunk and disorderly and battering old ladies and young, nervous-looking ones for their mobile phones and valuables.'

17

'Surely Scotland has nothing to do with this, though,' Joanna commented impatiently, tossing her auburn hair off her face.

Her husband gave her a look. 'No, of course not.'

I had an idea she was far more interested in the main reason for our presence as she had been working out in a gym during the afternoon, getting fit for her new career.

Patrick said, 'The elder Mackie's into protection rackets, running drugs and raiding post offices. He deliberately has a quick turnover of what he apparently refers to as "staff" to confuse the police and hires people from abroad who travel on false passports. The second, Matt Dorney, is the son of Len Dorney, who F9 finally managed to pin down a few years ago. He died in prison from natural causes. Matt's following in his father's footsteps by being responsible for most of the crime in his part of east London, adding his own particular brand of viciousness and greed. Apparently he brags that he can arrange the deaths of anyone as long as the money's forthcoming.'

I waved over a waiter, feeling a bit guilty as he was loaded with used crockery, and asked for menus.

Patrick continued, 'I couldn't find out much about the third in the time I had available. It's a cartel of various people with boxing backgrounds, not just the boss-man listed. They specialize mostly in cybercrime with armed robberies on the side for ready cash.'

'Now you mention it, I have heard of Len Dorney,' Carrick said reflectively. 'If the son's inherited his old man's malice and love of violence, he's not to be trifled with.'

Two

Commander Rolt continued to make good progress. Another development that took place during the next few days was that F9 made a formal request to Avon and Somerset Police that they carry on with the investigation on the grounds they were in possession of all available evidence. It seemed pointless, they said, for them to send someone from their HQ who might only replicate what had already been achieved. They nevertheless promised full cooperation. Put simply, Patrick told me, they were overwhelmed with work and struggling on account of their supremo being in hospital.

James Carrick, also overwhelmed with work, immediately made a formal request to Avon and Somerset's HQ to pass the case to the force's embedded NCA officer on the grounds that the NCA was already investigating cases involving a possible suspect for this crime. Not only that, the said officer's wife, who also worked for the NCA, had found the assault victim and was thus in possession of all visual evidence.

Patrick, also overwhelmed with work but subsequently ordered to take it on, sent the DCI what amounted to an electronic raspberry.

Rolt was now in a private hospital on the outskirts of Bath. He was still horribly black and blue and having more tests but was deemed to be out of danger. Medically, that is. An armed protection officer, a businesslike individual sweating in his body armour, was still stationed outside the door of the room.

'I'm sure you'll not be happy with the arrangement, sir,' Patrick began after I had made the introductions. 'But I've officially been asked to investigate your attack, a move initiated by F9.'

'I had been informed,' Rolt replied with a thin smile, reseating himself stiffly from where he had been pensively looking out of the window. 'But I'm a realist – I can't expect my personnel to prioritize an attack on me. And you needn't call me sir – I know more about you than you probably realize.'

Patrick handed him the list of three names without comment.

'Dorney,' Rolt said instantly, giving it back. 'He hates me, and what I represent, with an intensity that even I find disturbing. He wants me dead. We hounded his father for years and it was Piers Ashley who finally got the details of a big job they planned, a diamond robbery at an exhibition in London's West End. We grabbed them in the act.'

'And the other two?'

'They don't even know I exist, or shouldn't. Matt Dorney does – I interviewed his father personally, something I don't do normally, which now looks as though it might have been a serious mistake.'

'But how would he know who you are?'

'You'd be amazed how these details get out to the criminal fraternity.'

'Are you closing in on the son with regard to any particular crime?'

'There's no real evidence, no fingerprints and the gang wore masks, but a raid on a nightclub last month has all the hallmarks of his methods: the staff knocked about for no reason, one seriously so, a girl serving behind the bar raped, the proprietor shot and badly wounded. Just for the hell of it.'

'I take it you have a member of your team inside, or at least close to this lot.'

'Yes, I do,' replied the commander, without further explanation.

'Had he, or she, heard of anything planned against you?'

'No, Dorney keeps details of his plans very much to himself.' Rolt gave us another bleak smile. 'Call me what you like in these politically correct days, but I wouldn't send a woman anywhere near that odious rats' nest.'

'The price would be too high for her to pay,' I said.

'Yes, precisely,' Rolt replied.

Patrick said, 'I take it that your department will forward to me anything relevant about this character.'

'They will. Just let me have your details.'

Patrick gave him his card. 'I understand you told DS Outhwaite that you weren't aware of being followed that morning.'

'No, and you'll probably think me careless. But up there, miles away from it all, I have to say it

22

was the last thing on my mind. The rain, not to mention the wind in my face, made hearing anything pretty impossible anyway.'

'Who knew where you would be that day?'

'Only a lady friend. She's a lawyer and works in London. I keep in pretty close contact with her and must have mentioned my plans.'

'Are you sure you didn't tell anyone else?'

'No one that I can think of.'

'Where were you staying?'

'Ah. Oh, yes. At a pub in Bath that has rooms, The Lion and the Unicorn. It's on Wellsway. I suppose I might have mentioned it in passing there. People take an interest and you can't be churlish.'

'Have you been to this area before?'

'Only once, to Bath, but that was years ago.'

I was making notes of all this.

'Did you have the hood up of your anorak?' I asked.

'I did, but when I was jumped from behind I yanked it off so I could see what was going on around me.'

'Your hands are bruised,' Patrick said. 'You fought back. How many of them were there?'

Rolt hesitated. 'Three, I *think*. Then I was hit on the head with something and that was that.'

'Did you notice them carrying weapons?'

'No.'

'Your personnel, in disguise, sometimes carry out raids on dodgy premises themselves, especially if protection rackets are involved and the perpetrators are known to be on the premises engaged in heavy breathing.'

23

'Real crooks blurt all kinds of revealing information to people they haven't the first idea are police officers,' Rolt observed.

'I think I might turn myself into a counterfeit mobster,' Patrick said thoughtfully – no, blissfully.

'If you're thinking along those lines go and talk to Ashley about Dorney senior – he knows more about him than I do.'

I was impressed, and a bit annoyed, that he hadn't tried to talk Patrick out of it.

First, Patrick needed to visit the scene of the crime. We went on horseback as it had carried on raining on and off since I had found the commander and neither of us fancied a long walk through the mud. Katie's pony, Fudge, is too small for me to ride and, as I had no wish to repeat Padraig's amazing spectacle, I was permitted to borrow someone's grey Highland by the name of Haggis. He proved not to have the same references as Padraig's mount, that is, slow, and as soon as we entered the stubble field he thundered off with me, his long mane flying into my face, hooves half the size of buckets and all.

'I thought Highlands were supposed to be quiet,' I panted when I had finally managed to stop him before he jumped a gate right at the top of the field, my husband having cantered up, well in control of George. Natch.

'But they can carry a dead deer weighing around twenty stone,' it was pointed out to me. 'He hardly notices that you're on board.' Patrick laughed. 'You always get run away with.'

'Not *always*,' I retorted.

All evidence would have been destroyed by the subsequent activities of people and animals, not to mention the weather, but it is always valuable to see where a crime has been committed, especially if you are, like Patrick, an ex-special operations soldier. When we had ridden back the short distance, gone through the wood and arrived just short of the spot, he dismounted, handed me George's reins and gazed about. Then he set off, quartering the ground lower down the slope to the left of the old road. There was nothing of obvious value evidence-wise on the track itself, the ground really churned up by now.

'I wonder if Rolt, and presumably his attackers, came through the wood, as we've just done, or up the track,' Patrick called. 'I forgot to ask.'

'As they were almost certainly all strangers to the district I reckon they would have come up the track,' I replied. 'It's well signposted and features on maps.'

'And, as we know, his car was found in a lay-by not far from the village. It might be worth having a look round there for other tyre tracks.'

'I walked up there the other day. It's little more than a wide, muddy verge normally and, right now, is one huge puddle.'

He wandered around for another few minutes and, having hauled George out of a bush he seemed intent on devouring, I had no choice but to let the horses graze the lush grass.

'I'm asking myself how far they'd tailed him,' Patrick said, returning. 'It's obvious that whoever it was didn't lie in wait for him as it wasn't a

25

regular walk he took, and they couldn't have known his intended route.'

'They might have been shadowing him for days.'

'Depressing, isn't it?' He went into the wood, still examining the ground, and was gone for longer this time. When he came back and had remounted George he shook his head and muttered, 'It's rained too hard and too many people have walked through there.'

The lay-by was still boggy with a large puddle on the lower side, right by a hedge that bordered a field. We had come back down the track, our mounts on a loose rein, having settled down after a canter to the top of the hill. We had looked for anything that might help with the case on the return journey but there was nothing visible.

There was nothing of interest in the lay-by either but Patrick didn't give up, leaving me with George again to disappear over a gate into the field, which was down to pasture. He came back quite quickly – there was a bull in it – but had established that there was no sign of anything that could have been used as a weapon within throwing distance of the lay-by.

'If you're tailing someone and they pull over and stop you drive by to avert suspicion,' Patrick said, thinking aloud. 'But you don't go very far for obvious reasons. OK, let's ride by.'

We were able to stay on the verge, which was fortunate as there was quite a lot of traffic. Soon, a farmhouse in sight, we came to a semi-derelict barn that was in a field down a short track. It housed, towards the back, an ancient tractor and a lot of rural rubbish. Despite the rolls of rusting barbed wire, rotting wooden gates, an equally decomposed hen coop and old farm implements, there was room for a vehicle to be parked in front of all this. Several sets of tyre tracks were visible leading into it.

Patrick found his mobile and contacted James Carrick. 'James, old son, I can't guarantee anything but have a barn for a scenes-of-crime unit to have a rummage inside in connection with the attack on Rolt. Preferably as soon as possible. I'm not going to touch it as I'm not allowed to.'

I distinctly heard the DCI say, 'And when have you ever stuck by the rules?'

'Think,' Patrick said. 'This has to be handled like a crime scene and I've never messed around with those.'

After a short pause, 'OK. Give me the details.'

This Patrick did, commenting after the call, 'He must be having a bad day.'

I took the horses back to the livery yard, leaving Patrick waiting at the barn. Hopefully, with regard to the investigation, the morning hadn't been a complete waste of time.

'It was a billhook,' Patrick announced when he came home late that afternoon just as it was beginning to get dark, with more rain on the way. 'They might have found it in the barn and chucked it back in afterwards thinking it would never be found. I took it to the farmer, whose name's Colin Reed, and although he couldn't positively identify it as his, he reckons it was one his late father used for hedge-laying. Ownership's not really important. He was a bit shocked – there's blood on it and even a few human hairs – and said he'd get rid of all the stuff in the barn, sell it for scrap. I had to make him promise not to do it *yet*. The building's cordoned off.'

'Let's hope that cheers up James,' I said.

'He's gone home feeling ill. Lynn reckons he's got the flu.'

Lynn was quite correct and suddenly found herself with no one to refer to on this case, never mind several others. The following day, she appealed to HQ for assistance and was told that people were off sick and to carry on as best she could until someone could be found to stand in for the DCI. She had a nasty idea, she confided to Patrick, that it simply wasn't going to happen.

The force's embedded NCA officer moved into Carrick's office.

'I can do most of the other stuff online or over the phone,' he said to me when I met him in Bath for a quick bite of lunch. 'As, obviously, I can't just drop everything else. But I'll have to tell Greenway – and the other nicks I'm involved with at the moment.'

'Taking this on as well isn't really your brief, though, is it?' I said.

'I'm starting to realize that my brief is that of dogsbody. But it means I have a sort of base until Carrick's relief turns up – if anyone does.'

Anyone didn't and, two days later, Commander Greenway phoned me just as I had switched on the Mac to start a morning's work on my latest novel.

'This case, which, as I'm sure you know, has a top priority rating, is stagnating and I'd like you to give Patrick a hand,' he said after the briefest of greetings and sounding extremely put out.

My working partner, the man in my life, my spouse, had said not one word along these lines to me.

'Right,' I acknowledged briskly.

'F9 appears not to be able to deal with this, Bath CID's ill, Avon and Somerset ditto, so it seems that my department's the only one that can investigate a serious crime committed against one of the most senior and highly thought of commanders in the Met. Please get over to Bath nick as soon as possible.' And he rang off.

Roger and out, I thought.

Patrick looked very surprised to see me.

'Orders,' I said. 'Mike's in a strop about how bad it looks that the case is stagnating as Rolt's royalty.'

'It's not stagnating,' he protested. 'We think we know who's responsible – I've informed the Met as they're trying to keep tabs on Dorney too – we've found what was probably the weapon used and I'm awaiting results from the lab. Didn't you tell him that?'

'He rang off before I could say anything.'

He reached for his desk phone, muttering.

'Your oracle has reported for duty and I suggest you cool it,' I said. 'You need Mike completely onside and right now I think he's under pressure from several different directions, chewing up everyone and spitting out the bits.'

29

After hesitating for a few moments, Patrick sighed. 'You're probably right. Perhaps he's going down with the flu as well. OK, oracle, what next?'

'I take it you can't leave here at the moment.'

'No. Lynn's out with the scenes-of-crime people on another case.'

'Rolt suggested talking to Piers Ashley. Shall I do that tomorrow?'

News of the attack on Commander Rolt was finally released to the media. The next day, several newspapers had front-page articles about the attack on a senior police officer, no name mentioned, at a Somerset beauty spot. There were hardly any other details, or even whether the man had lived or died, but it was suggested the crime could have been the work of a London gang being investigated by the National Crime Agency. Someone had dug out a photograph of The Monks' Way but it was incorrect – pictured was a section of it on Dartmoor in Devon. There was even a tor in the background.

'So either someone in authority took the lid off the story or there's a mole,' Patrick commented. 'It's too late to worry about it and, either way, it might make something happen.'

This was soon to be proved correct.

I did some research just before I left for Ashleigh Hall at Ashleigh Coombe. It was in Sussex and open to the public for most of the year. At one time, I read, at the start of the building of the second dwelling on the site after a disastrous fire in 1672, it was referred to as Ashleigh Castle, possibly on account of the fact that the only surviving relic of earlier days was the barbican, or gatehouse, a forbidding-looking structure. Ashleigh Hall, as it stood today, their website stated, had the earlier barbican in its centre with living accommodation on either side in two wings. Included in the right-hand wing was a replica of the great galleried room that was destroyed in the fire, together with most of the original building. Fortunately, a good proportion of the contents had been saved.

Another nugget of information was that the discrepancies in the spelling of the names was thought to be due to a clerk's error in the eighteenth century while drawing up a legal document.

It seemed a little strange to me that a man – a young man, according to Rolt – who was now responsible for this beautiful mansion and the hundreds of acres of farmland that surrounded it, had until comparatively recently been a police officer. This was going through my mind as, the following day, I made my way up a drive marked PRIVATE. I had phoned and arranged a time with a woman, perhaps his secretary, who had given me directions, adding that I might have to search him out if he was somewhere on the estate. Mention of the National Crime Agency had been met with no surprise.

There was a large oak front door set in an uncompromising granite frame in the knapped flint wall where I guessed the portcullis had once been. No other hint of a martial past remained,

31

if the place even had one, as rambler roses framed it and clipped box in pots on either side replaced armed sentries. I pulled on a heavy ring attached to an iron chain and, somewhere within, a bell tolled.

The woman who answered the door instantly reminded me of Elspeth, Patrick's mother. My quick impressions were of someone with a lively wit, perhaps in her early seventies, slim, casually but smartly dressed, her face very pale and a little drawn, perhaps from a recent illness. Then I remembered: she had been widowed not all that long ago.

'Elizabeth Ashley,' she said, holding out a hand. 'Do come in. You're not *the* Ingrid Langley, are you, the novelist?'

I said that I was – Langley is my maiden name – and found myself in a high hallway that must have originally been the interior of the gatehouse. Again, other than a few ancient weapons and a couple of shields on the panelled walls, all evidence of grim times had been removed or, more likely, covered up, and my feet had sunk into a thick red carpet.

'It set me wondering when we spoke yesterday,' Mrs Ashley continued. 'And you also work for the NCA!'

'I'm a sort of adviser to my husband, who does.'

'Ah, that makes perfect sense. If all men had women as advisers the world wouldn't be in the wretched mess it is today. I did mention your visit to Piers and he promised to be close to home in order to speak to you. Would you like coffee while I ask my daughter to call him on his mobile and tell him you're here?'

I had left home late without a proper breakfast so this offer was very welcome.

'Come into the living room. Thea, are you there, dear? Ring Piers, would you?' she finished by calling.

There was the sound of quick footsteps and a young woman with blonde hair emerged from somewhere at the rear, wiping her hands on a towel.

'Sorry, a late breakfast, buttery fingers,' she said and we shook hands.

'Thea's having a break at home from working in London,' Mrs Ashley went on to say. She eyed me anxiously. 'I take it this is a police matter and you want to talk to my son in private.'

'It's about a case he worked on,' I replied.

'He's not going to get dragged back into it, is he?'

'I'm after information he might be able to give me, that's all.'

'Only we nearly lost him, you know.'

'But I was given to understand that his injury wasn't as a result of his job.'

Sharply, her mobile in her hand, Thea said, 'It seems you know everything about us.'

'I know nothing at all about you,' I replied, wishing I hadn't referred to it. 'That information was on a secure police website and we've met an old colleague of his. Police departments have to liaise.'

'Oh, right. Sorry. I'll make some coffee.' She went into an adjacent room, busy with her mobile.

I was ushered through a doorway on the opposite side of the hall into a large but cosily furnished room. Through an open door on the far side of it I caught a glimpse into what must be the galleried room referred to on the website. There was the distant sound of a vacuum cleaner.

'We're usually open to the public,' Elizabeth Ashley was saying as she closed it. 'Do sit down. But since my husband died I simply can't face doing it again. I'm sure you'll think me a bit silly and Piers says it doesn't matter and he'd like to make some improvements to the place anyway and have builders in . . .' Her voice trailed away sadly.

I reasoned that I would find it hard to get out of bed in the morning if Patrick died, never mind having hundreds of complete strangers traipsing around my house, and said so.

'But you have to carry on, don't you? I realize that it brings in a useful amount of money and don't want to be a pain to Piers now that he's running everything, but . . .' She broke off again for a moment, and then said, 'We discovered about the time that Piers was shot that the farm's manager was lining his own pockets, so we did without one altogether from then on and rented out the house he was living in. That was just about the only good thing that happened that year.'

Thea came into the room to say, 'Piers will be here in a few minutes,' and went out again.

'You mentioned a colleague of Piers in the police,' Mrs Ashley continued. 'He had been sent to prison for six months along with some of the members of the gang he'd infiltrated, although he didn't serve that long. He can talk about it a bit now, you see. Then he was shot and when he was here recuperating his boss came to warn him as it was thought the gang leader had suddenly found out who he really was and had set out to kill him.' She lowered her voice. 'I'll let you into a secret: Thea was really taken with him.'

'What was his name?'

'David Rolt.'

'Do you think he felt the same about her?'

'Well, he's an inscrutable kind of man. Senior policemen are – you must know that – but I have an idea he found her attractive too. Then she married a South African chap; it's all gone terribly wrong recently and they're getting divorced. This happened just after Mycroft had a heart attack and died.' She gave herself a little shake. 'I'm so sorry. I really shouldn't be bothering you with this.'

I made a suitably sympathetic remark, actually finding it all utterly fascinating.

'Where is everyone?' a male voice suddenly enquired loudly.

'Here,' Elizabeth answered. 'In the living room.'

A man who must be Piers Ashley entered. He still looked like a policeman, even though his feet were clad only in a pair of pale blue, fluffy socks.

Three

'You can talk in Mycroft's study,' said Elizabeth after the introductions. 'I'll bring your coffee in there.'

'*I'll* take the coffee,' her son corrected. 'Is there any of that fruit cake left?'

'Only if you didn't finish it yesterday.' This with a wink in my direction.

It turned out that he had.

The study was a rather dim room towards the rear of all that I could discern of the ground floor of the left wing. It smelled a bit musty. Ashley opened the curtains wide – they had been half-closed – but this did not improve matters much as creepers were growing across the window. Invited to make myself at home, I was about to seat myself on a sofa that looked as though it had been lived on by big dogs – that is, sagging – but he uttered an expression of alarm and directed me towards a button-backed chair.

'I ought to get rid of that but can't somehow,' he said, pouring the coffee. 'At one time we had three Labradors and a Border terrier but they gradually died of old age or had to be put down for other reasons. My father became very depressed about it, said he didn't want any more.'

'I understand that your father died very suddenly.'

'He did, but it might have been preventable.

He had no previous history of heart trouble but had been suffering from vague chest pains on and off and Mother made a doctor's appointment for him. The doc gave him some pills and said he'd arrange for a specialist to see him as soon as possible. Dad kept forgetting to take the pills and then forgot to attend the hospital for the appointment. Three days later, he died. Now, what can I do for you?'

He had seated himself in the only other chair available in the room – the one behind the desk – and was smiling politely. He was good looking, fair-haired like his sister and, oddly, today they were both dressed in similar fashion: pale blue jeans – only his were rather dirty as though he had been kneeling on the ground – and pale cream sweaters. Were they twins?

'Commander Rolt tells me that he was your boss.'

'He sent you?'

'He suggested we talk to you.'

'May I see your ID?'

I handed it over and, after a quick glance, he gave it back. 'Why?'

'He was the senior police officer attacked while on a walking holiday in Somerset.'

'*What!*'

'He's still in hospital but slowly on the mend. It's thought whoever did it hoped to kill him.'

'I'll kill *them*,' Ashley muttered.

You really must swap notes with Patrick, was the thought that immediately flitted through my mind, but I said, 'The NCA has shortlisted three names of serious criminals being investigated by both us and F9. Initially, you see, we weren't involved. But, due to circumstances, my husband, Patrick, has been given the case.' I quickly explained what these were.

'And the names?' Ashley queried. 'God, I can't get over this. I must go and see him.'

I gave him the list, saying, 'We showed this to him and he only picked out one, Matt Dorney.'

The man's face hardened. 'Son of Len Dorney. I cheered the day that little shit – sorry – died in prison.'

This was personal then. As a writer, I know enough about what makes people tick to realize that while working undercover Ashley must have suffered at the hands of this criminal. If I was his mother I would be glad he was out of it too.

Ashley handed back the list and said, 'Dorney senior never went on a job personally. God knows what Matt does now. Len only broke his golden rule once and that was because I persuaded him to as he said he was going to retire afterwards. That's when we arrested him, and then Rolt arranged for me to disappear. I sold my flat in London, got rid of the car I had and lived in a safe house for six months until the dust settled, during which time Rolt took me on as his personal assistant as I wasn't fit after being shot. Then, a year later, my father died.'

'Patrick's thinking of doing the same sort of thing as you did to ferret Dorney out – go right undercover.'

'He mustn't! It's too dangerous.'

'We are talking about an ex-special operations soldier here.'

'Nevertheless, it would be the death of him. I worked my way up the hard way – you have to, to be Dorney's right-hand man. Going to prison with some of his boys convinced him that he could trust me. But Matt's reputed to be brighter than he was – he probably won't fall for that kind of deception. Word has it he only hires people he knows or who are recommended by mobster associates. Even then, he insists on constant updates of what's going on when they're on a job – he doesn't trust anyone. He sold Len's house near Well Street Common. No one can find out where he lives – he probably moves around all the time. We don't even have a good mugshot of him, just a blurred photo when he was spotted leaving a strip club in Barking. It would be useless for identification purposes.'

'What's the name of this place?'

'Not known. And I have an idea the person who took the picture's dead – found dead.'

Which was discouraging, to put it mildly. 'Could you identify Matt?'

'Unfortunately not. But he might look like his old man.'

'I rather think Patrick's planning to set himself up as the boss of a new gang.'

'What, with cops pretending to be his heavies?' Ashley asked incredulously.

'No, real villains.'

'Can he do that?'

I knew exactly what he meant. 'Oh, yes, my husband would make a wonderful mobster.'

'I'd like to meet him.'

'That's easy. Come to Bath to see Rolt and I'll arrange it.'

We spoke for a little longer, then, having said goodbye to Mrs Ashley and Thea, I left.

Hopefully, this would be a man thing.

I was not ignoring the dangerous implications, however, and was hoping that Patrick would consider other tactics. On some previous occasions, when he had initially been determined to go for the no-holds-barred option and I had suggested a different approach, he had come to agree with me. The more I thought about this latest project and my writer's imagination kicked in with all kinds of ghastly scenarios, the more alarmed I became.

'You can relax,' Patrick said when he came home the following evening and, not for the first time, I had voiced my reservations. 'Greenway, he say no.'

'Oh. Did he give his reasons?'

'He said he couldn't authorize anything like that and he'd get it in the neck from those on high if it all went wrong.'

'Like all the wrong kind of funerals – yours, for example.'

'That too.'

'You could modify your plans.'

'Yes, I'm working on it.'

I decided to worry about that another time and said, 'Piers Ashley rang. He's visiting Rolt tomorrow. Discuss it with him.'

'Have you fixed up anything?'

'Yes, I've invited him to join us for an evening meal at the pub. He's staying overnight in Bath.'

40

Patrick poured himself a tot of whisky and turned to me with a sly grin. 'You quite fancy him, don't you?'

'I can't imagine what would have led you to think that,' I replied coolly.

'You have a little smile on your face when you mention him.'

'I always fancy good-looking men, including you – sometimes.'

Piers Ashley had arrived before the arranged time and rose and came towards us when he recognized me. He had been sitting on a seat on the village green that fronted the Ring o' Bells and which we have to cross in order to reach it unless we use a surrounding lane. The rain had finally cleared away and it was a fine, if chilly, evening and very quiet, the only sounds being an occasional car on the nearby road and rooks cawing in the large oak tree to the rear of the old inn.

I introduced Patrick and the two shook hands.

'I understand you intend to turn yourself into a mobster,' Ashley said to him as we approached the pub.

'I've done it before,' Patrick replied. 'More than once.'

'Do you have official backing?'

'No, not right now.'

'You don't make it sound as though that's too much of a problem.'

'I'll try to talk him round.'

When we had settled in the lounge bar – our table was booked for a little later – and the men had acquainted themselves with their pints of bitter, Ashley said, 'One thing I must point out is that I worked hard at this to earn credentials with Dorney. I went with his gang on jobs, drove getaway cars, was sent to prison, got beaten up on his orders if he thought I wasn't giving him the respect he deserved. You haven't the time to take months out to do that, even if you wanted to.'

Patrick smiled and said, 'How did you get him to take you on in the first place?'

'I lived rough, and I mean rough, for a while, hung around where I knew he could sometimes be found. Word from snouts was that he recruited from a certain pub in Dalston. When I finally came upon him he was looking for bruisers and, as by that time I looked like one, he took me on. I had to prove myself, go with witnesses and beat up someone, which I did.'

'Who?' I asked, really, really needing to know.

'A rival drug dealer who was refusing to get out of what Dorney regarded as his manor. It wasn't difficult as I happened to know that he was recruiting children and vulnerable people who he issued with mobiles to act as runners to look out for those who wanted drugs. I made sure, though, that F9 scooped him up later from where I'd dumped him.'

'Tell me about this manor,' Patrick said. 'I take it Matt's inherited it, if that's the right word.'

'It's in Hackney, east London. I wrote down the details.' He took a piece of paper from his wallet and consulted it. 'It's an area of around twelve square miles, roughly bounded by Graham

42

Road – the A1207, to the north and the Regent's Canal to the south. Queensbridge Road, the B108, bounds it to the west and Mare Street, the A107, to the east. It's a sort of upright rectangle.'

'May I have that?'

'Of course.' Ashley passed it over. 'Len used to have what he called his office over a shop in Mare Street which was a Chinese takeaway when I was first on the job. He reckoned that a business that purported on a brass plate by the door to be a distributor of educational videos wouldn't attract many casual callers. He installed plenty of lookouts, though – no one ever took him unawares. But that's history – nothing's the same now as someone firebombed the takeaway one night, destroying a good proportion of the row of shops as well. Initially, a charred body found roughly at the seat of the fire was thought to be Len's but it turned out not to be. We never found out who it was.'

'I understand Matt Dorney brags that he can arrange to have anyone taken out as long as the money's right. Is that just a lot of hot air?'

'No, apparently it isn't. He also said – joked, probably – that he would set up a website and call it murders dot com.'

I wondered how he knew that.

'Who does he use to do the dirty work?' Patrick went on to ask.

'No idea. Several hitmen, probably. He might hire from abroad, they pose as tourists and go home afterwards.'

Patrick held up his empty tankard. 'Another?'

'Better not, I'm driving.'

43

I said, 'I know it's a bit obvious to say this but the key to this is to discover exactly who tried to kill the commander. Was it the work of someone not actually part of Matt Dorney's set-up but hired – if indeed Dorney's really behind it? Has whoever it is left the country? Have they been paid? Hardly any details have appeared in the media so Dorney will have no proof as to whether they succeeded or failed.'

Thoughtfully, Patrick said, 'The hitman, or men – Rolt thinks there were three of them – wouldn't have known initially that they'd failed but will have gone to collect their money anyway. Or does he pay for jobs upfront?'

'No idea, but Len never did and always wanted proof before he handed over the money.'

'Suppose someone turns up and shows him a picture of Rolt as large as life in hospital. That someone could offer to track down the failed hitmen and, if the money had been paid, get it back or even volunteer to do the job properly.'

'And if Dorney says in believable fashion that he had nothing to do with it?' Ashley queried.

'Plan B.'

'Which is?'

'I'll think of something.'

'You'll have to find him first.'

When he worked for MI5, Patrick had carte blanche, but these days he's a police officer so has no choice but to get permission for what he wants to do. As a courtesy, he first consulted James Carrick, as it was his case. But the DCI, or rather the husky wreck on the other end of the

44

phone that Joanna insisted was her husband, confessed to not being in any fit state to even make useful suggestions. Having a jaundiced view of chasing it through Avon and Somerset's HQ, being embedded in the force or not, Patrick came to the conclusion that there was nothing for it but to get the train to London early the next morning to tackle Michael Greenway face-to-face. I was requested to go along to exert a little charm.

'Mike isn't at all susceptible to charm,' I argued in vain.

During the journey, Patrick was very quiet, perhaps working out his strategy with Greenway. In my mind, I kept going through what we knew already. Nothing had been found either on or inside Commander Rolt's car that would provide evidence in connection with the attack on him. No one had tried to break into it even though he had left his rucksack on the back seat. So it had been decided that after he had been given what personal possessions he needed from it, the vehicle would be taken to F9's HQ for safe-keeping. Rolt didn't want it to be parked where he lived, a townhouse in Woodford Green, but kept the reasons behind this to himself. Not wishing local attention to be drawn to it and start tongues wagging, perhaps. I had an idea he went out in the mornings giving every impression of working in the City.

'I find very alarming the suspicion that Rolt was followed when he went on holiday,' Patrick said as we entered the NCA building. 'The location of F9's HQ is practically a state secret – I don't know exactly where it is – and his private address is kept quiet too. How did they locate him and know what he was going to do?'

'I can't believe it was just a casual mugging either,' I said. 'It was a filthy day and someone could have waited up there for a victim until they died of exposure. Nothing was stolen, was it?'

'No, not even the money in his wallet, although it must be borne in mind his wallet was in a concealed pocket.'

'Which is surprising as one would have thought that in order to avert suspicion from themselves they'd have tried to make it look like a mugging carried out by local yobs.'

'They might be stupid. And we must face the possibility that everyone's completely wrong about Matt Dorney being responsible. There's absolutely no evidence yet to connect him with the crime. The case was only raised as a priority because of Rolt's position and because the commander's fairly sure Dorney was behind it, so he's the chief suspect. That line of enquiry might be a complete waste of time.'

'But Dorney is on the Met's Most Wanted list,' I reminded him. 'He needs to be grabbed anyway.'

'Good point.'

Greenway was in a meeting and we had to wait in the corridor outside his office. Patrick endeavoured to access the one he had used when he worked there but someone else had it now, a small detail that I think finally drove home to him that he was now outside the heart of the organization.

'This looks like a deputation,' Greenway said

46

when he finally turned up and went into his room, momentarily out of our sight. There was a crash as he must have dropped the files he was carrying into a tray on his desk. He reappeared and glanced at his watch. 'Lunch. Please join me.'

An hour later, Patrick was no closer to getting what he wanted, despite having presented his case persuasively. This investigation, Greenway insisted, would be handled using established police methods and protocols. There would be no 'iffy' contrivances, schemes or intrigues.

'Evidence,' the commander said, not for the first time. 'There aren't any leads at all yet to connect Matt Dorney to the crime and Rolt's theories can't be used as the basis for our investigation. We can't be seen to be using his department's unorthodox methods.'

'Why not?' I asked before Patrick could react in a more robust fashion.

Greenway put his coffee cup back in the saucer with a loud clatter. A big man, he tends to be noisy anyway. 'Because while what Rolt does is perfectly acceptable in a small way, you have to be careful that it doesn't get out of hand so everyone wants to give it a try. It simply can't be allowed to replace careful and accurate conventional policing. Not only that, think of the fallout if Patrick was hurt or even killed.'

Shortly afterwards, we thanked him for lunch and left him finishing his coffee.

'No gunpowder, treason and plot,' Patrick muttered when we were outside. 'What did you make of it?'

'He doesn't approve of F9 and gives the

impression that he doesn't like Rolt much either. Is Rolt senior to him in some kind of way?'

'Only in the sense that he's more highly thought of. F9 was the brainchild of an extremely senior Met officer who's dead now but had connections with what I'll call the right people. I've been told that Rolt has connections with the right people. Mike's worked his way up and has succeeded because he's damned good at what he does, but that's it. It's unfair on him but I think the answer to the question is yes, and, as you yourself said, Rolt's royalty. Mike resents it and is determined to carry out the investigation méticulously, with none of my previous loose cannon stuff.'

Although I basically approved of the commander's thinking, it did sound like male point-scoring. I said, 'So, on the one hand he's saying he wants progress and on the other insisting that you don't do it in the way that's been so successful in the past.'

'Any references to rocks and hard places right now will have me chucking myself off the Shard,' Patrick replied absently. 'What does the oracle think?'

'I've told you what the oracle thinks. Your *wife* thinks exactly the same – that you shouldn't necessarily follow your instincts. You wanted the potentially safer West Country job for your family's sake. You can't have it both ways, either.'

He flagged down a taxi. 'Shall we stay the night and think about it?'

We didn't. A little later, Patrick got a call from Acting Detective Inspector Lynn Outhwaite to say that two men had been found hanged in the wood near where Rolt was attacked.

The bodies were still in situ, the area cordoned off, scenes-of-crime personnel in their protective clothing moving about beneath the trees, the normal dimness banished by rigged-up lights. A pathologist had already taken a quick look at the corpses and his first impression, he had told Lynn, was that the men had been alive immediately before being strung up – in other words, someone had not merely hung up dead bodies. Also, in his view, they had put up a fight either shortly before this occurred or at some time previous to that. Obviously, he would know more when he performed the post-mortems.

'It looks as though they might have driven up in some kind of 4x4,' Lynn said. 'Which, of course, we've all had to do.'

'Obliterating any other tyre tracks,' Patrick observed, gazing around at the various vehicles.

'Surely you didn't expect everyone to walk,' she countered, brittle with nerves in the face of so much responsibility having been thrust upon her.

Patrick placed a conciliatory hand on her arm. 'No, we drove up too. I'm just thinking aloud.'

'Not exactly the kind of place where there would have been many witnesses.'

'Probably just as well or they might have ended up dead too.'

'Surely this is connected with the attack on Commander Rolt.'

'It would be an amazing coincidence if it

49

wasn't. Two serious crimes committed in the same fairly remote vicinity in the space of just a few weeks? Do we have any idea yet who they were?'

Lynn shook her head. 'Not with faces like that.' She took a deep breath. 'I've never seen anyone who's been hanged before.'

Gently, Patrick said, 'Seeing that there's every chance of a connection with the Rolt case, which appears to have landed in my lap, would you like me to carry on here?'

She gave him a grateful smile. 'I've a serious rape and a couple of break-ins to deal with back at base.'

When she had gone, he said to me, 'You do realize that I've never been in charge of a murder inquiry before. Just as well I attended a really boring lecture about procedures recently. Will you do something for me?'

'Of course.'

'Skirt the cordoned-off bit and take a look to see if there are any tyre tracks in the field on the far side.'

In the failing light and glad that we keep boots in the car, I made my way through the trees and wandered around the field, which was still just down to the stubble of the harvested cereal crop, being careful not to tread on anything that might turn out to be evidence. There were plenty of footprints from dog-walkers and ramblers in the damp ground and an even greater number of hoof-prints. A series of tracks, coming and going, led towards the centre of the field. I abandoned following up those when I belatedly realized that

that was where the rescue helicopter had landed when I found Rolt. There were also the cloven hoof-marks made by a cow, an escapee perhaps, and those of deer. I found no vehicle tracks until I widened my search and then came upon tyre marks made by something with a very narrow wheelbase, possibly a quad bike. There appeared to be two sets. Two quad bikes, two journeys or, come to think of it, four trials bikes? Walking well to the side of them, I went downhill and eventually discovered that they led to the gate at the bottom. Perhaps this was nothing more sinister than the farmer inspecting his land on more than one occasion recently. I retraced my footsteps and found that the tracks went very wide before becoming lost in the rough vegetation on the edge of the wood. Some of the tyre marks, I reasoned, might have been made during a return journey. What I needed was someone good at tracking.

By this time Patrick was clad in an anti-contamination suit, inspecting the bodies. I had no wish to do that so called to him from the edge of the taped-off area. He waved and said he wouldn't be very long.

'It might be absolutely nothing important,' I said when he joined me about five minutes later.

I waited – one set of footsteps less to confuse any further investigations – while he walked around the area I had indicated, pausing now and again and finally doing as I had done, going down the field to the gate. He took what seemed a very long time over it and I began to shiver in the chilly north-easterly breeze.

He came back. 'Two quad bikes, both quite heavily loaded on the way up but with a lighter load on the way back. Can you see if they were parked up here?'

'It's just a mass of rough grass and squashed greenery near where people and animals go through the gap in the fence,' I told him.

'They were left here for a while,' Patrick said, having bent down to take a closer look. 'One has a bit of an oil leak. We need an expert to look at this but not today – it'll be dark soon. I'll ask them to cordon off this area as well.'

'It might be worth asking Colin Reed, the farmer, before you do anything,' I suggested.

'Good idea. I made a note of his number.'

We quickly found out that, early that morning, Reed had discovered his two quad bikes were missing but they had been found on the edge of the wood at around eight thirty a.m. by a neighbour walking his dog. He and his son had ridden them home. There was no apparent damage so he hadn't reported the incident to the police.

'Young tearaways, no doubt,' Reed had concluded dismissively.

He was told that the machines, plus the clothes he and his son had been wearing, would be taken away and sent to a forensics laboratory.

Four

'Reed and his son didn't go into the wood,' Patrick said after getting a phone call with a report from someone he had sent to the farm to ask more questions and organize the removal of the quad bikes. 'The neighbour's not at home right now but will be questioned later.'

'Who found the bodies?' I asked. By this time we were standing under the shelter of the trees.

'A woman also walking her dog at just before ten this morning. Apparently she's a fan of *Midsomer Murders* so didn't go near them in case she destroyed evidence.'

'There won't be much evidence on the quad bikes now they've been ridden by others,' I commented.

'I can't imagine a richer source of DNA than farmers' overalls,' Patrick said with a groan. 'Even if they'd put on clean ones.'

'It was interesting, the pathologist remarking that it looked as though the deceased had put up a fight either just before they were hanged or at some time previously.'

'That may be a significant clue.' He gazed at me. 'Why don't you go home? You look frozen – I can get a lift.'

I gladly did so.

It was quite late when Patrick got back and, having had no chance to change out of lighter

53

city clothing, he too was cold by this time. And wet, as it had started to rain. Pausing only to say goodnight to Justin and Vicky, he then headed for a hot shower. A tot of whisky was deemed vital to restore normal functions.

'There's blood on one of the bikes,' he reported. 'Nothing to do with injury to any of his stock, according to Colin Reed. The quad bikes are kept in an open barn but with metal field gates across the front. No animals wander around there except the farm cats and the odd rat.'

'I take it the gates weren't padlocked.'

'No, I seem to remember they were just leaned across and fixed with baling twine.'

Patrick's work mobile rang and he swore under his breath. 'That was Rolt,' he said, finding me in the kitchen a few minutes later. 'He's going to Ashleigh Hall tomorrow to stay for a while. Someone's driving him there – he didn't say who. I told him the latest developments and he said that's how Dorney works. People don't screw up with him.'

'Releasing the story has made things happen, then.'

'Rolt's just told me that he requested it was. I can't believe he imagined it would result in the murders of those who failed to kill him, though.'

I wasn't so sure about that.

The bodies of the two men, who had been in their mid to late thirties and of similar height and build, had nothing on them to indicate their identities. The only possible means of identification of one was the fact that his arms and torso were quite heavily tattooed, and on his hands were the words CHAMPION and INVULNERABLE.

'The tattoos sound like something from computer games,' I observed as I went through the pathologist's report that Patrick had brought home the following evening for me to read.

They had both been subjected to what was described as a 'severe beating' before being hanged. The body without tattoos had a wound to the head that had bled quite profusely. A scraping of dried blood taken from the quad bike had been sent for DNA testing, together with blood samples from both bodies as the pathologist believed, due to physical similarities, that the two men might have been related.

'Did you go to the PMs?' I asked.

'Yes, I did. They didn't reveal anything in the way of useful evidence.'

I made no further comment just then. We were speaking quietly as Matthew was doing his homework, also reading, the book flat on his lap, in the conservatory with us. I saw that my adopted son, who has more than a passing resemblance to his uncle at that age, was interested and said, 'Champion and Invulnerable, Matthew? Or perhaps Invulnerable Champion. Mean anything to you?'

'I think it's the name of a plastic robot thing that you build. It's supposed to be for kids but not my kind of thing,' he immediately said. 'And there's a computer game connected with it that's for kids too.'

That didn't sound too promising, unless one of our corpses had been in possession of fairly basic thinking processes.

'They're also the names of two of the Royal Navy's destroyers,' Matthew added.

'Ah, that's better,' Patrick said. 'Odd though to have the name of the ships you serve in tattooed on your hands.'

'Perhaps his chums fixed it up one night in a port somewhere when they were all drunk,' Matthew suggested.

I wondered which books he was reading but, again, said nothing. On the other hand . . . 'What's the homework about then?' I asked him.

He went a little pink. 'We were told to take a book out of the bookcase at home and read the first chapter. Just pick one, she said, and then write about it. My friend Jake's really stuffed – there are no books at his place.'

'And yours is?'

'It's by someone called Stieg Larsson.'

'Did anyone say you ought to check with your parents if your choice was OK?'

'Yes. She said that twice.'

'I don't recollect you asking us.'

'No, you weren't here. I asked Grandad.'

Who hasn't the first clue about modern fiction and was probably composing his next sermon at the time.

'Are you enjoying it?' Patrick enquired.

'No. It's a bit complicated and the people in it are really weird. There's this woman and—'

'I'll find you another one,' Patrick interrupted, getting to his feet.

Enquiries Patrick made the next morning to the Ministry of Defence elicited the information that among others who had served on the ships was a seaman who had been given a Dishonourable Discharge. He had struck an officer, a sub-lieutenant, and had been found to have Class-A drugs in his possession. Asked for a description, the MoD forwarded this in an email – tattoos were mentioned, together with a photograph. Even though the features of the hanging victim had been distorted, Patrick said it was clearly the same person.

Digging a little deeper, in police files, he then discovered that the name the man had been using for his RN service was not genuine and his birth certificate forged. He had a criminal record. Known in his navy days as 'Spike' on account of his bad temper, he had actually been half-Polish and had several assumed names, thought to be stolen identities, one of which was Steve Biddulph. It was this name that he had used mainly, the others having been utilized in connection with benefit fraud.

Another detail useful to the investigating officer was the fact that he had had a brother, Kyle, who also had a criminal record. This individual had specialized in car crime and drug dealing and he, too, had used several aliases.

'Shall we refer to them as the Biddulph brothers until we know better?' Patrick said. 'Otherwise we'll really get tied in knots and it's not as though they're going to get up to anything else, separately or together.'

'The second man's identity will still have to be confirmed,' I pointed out.

'We'll know more when we get the DNA results.'

James Carrick was slightly better, although weak and with a bad cough, and able to advise Lynn Outhwaite over the phone. Following a tip-off from a reliable source, she had already arrested the previous boyfriend of the woman who had been raped – her attacker had worn a mask – as, drunk, he had been bragging about it. Apparently there were several witnesses to this. With regard to the murder case, the DCI suggested that until he himself was back on duty – he hoped to return to work the following Monday – Lynn should liaise with the NCA officer investigating the attack on Rolt – Patrick.

Despite the promise of full cooperation, tracking down someone to talk to within F9 proved to be difficult. Rolt had said that they would send any useful information but, three days later, nothing had been forthcoming. As far as evidence was concerned, the immediate area surrounding where the men had been hanged had yielded nothing of value due to the bad weather and the fact that the trees were shedding their leaves. The only fact to emerge from lab reports was that DNA in the smear of blood found on one of the quad bikes matched that of the man who had called himself Steve Biddulph. The other man's DNA results suggested that they could be related. There was a lot of detail in the report that I had to admit to myself I simply couldn't understand.

'It could still be the brother, Kyle,' Patrick said, having ploughed through it to the end. 'If they had different fathers.'

We were both in James Carrick's office. Rain sluiced down the window.

'Nothing positive, though,' I said.

'No. We'll have to go to the last known addresses of these people.'

'In London?'

'Yes.'

'I hope in reality that you're going to ask the Met to do that.'

'Indeed I am, ma'am.' This with a big smile.

'So we're assuming that persons unknown rode the quad bikes up the field with the men they were going to kill on the back. That would explain the deeper tyre tracks. But were they just sitting there, like lambs to the slaughter? Surely not. But if they were unconscious they would have fallen off. I don't know much about quad bikes but they only have a sort of rack at the back, don't they?'

'Colin Reed's are Honda utility models. So yes, those have a rack where you can put a box or a short plank of wood for a person or a dog to sit on. If the men were unconscious they could have been tied on somehow. Or they could have got them up there on some kind of pretext.'

'So how did the third man get there? If there was a third.'

'Perhaps someone made a trip back for him. It's very difficult to tell exactly how many journeys were made as the field was so churned up with the tracks of those, plus animals and people.'

'And no one noticed all this going on? I find that difficult to believe.'

'I suppose that if they did it at first light . . . It was a wet morning, too.'

'We're not really getting anywhere with this, are we?'

'No, we're not.'

The next morning, Saturday, Commander Rolt phoned Patrick's work mobile. It was quite early, just before eight, and I answered it as he was having a wash and a shave.

'I've fixed up something for you,' he began. 'My man on the ground with regard to Matt Dorney will meet you if you so wish. You realize that this is extremely hazardous for him so the last thing you must do is turn up looking like the police. There's an outside chance he'll be followed. If you want to talk to him he'll be at The Barge public house at Acton's Lock on the Regent's Canal, Hackney at eight thirty tomorrow evening. He can't manage tonight as he has a getaway car to drive.'

'We'll be there,' I said, somehow managing not to ask questions about that last statement.

'Good. I'll confirm that with him.'

'What does he look like?'

'Right now he's telling me his hair's dyed a kind of dark red. And, take care.'

It wasn't raining in London but a mist hanging over the canal was clinging in tiny droplets to my hair as we approached The Barge along the towpath. It had been a fair walk as finding somewhere where Patrick felt at ease leaving an expensive car had been difficult. Finally, running out of time – we had been held up by an accident on the motorway – he had opted for the three hours' free parking available at a supermarket.

60

The mist was giving a Dickensian ambience to the area, swirling in the light breeze around an old-fashioned lamp post and under the humped road bridge over the canal near which the pub was situated. We had passed several moored narrowboats, their stove-pipe chimneys smoking, the interiors cosy where they could be glimpsed through windows where the tasselled curtains had not been drawn.

Patrick likes nothing better than not to resemble a police officer when on the job and, out of a modest repertoire of personas, had chosen that of mostly cleaned-up jobbing builder. This merely entailed donning the clothes he wears for decorating, faded and with streaks of paint here and there that won't come out, hopefully giving the impression that he was calling in for a pint on his way home from work, having finished late. I had an idea that a smart-arse smile might embellish the outfit when we reached our destination.

He still looked good enough to eat.

I was his girlfriend, who might have a job scrubbing floors but was obviously not capable of anything that required greater intellect. Leaving one's mouth open for most of the time and/or chewing gum ditto helps. You can do a lot with your hair and make-up as well to achieve this effect, partly by making yourself look approximately ten years out of date. It applies to clothes too and I'm always a keen rummager at village jumble sales and in charity shops. I once bought Patrick a clove-pink linen shirt, good quality and brand new, in one of the latter for his own undercover collection, thinking he might one day want

61

to look a bit, well . . . gay, and he fell upon it and wears it for best smart casual.

'I don't advise too much alcohol,' Patrick said to me out of the corner of his mouth as we entered the public bar of The Barge at a little before eight fifteen.

'Is it OK then if I just have a *small* glass of wine?' I enquired loudly, well in character and having decided that very second to be slightly tipsy already. 'And when the hell do I ever binge drink?'

Fleetingly, he looked taken aback and then chuckled. 'All right, darlin'.'

I had meant every word of it, not at all sure why he had uttered the remark. A bit worried about our planned encounter? Surely not.

Those who had overheard me were smiling and one man gave me a wink with leery overtones. Don't, I inwardly begged him, or you'll be in A&E while they dig your front teeth out of your tonsils. But, thankfully, Patrick hadn't seemed to notice.

The place was very busy. It was not a rough establishment by any means, and, through a wide archway, there was a restaurant area. The decor was mostly in several shades of green and there was a lot – too much – of highly decorated metal barge-ware, jugs in several sizes, buckets and so forth, on shelves and hanging from hooks. A small jazz band, rather good, was playing out of sight from us around the corner of the L-shaped bar.

My insides grumbled as we hadn't had time to stop for refreshments. I eyed the specials board on the wall at one end of the bar. Yes, afterwards, pork fillet in a sherry and cream sauce with rice would be lovely. With perhaps sticky toffee pudding to follow. To hell with calories.

When we had our drinks Patrick surreptitiously scanned the throng for the man we were supposed to be meeting. We had realized that he might not turn up if the auspices at his end were not good. I was aware that my companion was carrying his Glock in its shoulder harness – it was simply too dangerous not to. This was the first time he had done so, to my knowledge, since he had taken the new job.

'Crisps,' I pleaded during a break in the music several minutes later, wine on an empty stomach making me feel light-headed. The only event so far had been a waitress dropping someone's dinner on the floor.

Patrick regarded me as if weighing up whether what I might provide him with later would be worth the investment, came to a reluctant conclusion and went back to the bar. Then called, 'They've only got cheese and onion.'

'That's fine,' I told him.

A study of tragic self-sacrifice, as he actually hates the smell of them on my breath, he bought me a packet. It does have to be said though that the pair of us thoroughly enjoy this play-acting. Perhaps we should have gone on the stage.

Half an hour later, there was still no sign of our man. Ostensibly searching for the loos, we separately looked round the building but there was no one with hair that could be described as 'a kind of dark red' except a middle-aged woman having a meal in the restaurant with her family.

63

Then, after another ten minutes or so, the door behind us, which my partner had been quietly keeping an eye on, burst open and a man hurried in. He tossed off the hood of his dirty anorak to reveal rather greasy, dark auburn hair and headed towards the gents'. Not our man, I thought. He had coarse features and, frankly, looked somewhat stupid.

Almost immediately, three other men entered and then stopped, the one in front sending the other two off with jerks of his head in different directions, obviously searching, and then staying where he was to stand guard by the door.

These were not tooth fairies.

Patrick peeled himself off the panelled wall and, following a signal from him, I 'accidentally' dislodged a large and rather ghastly pottery plate from the wall behind me. It crashed down and shattered on the wooden floor where the carpet didn't cover it right at the edges. Everyone's attention nearby momentarily on this, he slipped away to grab the man standing by the door, taking him completely by surprise, and frog-marched him outside. Less than twenty seconds later, while I was picking up the pieces of the plate while keeping watch on what was going on, he was back, pulling his sweatshirt straight.

'Wait here,' was the whispered instruction as he went by and disappeared.

Another twenty seconds elapsed – ridiculously, I found myself counting – and then, after what sounded like some kind of minor demolition in the gents', though no one took the slightest notice, he returned with the somewhat stupid-looking

64

individual, who was staggering slightly. They headed for the door and, given a little nod, I followed, leaving the bits of broken plate on a window ledge.

'There'll be more of them!' the rescued one was saying urgently. 'He always sends back-up.'

'Are you all right?' Patrick asked him.

'Yeah, probably.'

'What do we call you?'

'Dark Horse.' As if expecting disbelief, he added, 'We have code names. The other guys sometimes call me Geegee.'

A woman who had been serving behind the bar pursued us. 'Oi! You'll have to pay for that plate!' she shrilled breathlessly at me.

'Forget it! It should've been fixed up better!' I brayed back at her, paying full attention to glottal stops.

She retreated, tottering on her impossibly high heels and my husband turned to me, eyebrows raised in mock horror.

Another three men stepped out from beneath the bridge and came towards us. It was bad timing on their part and they were at an immediate disadvantage as they had to climb the short flight of steps at the side of it.

'He wants words,' said the man in front to Dark Horse when he had reached the top of them. 'Who's this?' He pointed a knife he was carrying at us.

'Friends of mine.'

'I think he wants to tell you that you're suspect. We were told to follow you as he wants to know who you knock around with.' And to us, 'Get out unless you want trouble. Go on! Git!' When nobody moved he said to the other two with him, 'They're just punters. Chuck 'em in the water.'

The tall, dark-haired punter underwent a rapid change of persona, lunged at him, seized the wrist of the hand holding the knife and then clipped him on the jaw, hard, when he had no choice but to go in the direction that his arm was now being wrung. He went over backwards, taking one of the others with him and the pair rolled down the steps, ending up right on the edge of the towpath. The remaining man ran off.

'Some of us are getting sick to death of Dorney, including me!' Patrick bellowed at them. 'Tell him that! Make sure you curtsey as you do it!'

We returned to the car and the response to my query regarding the fate of the man by the door was that he was now polluting a waste food bin.

'I don't have to tell you this but I screwed up,' said Dark Horse when we were seated inside the Range Rover.

'You don't have to tell us anything,' Patrick responded. 'But I get the impression that something went wrong last night.'

'The boss'll kill me,' Dark Horse continued, as though he hadn't spoken.

'What happened?'

'My brief was to let them attempt a raid on an off-licence as planned to give Dorney a sense of security – that he could get away with anything he liked. It was arranged that the place would close early and, as it has metal shutters, it was reckoned to be safe. But for some reason known only to himself, he decided to go along. Dorney *never* goes on jobs. It was too much of a temptation and I tipped off the local cops. They arrived too early, someone glimpsed a police car and the gang turned tail, me included. I had Dorney in the car with me.'

'Why did he suspect you?'

'After what's just happened I can only think he hadn't told anyone else he was going to be there. Thanks for trying not to bust my cover, by the way.'

Five

We drove what was reckoned to be a safe distance away from Hackney, westerly in the direction of the centre of London, added a couple of miles for luck and then parked at a large Thames-side pub called The Old Water Mill. That this was fact was celebrated within, a large, plastic-looking waterwheel dominating an entrance vestibule that was draped in swathes of plastic greenery and flowers. The wheel was not moving but water dribbled tiredly over it into a small pool containing different coloured underwater lights that illuminated artificial water lilies and all the wiring.

Our passenger had remained quiet during the journey and Patrick had whispered to me that he had been knocked down and kicked in the gents' toilet at The Barge by the two who I guessed were now stashed away tidily in cubicles. I, for one, thought we ought to get some food inside him. And ourselves.

'That was neat,' Dark Horse said, halfway through his steak pie and chips. He had not offered us his real name and we were not going to ask him for it.

'What was?' Patrick enquired through a mouthful.

'Your handling of Stu. He really fancies himself as a hard man.'

68

Patrick offered a contemptuous comment about that individual which I won't repeat.

'I think you ought to understand,' the F9 man went on, 'that I'm really only on the edge of that lot. An errand boy, to be called upon to drive cars – clean cars, for that matter. Do the shopping. The idea was that I'd be promoted, gradually work my way in. Then I'd really have had something to report to Rolt. Now I've screwed it.'

'Where does all this happen?' I asked him.

'All over. Places where his boys hang out or they meet Dorney in someone's lock-up garage. A lot goes on in lock-ups, some on estates that are due for redevelopment or in derelict warehouses. There's always a lot of booze and drugs. They don't care what they do when they're on drugs. As I'm sure you know, it's how some of these mobster bosses keep control.'

'Did you make a note of these meeting places?' Patrick wanted to know.

'Yes, I forward everything like that back to base.'

I expected him to give us a few details then but he didn't. Was he aware that Rolt had been attacked? Did he know about the hangings? Surely the commander had briefed him when they made contact. But nothing had been said about it and I was finding the fog in which this department appeared to operate a bit trying. I suddenly had some sympathy with Michael Greenway's thoughts on the matter.

'You agreed to talk to us,' Patrick said, showing signs of impatience as well. 'What has Rolt told you?'

69

'He said you were investigating an assault on him when he was on leave in your neck of the woods as you're stationed within Avon and Somerset. F9 HQ's not doing it so I'm assuming it has a low priority.'

'Never assume,' Patrick remarked mildly. 'The man almost died. Was a later crime mentioned by him when two men were hanged in a wood close to the scene of the attack?'

Dark Horse nodded. 'He reckons Dorney's responsible on both counts.'

'Did you get wind of any of this?'

'No, as I said, I'm just on the edge. Dorney keeps his big plans to himself.'

'But you found out and reported that they planned to raid the off-licence.'

'That's just keeping the cash flow healthy, not what he regards as big time or personal. Rolt is personal. He holds him responsible for the death of his old man after he died in jail.'

'I can't believe that he achieved hanging two of his mob and no one else knew what he intended to do. He had help to do it, for God's sake!'

'Well, if anyone knew about it they didn't tell me. I'm – probably was now – just a Bloke Friday, considered not senior enough to attend the meetings.'

For a moment, I questioned this as not seeming quite credible but dismissed the thought.

As if reading my mind, Dark Horse said, 'The gang's split into groups. Dorney works on a divide and rule principle. I don't even know who some of the other guys are.'

Patrick said, 'We spoke to Piers Ashley about any info he might be able to give us about Dorney.'

'He was called Homage. Rolt hands out all the names and I suppose it was an ironic reference to his background which I understand is upper class. He spoke like someone from the upper classes but could roughen off his voice if he needed to. Rolt called me Dark Horse because I look thick but I came top in the entrance exams. We all start off as ordinary constables in the Met. Was Ashley able to give you any leads?'

'No.'

'He never said where he lived and I didn't ask.'

'We met him in our village and didn't ask either. What are you going to do now?'

'I'm banking on Dorney not knowing where I live. I'll head there and then call HQ in the morning and get them to sort something out for me.'

'In return for possibly saving your skin I want the list of meeting places that you forwarded. Just in case I don't get full cooperation from F9.'

'How do I contact you?'

Patrick wrote down his work mobile number and then offered to take him where he wanted to go.

'No, it's OK, I'll get a bus.'

'D'you need money?'

'No, that's OK as well, thanks.'

'You can call me at any time.'

He thanked us again, said he didn't want coffee

and that he had better be going. Then, over his shoulder as he was leaving, he asked, 'Any idea where Rolt is now?'

'The last thing your lot would reveal is where the boss is,' Patrick replied with a smile.

'You're right,' was Dark Horse's parting remark.

As soon as he had gone from view, Patrick shot to his feet. 'Please settle up. I'm going to follow him. D'you reckon you can find your way back to the hotel all right?'

'We do have a satnav,' I reminded him. 'And for goodness' sake, be careful.'

He blew me a kiss, and then was gone.

This case was definitely getting curiouser and curiouser. But I had to postpone thinking about it too deeply, forcing myself to concentrate on London's appalling traffic instead. It was getting late by this time, just after ten thirty, and it seemed that half the city was on the move. It occurred to me that one way or another we were always being drawn back to the capital. Perhaps this would be the norm until Patrick retired. I did not feel particularly cheerful about it but, then again, it might just have been a long day.

He turned up at three a.m., humming tunelessly and clutching what turned out to be a battered red rose, one of those long-stemmed scentless ones people sometimes hawk around pubs and restaurants.

'Where on earth did you get that?' I asked a couple of minutes later after he had sort of crash-landed, fully dressed, on to the bed.

'What?' he mumbled.

72

'The rose.'

'Oh . . . dunno.' And went to sleep.

Enlightenment, along with a hangover, arrived when he awoke four and a half hours later. I made some tea, found a couple of strong pain-killers in my bag and handed them over. I'm not the sort to nag and rationed myself to pointing out to him that he himself had advised against too much alcohol. Patrick's reaction to this was a hollow groan before he took himself off, together with the tea and pills, into the bathroom for a shower and a shave. The combination restored him sufficiently to a state where he could contemplate having breakfast.

'The rose,' he said over a full English and as though it hadn't been several hours since the original conversation had taken place, 'came from a flower stall manned by a disabled man on the corner of Bush Road in Hackney.'

'Is that anywhere near Mare Street where Len Dorney used to have his HQ?'

'Yes. I slipped him a tenner and he said Matt Dorney's still in the immediate area.'

'I get the impression that you went in every pub looking for him.'

'No, I met Tim Shandy back in The Barge. I fancied a pint by that time and he insisted on buying me a whisky. Then I bought him one and . . .' He shrugged.

'What was a retired brigadier doing there?'

'Apparently looking up old haunts on the way back from delivering his sons to university. He's always insisted that he's a Londoner to the core.'

It appears to be one of the laws of the solar system that every time the two bump into one other they get plastered. This has punctuated, but not frequently, most of our married life.

'Those men might have come back,' I agonized.

'We'd have minced them.'

There being a lot of truth in this, I let the matter rest, saying, 'Before that, what about Dark Horse?'

'I caught sight of him as he got into a taxi – a taxi, mind you, not a bus – and managed to hail another. He went back to Hackney, around a quarter of a mile from Mare Street, and entered a terraced house near to what appeared to be a defunct printworks. I waited around for almost half an hour but he didn't emerge, so I can only guess that's where he or a friend he might have decided to stay with lives.'

'Something's not quite right.'

'No, and you must have realized when we were talking to him that I thought so too. I'm concerned that he went back after what happened. One would have thought he'd put as much distance between himself and that area as possible, even though he has a home there.'

'All he has to do, as he said himself, is phone HQ and be taken to a safe house.'

'Quite.'

'He asked us about Rolt's whereabouts, and was angling after knowing where Piers Ashley lives.'

'I'm extremely concerned about that. Is it a civilized time to phone Rolt?'

I glanced at my watch; eight fifteen. 'Bearing in mind that he's convalescing, leave it for half an hour.'

Rolt was very interested in what Patrick had to say but noncommittal, which was understandable in a way, and also gave the impression that he didn't want to talk about it over the phone.

'I can't work like this,' Patrick unsurprisingly said after the call. 'He said he'd deal with it – whatever the hell that means. Meanwhile, I'm still left the poor sod trying to solve an assault case with a double murder tacked on for good measure. As I've just said, I can't work like this.'

Caught between two police departments who seemed more interested in scoring points than solving a crime? No.

'Right,' Patrick said a couple of minutes later, pouring us both more coffee. 'I work for the NCA and that's where my loyalties lie. I was hired partly because I'm a loose cannon. Bugger F9. I shall find and grab this man called Dark Horse and make him tell it like it really is.'

When I first worked with Patrick for MI5, I accompanied him on all aspects of the job. It was a requirement. There were extremely dangerous moments when the pair of us could easily have been killed. Then Justin came along, a real surprise in view of the fact that Patrick had been told, following injuries while serving with special forces, that he probably would not be able to father children. The accident with the hand grenade – not his fault – had shattered his legs and caused genital injuries. Further confounding the medics had been Vicky and Mark when they had come along, but nothing at the time could be done with the lower part of his right leg, and this is now represented by a man-made version with its own tiny computer powered by lithium batteries. It cost a small fortune. Other than limping slightly when he is tired, no one observing him would guess, unless he is wearing shorts, the real situation.

The children. Because of them everything has changed, especially now Patrick has a new post and our working agreement means that I do not set off with him on the kind of venture that, right now, he had in mind. I went home, but was prepared to go back to London should the situation demand my return. It has to be said that, on occasion, I have thrown all of our working agreements, official and otherwise, out of the window. But, for now, I returned to Hinton Littlemore.

The phone call from Elizabeth Ashley the day after I arrived at the rectory came right out of the blue.

'I do hope you don't mind my asking as you must be an extremely busy lady and it's dreadfully last minute,' she began, 'but I'm president of the local WI and was wondering if you'd be prepared to come and give us a talk the day after tomorrow about your writing. The arranged speaker has badly sliced into her arm cutting a cabbage in the garden and can't drive. We'd pay whatever fee you normally charge plus expenses and you'd be more than welcome to stay here overnight.'

I practically kissed the phone.

Ashleigh Coombe had not escaped the endless rain but the village hall was warm and welcoming and there were a gratifying number of members present. I have a small collection of talks and usually try to make them as amusing as possible. This can be quite difficult as writing crime stories – I started off with romantic fiction and even wrote a couple of sci-fi novels but my characters developed a nasty habit of getting murdered – is a lonely occupation. All writing is. I was impressed when, during questions afterwards, a woman who had obviously done some research asked me if my husband had been the inspiration for *A Man Called Celeste*, which had been made into a film. Not a very good film, actually. I told her yes, he had.

'He must be quite a man,' she commented, and there was general laughter when she added that it was a shame I hadn't brought him with me. I could hardly say that it would have been a damned sight safer for him if I had as right now he was endeavouring to get an undercover cop by the short hairs.

Over tea, Mrs Ashley thanked me again. 'You are staying with us tonight, aren't you?' she finished by enquiring anxiously.

I said that I would be more than happy to. I had wondered if there was another reason for her invitation other than kind hospitality but reasoned that she might want another woman to talk to as a soon-to-be-divorced daughter might not be very

77

good company. As far as I was concerned, nothing would have kept me away as I really needed the opportunity to talk to David Rolt face-to-face.

One initially had to play this coolly, I decided, and not mention anything remotely connected with policing unless someone else brought up the subject. Especially during dinner.

I now knew that Thea and Piers, who were not twins, had a younger brother, Giles, who had left university with a degree in art history and wanted to be involved with the stage. Which direction this might take, his mother informed me a little wearily, was anyone's guess, and he was at present working 'as a kind of handyman' at the Savoy theatre in London. I had noticed a portrait of an ancestor, Sir Richard Ashleigh, who had apparently been knighted, on the spot, by Queen Elizabeth I after he had run through, with his sword, a man who had attempted to assassinate her. Sir Richard looked of quite delicate build and fastidious and stylish appearance, so perhaps Giles had taken after him.

With a little time to spare before pre-dinner drinks, I wandered in the great beamed hall, a reconstruction of the original that had been destroyed in the fire of 1672. On one panelled wall hung Sir Richard's sword. There was a small explanatory brass plate but no scabbard, and the blade glittered in the illumination provided by around a dozen wall lights. Surely, I thought, it would not have hung here like this when the place was open to the public; it was too valuable, too dangerous. It crossed my mind that its presence might indicate that a decision had been made that Ashleigh Hall was now closed permanently. One could hardly ask.

I heard footsteps and there, behind me, was David Rolt.

'You look a million per cent better,' I told him.

He smiled, a happier one than previously, which of course was perfectly understandable. 'How did the meeting with Dark Horse really go?' he then quietly asked.

For a moment, this blunt approach rather took my breath away. 'Patrick did report to you,' I replied.

'Were you present?'

'Yes, I was.'

'How did it *really* go?'

'Do you mean after Patrick had disarmed a man called Stu and he and another man rolled down the steps and almost went into the canal?'

'How interesting. Your husband is an ex-army officer so only presents the bald facts. He just said that there was resistance to the meeting from some thugs sent, according to Dark Horse, by Dorney, so you took him to a safer place. The things Dark Horse went on to say, particularly asking the whereabouts of both Piers Ashley and myself, aroused both his and your suspicions.'

I had been giving this some thought and said, 'That's right. Dark Horse was knocked around in the gents' toilet in the pub but Patrick got him out and when we were outside three more men approached. The talk was that your man was under suspicion and he would be taken off to be dealt with appropriately. Why did Dark Horse ask us where you were and hint that he didn't know where Ashley lived? Is he on the line? Frankly, Patrick can't investigate who's responsible for the attack on you when everything's so unclear.'

Rolt came closer to gaze at the sword. 'I understand from Thea that Piers once had a sword fight with his father in this room – a real one. It stemmed from Mycroft refusing to have him in the house when he came out of prison as the family was in complete ignorance of his real profession. Piers knew his mother wanted him at home as she had problems of her own. Mycroft armed himself with this and Piers grabbed the only other similar weapon, that early nineteenth-century naval officer's sword on the wall over there. Apparently Piers was winning easily when Giles came up behind him and hit him on the head with an oak stool, knocking him out. Elizabeth then threatened to leave Mycroft if he carried on behaving the way he was and they somehow sorted it out. My point in telling you this is that undercover jobs can create mayhem if not handled carefully.'

I recollected that Patrick and I have suffered some serious glitches in our relationship when he was taking on some of his more unsavoury roles.

'Did the men from Dorney say that he was suspected of being a police officer?' Rolt went on to ask.

'No.'

'Did your husband at any stage say that he was police officer?'

'No. As you'd requested, we'd dressed rough,

and Patrick gave them the impression that he was somehow part of the criminal scene and that he was sick to death of Dorney.'

'That was good thinking. Dorney's paranoid about other crime bosses invading his patch or stealing his gang members. He doesn't know Dark Horse is a police officer. Nor can he have known that he was meeting people from the NCA.'

'If that's the case why did he send those yobs after him?'

'According to another gang member Dark Horse has since spoken to over the phone, it was because of the failed job the night before. Dorney blamed him and said he was in the pay of someone he knows is trying to take over his manor and Dark Horse had hoped he – Dorney – would be arrested.' He smiled again, his bleak professional one this time. 'With a bit of luck he'll think it was someone your husband's working for.'

'Patrick followed Dark Horse when he left us and, having said he'd catch a bus, he took a taxi straight back to a house in Hackney. Disingenuousness apart, wasn't that rather dangerous in view of what had happened?'

The man actually uttered a quiet chuckle. 'I'm sure you both know everything about not necessarily telling people the absolute truth about your planned movements. He and a chum who sometimes helps on a flower stall on the corner of Mare Street share a house there.'

'Dark Horse seemed confident that Dorney didn't know where he lived. But someone could have followed him home – followed either of them, for that matter.'

'They're both extremely careful about that and are very experienced. The chum tells people he's the disabled man's brother and is giving him a hand but the real story is that he does it so he can keep an eye on what's going on in the area. There's no reason why anyone else should know about those arrangements either.'

'He works for you too?'

'He's a retired police officer who's glad to keep his hand in. I have several of those and they're on a confidential payroll. Some work normal hours, others part-time, the rest I call on sometimes. I refer to them as my ghosts.'

I knew I shouldn't ask this kind of question but did anyway. 'Are you absolutely sure of Dark Horse's loyalty?'

Rolt didn't seem to mind. 'Quite sure.'

'What is he going to do now?'

'Lie low. I need to think of the best way forward for him but I've a mind to pull him out altogether.'

I decided not to tell him that Patrick was hunting for him, and said, 'Have you any idea why he asked us where you are now and hinted that he didn't know where Piers lived?'

'That was clumsy. He knows where Piers lives – he's been here, to this house, because the Ashleys threw a big party when he left F9. Unfortunately I couldn't be present as I had no choice but to attend some wretched conference. But sometimes it's better to let your staff enjoy themselves without you. Perhaps he was testing you, seeing how much you knew already, how deeply involved you really are. You mustn't go by this man's appearance, you know. He's one of the best I have.'

I thought there was a distinct lack of proof in all this but, whatever the truth, it led us nowhere.

Six

The next morning, I again returned to Hinton Littlemore feeling that although I had enjoyed a pleasant day I had achieved little. The commander had finished by telling me that his doctor – in Woodford, that is – having been in contact with those who had treated him in Bath had forbidden him in a telephone conversation from going back to work for at least another week. Rolt had not seemed to be too worried about this and would obviously be briefed by his staff if and when necessary.

The Metropolitan Police had meanwhile reported that the men we were referring to as the Biddulph brothers had been of no known addresses, although Steve had lived rough but was thought at one time to have shared a bedsit in Bethnal Green with Kyle, his half-brother. The Met had lost track of the pair of them after they had been evicted for not paying the rent. Both had been known to have drink problems and prepared to do just about anything to get hold of it.

'They were probably regarded as expendable,' Patrick said during a phone call to me that evening. 'I reckon Dorney got them to do the dirty work with someone else – if there were indeed three of them. They probably got a couple of bottles of whisky each. Then, when he discovered, somehow, they had failed to kill Rolt, he got a kick out of stringing them up. But it's all conjecture – I might be quite wrong.'

'Surely the third man would have been the brains behind it as it doesn't sound as though they would have been that intelligent,' I said. 'And we still don't have the first idea how they knew where Rolt was going to be.'

'Perhaps you'd better go and ask at that pub where he stayed, The Lion and the Unicorn. Make it official.'

'Have you located Dark Horse?' I asked.

'No. It looks as though he's gone to ground, as he said he would. But he doesn't appear to be at the house I saw him enter – no one is. I'll give it another twenty-four hours – I can't spare any more time.'

The pub had obviously been built some time during Queen Victoria's reign and, from the outside at least, looked as though little had been done in the way of refurbishment since. But when I arrived at lunchtime the small car park was full and I was forced to leave the Range Rover half on a pile of gravel in one corner, something that these particular vehicles do not find a problem.

Within, it was warm and clean, a log fire crackling. The throng of customers all appeared to be eating and lunch suddenly seemed a very good idea after my frugal slice of toast, marmalade and coffee breakfast. I managed to find a small table and had a look at the menu. Pheasant casserole, chicken and mushroom pie, venison sausages, cold game pie and salad, and roast pork with all the trimmings were on offer. Little wonder Rolt had come here, for the man-food.

After relishing the said chicken and mushroom pie, I went to settle my bill and asked to speak to the manager. This request seemed to fluster the girl behind the bar and I had to assure her that I wasn't going to complain about anything. She told me that she would fetch Mr Fielding, who was actually the owner.

A man, probably in his late thirties, appeared from somewhere at the rear and, oddly, seemed to be immediately on the defensive as he said, 'John Fielding. What's the problem?'

'National Crime Agency,' I said, producing my warrant card. 'Congratulations on a wonderful pub.'

'Oh,' he said, looking relieved. 'Thanks.'

'On the twenty-third of last month a man was staying here and I'm not sure if he actually checked out, although I should imagine that all accounts would have been paid to you by now,' I began. 'Would you be good enough to check as I'm not sure if he was using his real name.'

'Dodgy then, eh?' Fielding replied with a knowing look.

'Far from it.'

He went away and came back with the register to ask, 'Was he on his own?'

'As far as we know.'

'Yes, here we are. There were two couples staying on that date and one bloke on his own. A Mr D. Rolt.'

'Had he stayed here before?'

'He can't have done as we've only just started

86

having paying guests and the previous owners didn't. I only bought this place a few months ago. It was pretty rundown – the kitchen contained just a filthy deep fat fryer and several microwave cookers.'

'So he might have found out about it on the Internet then.'

'That's perfectly possible as we have a good website. I've remembered what happened now. He'd been here for two nights and then went out one morning and we didn't see him again that day, or ever again for that matter. The next morning a man and a woman arrived, settled his bill and said that he'd been taken ill. They took his possessions with them, something I wasn't very happy about, but one of them showed me a police ID.'

'That was all perfectly OK,' I assured him as he still seemed to be uneasy. 'Were you aware of anyone visiting him here? Did you notice him talking to anyone or did anyone sit with him at mealtimes?'

Fielding shrugged. 'This is a very busy pub.'

When I merely smiled, he added, 'I'll ask the staff but I can't be sure exactly who was working during those days as they're mostly students.'

'But you must have records,' I said as he turned to go.

He gave me a crooked smile. 'They come, they go. Sometimes they turn up, sometimes they don't. I'm always on the phone begging someone to come to work.'

'Please also ask them if he mentioned where he was going or what he intended to do.'

He went away again and was gone for quite a while but had nothing to tell me when he returned.

'Did he tell *you* where he was going?' I persisted.

'No, but I'd noticed that he was wearing hiking gear at breakfast so assumed he intended to go walking.'

'And the previous day?'

'Er, yes, I think so.'

'Please try to remember. It's very important.'

Fielding stared into space for a few moments, and then said, 'Yes, I'm fairly sure he was now.'

'Sorry to go on about it, but he thinks he may have mentioned what he intended to do that day to someone here.'

'If he did I haven't a clue as to who that might have been.'

I had no choice but to leave it there and, a bit depressed that once again I had achieved nothing, I drove back home. Much later that day, Patrick arrived, having failed to locate his quarry even though he had worked most of the night, as he put it, 'dredging Hackney'.

Michael Greenway had been right: the case was stagnating.

James Carrick returned to work and perhaps due to *après*-flu depression was driven to make up for his absence by going through the nick and all cases outstanding therein like a firestorm. Lynn Outhwaite was almost reduced to tears after one such sally in her direction. Other personnel, I was given to understand, were going about their duties tight-lipped. I stayed away following a tip-off from my partner, who seriously fell out with the Scottish DCI – thankfully, in the comparative privacy of Carrick's office, Patrick tending to counter bad temper and unreasonableness with carefully selected blistering nouns and adjectives. Which always makes things worse.

This couldn't be allowed to continue.

An hour after Patrick had departed for work, his intended venue for this not mentioned, I borrowed Elspeth's car and drove into Bath not knowing, frankly, what I was going to find in what was supposed to be a powerhouse of keeping law and order.

I knocked, briefly, on the DCI's office door and, without waiting for a response, went in. I already knew he was there as I had heard him coughing as I approached.

'Good morning,' I said, having seated myself. Then, bloody-mindedly ignoring the fact that he looked pale, was thinner in the face and obviously still downright unwell, continued, 'If you don't sort this out – alienating all your loyal staff – I shall contact Commander Greenway and suggest he pays a visit and gives you and Patrick what would amount to a kick up the backside.'

OK, I had absolutely no idea about the protocols involved with this threat but it had sounded good to me.

Carrick stared hard at me for a moment and then glanced down. I detected a fleeting smile on his face.

'I should have expected something like this,' he murmured, running his fingers through his thick fair hair.

'I'm not taking sides,' I told him.

'No,' he agreed. 'You're always even-handed.'

I took this as an attempt to mollify me but, under the circumstances, could hardly blame him. There was a short silence, and then he continued, 'The Met has traced the next of kin of the hanging victims, Steve Biddulph and his half-brother, Kyle. Patrick's trying to find out a bit more about them in police records. The mother, plus a full brother to Steve, and a daughter, all have form and appear to live, on and off, at the same address in Bethnal Green – a rented flat over a dry-cleaners. I have an idea that man of yours is keen to undertake some surveillance on them and while he's in London have a last-ditch look for the F9 man.'

'Can I get you anything from the chemist's?' I asked.

'Thanks, but I'm up to my ears with all kinds of stuff already.'

'I could drive you home.'

'No, but thanks anyway.'

There seemed little point in staying longer so I rose to go.

'Ingrid?'

I turned.

'I'll try to fix things.'

Patrick was in the general office, having borrowed someone's desk who was on leave. At least, I hoped that the framed photograph of the busty young woman not wearing much on it wasn't his.

'That's Amethyst,' he informed me, seeing the direction of my gaze and speaking quietly

ut I'd rather thought my
ke that were over.'
try again?'
vords, and he can't really
got the impression he wants

g partner?'
lier in the week still applies.
difficult, you must bale out.'
greement.
hecking on Dark Horse – not
and raking Matt Dorney out of

s was a reminder to himself rather
to do with me.

into our usual hotel in the West End
ick jokingly put it, there was little
r camping out under a canal bridge.
went out a short while later we were
the same clothes as when we had
nconspicuously, like tourists. Patrick had
a camera with him to enhance the impres-
small one which could be slipped into a
pocket so as not to be an encumbrance.
had left the Range Rover at home and
led up by train as it is sometimes too
picuous. Taxis are anonymous and we took
to Hackney, asking to be put down near the
n hall. We would walk from there and planned
st to check on the house Patrick had seen Dark
orse enter. By this time it was a little after three
hirty and would get dark early due to a heavily
overcast sky.

as others were working in the room. 'I think they're getting married soon. He's booked the bouncy castle.' He then had a brief attack of man-giggles.

We were under serious pressure from the older children to arrange one of these as it was Mark's first birthday soon and they wanted to have a party. I was not winning the argument that he was far too young for that kind of thing.

'Have you seen Carrick?' Patrick went on to ask, cautiously.

I nodded. 'He's too ill to be at work.'

'I think everyone's agreed on that.'

'He intimated that you might be going to London to check up on the Biddulph twos' next of kin.'

'Well, nothing's being achieved here – there's no evidence locally.'

'I'd like to come with you this time.'

This was given consideration.

'I'm not even earning my part-time salary,' I pointed out.

'Just think of it from the point of view that your husband gets paid neither overtime nor danger money,' Patrick whispered with feeling.

I ignored the remark. 'Besides which, your battleaxe is bored on account of not having shot up any mobsters lately,' I added.

He gazed at me for a moment as if wondering if I was being flippant, a bad failing of mine, and probably decided that I was. Then he said, 'All right. Providing things don't get too hazardous – and you'll have to promise that you'll clear out if I tell you to.'

I promised and pulled up a chair.

'They're an obnoxious bunch,' Patrick went on to say, his eyes on the computer screen in front of him. 'As well as having had a half-brother, Kyle, Steve Biddulph had a full brother, Wayne. No one's quite sure but there's a Polish father in there somewhere who appears to have nothing at all to do with crime and probably bolted back to his native country when he saw the way things were working out. Wayne's been in trouble with the police for most of his life. Rumour has it that he's a member of a London gang. His sister, Ravenna, has done time for shoplifting on an industrial scale with a bunch of other women and was in trouble before that for being drunk and disorderly and assault. The mother, Donna Black, ran the shoplifting business and they sold the stuff through a market stall that also had legitimate stock – or at least it couldn't be proved that it wasn't. She was thought to be behind an acid attack on another stall-holder after some kind of disagreement, but again, nothing could be proved.'

'They're not going to take kindly to being questioned about the deaths.'

'The Met's already questioned them and the mother's upset and spitting mad about it but said she doesn't know anything. Whoever spoke to her thought she was lying, possibly out of fear. But she was adamant that she hadn't seen either Steve or Kyle for ages. As far as Wayne goes, she says she hasn't seen him for even longer and in her words "he's a good boy, really".'

'And the daughter?'

'Not around. Black said she didn't know where

she was. It w

one other

voices a

have a se

been a rad

'Are these

'No idea.'

'We could h

'There's mor

east London.'

'The nearest on

But there were

had to give his atten

said, he couldn't jus

leave others to deal w

this – much of it was v

of us plodded along w

week. Then, on that Frida

home and announced tha

weekend if necessary to fi

having just rung him to say

contacted.

'Rolt finally, *finally*, sound

Patrick added. 'He said he'd re

contacts in that area keep an eye

they haven't seen him either. The

helps on the flower stall as his

Rolt's "ghosts", also seems to have

map.'

'So?'

'So the bloke who just failed in c

couple of Dorney's mob into the Reger

will have to have another go at locating t

I appear to be the only person on the planet

'At the most, we have an hour and a half of useful daylight left,' Patrick commented as we walked, his thoughts uncannily echoing mine.

I tucked an arm through his. 'How are you going to refer to this man if you ring the doorbell and someone we don't know about answers it?'

'I mentioned that to Rolt. He said just ask for Phil.'

'And if they say he's not there?'

'How I play it depends on who answers the door.'

The shutters on the little flower stall were down and padlocked and it was comparatively quiet for London, the lull before shoppers and workers went home and then possibly got ready to go out again for the evening. We walked for fifteen minutes or so and then took a right turn into one of the thousands of practically identical residential roads of the capital. An unremarkable scene: terraced and semi-detached Victorian houses, pollarded trees, a fairly modern block of flats that had perhaps been built on a wartime bombsite, the defunct printworks Patrick had mentioned. It was still oddly quiet. A couple of cars went by and just a few pedestrians were in sight.

'Number twenty-three,' Patrick said.

As is our practice, we first went right by and carried on walking with no more than a passing glance. Nothing out of the ordinary could be seen. The place looked tidy if a little tired and in need of a coat of paint, but someone had recently cut the grass in the tiny front garden. Gardens say a lot about people, but then of course the landlord might have seen to it.

'For once in my life, I am going to be polite and ring the doorbell,' Patrick said when we had turned and were going back the way we had come. 'For one thing, it's a mid-terrace, there's no sideway and I'm not going to start poking around to find access to the rear.'

There were two doorbells for upper and lower flats but no nameplates to give an indication as to which one our quarry lived in. Patrick rang both twice and there was no response from either. I stepped to one side and, almost avoiding a variegated holly bush, looked through the only window on the ground floor at the front of the property. There was nothing to be seen in the dark interior except for the vague outlines of a sofa and a couple of armchairs. 'We can't just break in,' I said, rubbing my prickled arm.

Patrick was studying the locks on the front door. 'No, but I think I can open these without breaking anything.'

He has a set of what I call his 'burglar's keys', which successfully deal with everything but the most modern locks.

I said, 'I don't like it that Phil's chum seems to be out of circulation as well.'

'Neither do I and, as we know, they share this house.'

One of the locks had yielded to Patrick's efforts when the front door of the house to our left opened and a middle-aged man came out. 'What the hell are you doin'?' he demanded to know, hitching up the waistband of his sagging tracksuit bottoms over an impressive beer belly.

'Good afternoon,' Patrick said. 'Police.' He

produced his warrant card and gave it to me to show the man. 'Have you seen the people who live here lately?'

The man hardly glanced at it. 'Not for a coupla days. Can't say I'm surprised you're checking up on 'em, though. A right pair of dodgy characters.'

'Who did you see?'

'I don't know their names. The younger, ugly one.'

'Can you remember exactly which day it was you saw him?'

'It mighta bin Sunday – no, Monday.'

'And it's Saturday now, so that's actually about five days ago.'

The man shrugged disinterestedly. 'Time flies, dunnit?'

'Have you noticed other people going in and out?'

'No.'

'No one hanging around in the past few days?'

'No. I've got better things to do, ain't I, than snoopin' on the neighbours.'

'OK, thanks,' Patrick said and proceeded to stare him right off his own threshold and back indoors. The door slammed.

After a little more careful wrangling, the second lock opened. Patrick pushed the door wide without entering and hot air with an unpleasant musty smell gusted out. We exchanged glances and he moved to go in but paused to signal to me to stay where I was.

I didn't have to be asked twice: I had a horrible feeling what the smell was.

About half a minute later, Patrick came out, looking rather pale, took a deep breath of fresh air and went back in again. After another short period of time had elapsed, I looked through the open doorway and heard a faint hissing sound, seemingly coming from upstairs. But there was no smell of gas, and I then saw that water was running down the stairs to form a small lake in the hall. I took hold of my mobile phone in my jacket pocket.

Patrick reappeared from the direction of what was presumably the kitchen. 'One in the bathroom of the upper flat, hanging from the shower – it's been torn out of the wall with the weight of the body – and one just outside the back door strung up from a pergola,' he said, coming right out into the open for more fresh air. 'They'd been shot before they were strung up and have been dead for days. The heating seems to be on full blast.'

To make sure that the corpse inside the house started to decompose? This was utterly horrible.

Commander Rolt had been immediately notified and announced that he would return from Ashleigh Coombe without delay, arranging for someone to bring him to London as he was not yet permitted to drive. Although Patrick met him there, I was not present when he visited the crime scene later that night as I had made a short statement and returned to the hotel.

'Against what I gather was fairly fierce female opposition, Piers Ashley did the driving,' Patrick told me when he arrived in our hotel room. 'Must have a shower – I can still smell those bodies.'

So could I, on his clothes. I put everything he

had been wearing in one of the large plastic bags we carry for that purpose and secured the top. Then I contacted room service and ordered some food for him. Only sandwiches were available at this time of night.

'The Ashleys simply can't face the thought of Piers getting involved again,' I said, carrying on with the conversation when Patrick appeared in his bathrobe.

He tackled the sandwiches. 'Thanks for getting these. His mother in particular can't. Thea wanted to bring Rolt in her car but big brother said no.'

'Poor Thea. She's actually four years older than Piers. Elizabeth told me.'

'I honestly don't think he was being controlling. Just doesn't want her to be exposed to any danger, not even London's traffic system.'

'*And* she has her own business in the city.'

After a pause, Patrick said, 'D'you mind if we talk about these latest murders in the morning?'

I told him that I would rather not have to think about them again tonight either.

Seven

'Perhaps it was unwise for Rolt to visit the crime scene personally,' I commented as we were going down for an early breakfast. 'Someone might have been watching the house, I mean.'

'F9 had thought of that too and there were a couple of hefty armed minders with him,' Patrick replied. 'He'd gone to HQ first.'

'I should imagine that he was pretty upset to have lost people in those circumstances, never mind having described Dark Horse – Phil – as being one of his best men.'

'Almost certainly, but no one last night would have guessed – he could have been carved from granite.'

'It's absolutely ghastly,' I murmured.

'The worst thing is that the perpetrator – Dorney? – knew where they lived. And why kill them? Did Dorney, if he was responsible, suspect Dark Horse of being an informer, or a cop, after all, and the other man just happened to be on the premises and had to be dealt with too? There'll be a massive manhunt set in motion now, of course, but that doesn't make it any easier for Rolt. His whole department's on the line.'

'But where does it leave you?'

'Well, I've found him, end of mission,' Patrick replied sadly. 'But, forcing myself to be practical, this latest crime is just an added incentive to catch those who attacked Rolt. That was my original brief and there has to be a connection. It's not my job to investigate these latest murders, although I'm sure I'll occasionally bump into those who are. My regret is that I didn't break into that house when I was here before.'

'I think the man next door knows more than he made out.'

We were directed towards a table by a window and Patrick immediately requested another in a corner of the room. A very slim chance perhaps but there is no point in offering yourself as a target to any particular member of the criminal fraternity who has a grievance.

'The Met are bound to interview him,' Patrick said when we were seated, gazing at the menu. 'Kippers,' he announced before glancing across at me. 'What are you having?'

'You need to go back there and pin him to the wall by his ears.'

A husbandly frown. 'Figuratively speaking, I hope.'

'You're perfectly entitled to,' I persisted.

'I'll think about it.'

'Or we could question Donna Black about her horrible brood.'

'I think it would be preferable to undertake some surveillance first as I have an idea questioning them again will not yield anything new. And I'll probably ask the Met to do that – but not this weekend.'

'So your next line of investigation is what?'

Patrick was rescued from responding to my, on

reflection, very unfair badgering of him so early in the morning by his mobile ringing. He left the table, and the dining room, to speak to whoever it was. We both dislike people who conduct conversations on their phones in public places, especially restaurants, and avoid doing so whenever possible.

'That was Carrick,' Patrick said when he returned. 'There's been what might be a breakthrough. A man was arrested in Bath city centre last night for committing criminal damage – he'd wrenched a litter bin from its fittings on a lamp post and thrown it through a shop window. Drunk, I gather. This character has been used as a snout in the past, quite a good one apparently as he's prepared to sell anyone and everyone down the river for a few quid. He's trying to buy his way out of being charged – seems quite keen to talk, in fact – by offering details of someone he knows who heard news of a senior cop in a pub in the city and told a mobster chum in London. It's all a bit vague but someone on Carrick's team got out of him the name of the pub: The Lion and the Unicorn. Carrick suggested leaving him to sleep it off today and we can question him tomorrow morning.'

'You've made it up with him over your disagreement, then,' I said hopefully.

'We're going to buy each other a tot. He said I could swear almost as well as he does.'

I wondered that if the senior cop in question had been Rolt, how had this 'someone' known his identity?

* * *

102

It was a dull, chilly morning, even in the interview room, and I shivered.

'Litter bins through shop windows are not my concern,' Patrick was saying, having formally opened the interview. 'I can't do any deals with you either as that's the responsibility of the senior officer here, the DCI. I can only recommend leniency if I think you've offered us valuable information. And be warned, I'm very good at recognizing a load of horse feathers.'

The man in front of us, one Bernie Mason, didn't look as though he had lost his hangover. I supposed he was in his fifties but could have been older. The several days' growth of beard, bloodshot eyes and general appearance of needing a thoroughly good scrub with strong disinfectant intended for drains said it all really. But he appeared to be no fool and was openly eyeing up Patrick, assessing his chances with him. I got the impression that his findings improved neither his mood nor his headache.

'I don't remember the bin bit,' he said after quite a long pause.

'The CCTV camera has a good record of it, though,' he was coolly told.

'Oh.' Then, 'Bloody things are everywhere these days.'

'They can be inconvenient,' Patrick conceded. 'Tell me about this chum you say heard about a top cop staying in a pub.'

'I don't remember saying that either.'

'Well, you did, last night when you were arrested for causing criminal damage.'

'Oh.' He rubbed his hands over the stubble on

103

his face. 'God, I'm a mess. That was really stupid – I don't usually do stupid things like chucking bins around.'

'And I have to tell you that the top cop in question *might* be the victim of a local attack, someone who was almost killed not all that long ago. If it is and you withhold information, we're straying into the territory of your being an accessory to attempted murder.'

'Hey, it's nothing to do with me and the bloke I'm on about isn't a chum of mine at all! He owes me fifty quid!'

Presumably that made dropping him in it all right.

Patrick continued, 'You also said that he'd contacted a mobster associate in London. I want your source's name and also the name of the person he contacted.'

'I haven't a clue who he spoke to. He didn't say.'

'So this isn't hearsay – you got this information from him personally.'

'Yeah. I looked him up and asked him for the money, didn't I? He said I'd get it when he got paid for the tip-off about the cop.'

'Has he paid you?'

'Nah, the bastard's gone off somewhere.'

As is our normal practice, I had been introduced as a note-taker but so far there had been nothing interesting for me to jot down. Right now, I wasn't looking at Patrick, but was sure that he was giving Mason a 'you don't have to feel guilty at making life a bit uncomfortable for him then, do you?' smile.

'He owes me,' Mason said dully, staring at a point somewhere in the middle of the table between us.

'Why did he tell you about it?' I asked.

Mason looked at me for the first time. 'He thought I might be able to use the info and get something from you lot when I needed to – currency, if you get me – and would forget about the money he owed me. Fat chance. I don't operate like that. And from the way he spoke, I got the idea that he had some kind of grudge against this London mobster, perhaps for not paying him for the last time he did something for him.'

'You reckon he works regularly for this man?'

'I think he might have been more active, like, in the past but had packed it all in and moved out. God knows and that might be all wrong. I'm guessing. A man of few words is Wayne.'

'Wayne?' Patrick repeated.

Mason groaned. 'Didn't mean to let on yet. Yeah, Wayne.'

'Surname?'

'Dunno. Someone said he has several names. Fancies himself as some kind of big man – a crime lord, for God's sake. Really thick – just like the other bloke he had with him once who he said was his half-brother, Kyle. Not a brain cell between 'em.'

Patrick leaned forward and stared intently at him. 'Do you know how he had a good idea this man he'd seen in The Lion and the Unicorn was a police officer?'

'You will put in a good word for me, won't you?'

'Yes, I will.'

'Only cops don't always do what they say.'

'You have my word.'

'The barman told him. He'd overheard a mobile phone conversation or something like that. I'm guessing again. Dunno what it was, really.'

'It was a man, not a girl?'

'Yeah, a bloke.'

'D'you have anything else to say?' Patrick enquired when Mason had gone quiet but looked uneasy.

'Yeah. But . . .'

'But what?'

'There's no guarantee there's any truth in it.'

'Let me worry about that.'

'It's just a rumour – rubbish, most likely.'

'Spit it out.'

In an undertone, Mason said, 'Word has it that Kyle and another member of his family – could've been another brother – did a job for this mobster not long after Wayne blabbed to me. But they screwed it up and it was them what got strung up in the hills somewhere. I don't believe it but it never said in the papers who the bodies were, did it?'

'No,' Patrick agreed.

'Was it them?'

'I'm afraid I can't discuss another criminal investigation with you.'

'It was them then. God. And Wayne's gone to ground. I'll never get my dosh back now, will I?'

* * *

106

'The three of them,' Patrick muttered as we were making our way back down the stairs, having given James Carrick our immediate findings. 'Steve, his brother Wayne and half-brother Kyle. Steve and Kyle are dead. Wayne must be hiding out somewhere locally as I can't believe he has the money to go anywhere else. It's imperative we find him.'

'Before Dorney does,' I said.

'That too. Although I can't imagine what grounds he'd have for getting rid of him if he gave him the tip-off about Rolt in the first place.'

'Just to tidy things up, then.'

'You're probably right. And as far as the barman goes, it's not a crime to whisper in the ear of a local villain that one of the customers is probably a police officer, is it?'

'Probably not,' I replied.

'Pity.'

Over the phone, it was quickly established from John Fielding, the owner of The Lion and the Unicorn, that he did employ a part-time barman, Paul Bradley, a fact he had omitted to mention to me, he had said, due to an oversight. It was arranged that we would talk to this man when he was next on duty, that same evening. I had a feeling his meeting with Patrick would not be a happy one.

We were having coffee in a nearby bistro when Patrick had a call from Commander Greenway. Patrick said little and, from what I could hear, Greenway sounded angry. Finally Patrick rang off and smacked his phone down on the table.

'Does he want you back there when we've only

just returned?' I said, preparing to get very annoyed.

'Apparently Rolt is demanding a face-to-face, detailed breakdown tomorrow morning of where I looked when I was searching for Dark Horse. He seems to be blaming me for his death as I failed to find him until it was too late.'

'But you were looking for him before Rolt asked you to as you were going to get the real story out of him.'

'That's exactly what I intend to point out.'

'You did go to the house where they lived.'

'Yes, and although there was no sign of anyone being there I didn't feel then, as I've said before, that the situation demanded that I break in. Perhaps I should have done.'

'Patrick, these people should look after their own personnel!'

'I got the impression that's exactly what Greenway said to Rolt. However . . .'

'And I really don't see why you should have to suffer two men with ego problems.'

'No chance. I shall have to catch a train. Please go and talk to that barman later. Give him hell and, if you think he's bent, tell Carrick.'

The pub was as busy at eight thirty that evening as it had been on the previous occasion I had been there. Deciding, regretfully, that it would give the wrong impression if I had even a small glass of wine, I waited until he was free and then approached the unsmiling individual behind the bar.

'Paul Bradley?' I enquired.

'That's me,' he answered, wiping the counter with a cloth without looking up.

I put my ID under his nose. 'I'd like a word with you.'

He gave me a look that slid away and said, 'Can't you come back when I'm off-duty?'

'No. Besides which, if you were off-duty you wouldn't be here, would you?'

'You can find me at my flat in Oldfield Park. I finish at ten thirty.' This with an infuriating smirk.

'I'll make you an offer. We can talk here or down at the nick.'

His pale blue eyes bored into me for a second or so, and then he said, 'I'll have to find someone to take over for a few minutes.'

When he had done this, the young woman appearing who had been serving behind the bar the first time I had visited the place, he led the way to a small storeroom next to the kitchen and closed the door behind us. I opened it again as I never like being shut up with men who are regarded as potential suspects.

'I don't want anyone to hear our conversation,' Bradley said.

'Why not?' I snapped. 'What do you have to hide?'

'Long ears work here, that's all,' he muttered.

'I want you to think back a few weeks,' I said. 'We're investigating the circumstances surrounding a serious assault near Hinton Littlemore. Someone we've interviewed since then has said that a man he knows was told, by you, that a customer here was a police officer.'

'No, not me, I don't gossip.'

'He has nothing to gain by telling us this and I believe him. Were you given money in exchange for the information?'

'I've just told you, it wasn't me!'

'So are you particularly good at guessing people's professions or did you overhear a phone call?'

'You're not listening to me!'

'I am, and you're lying.'

'Just go away and leave me alone.'

'Been had up recently for speeding lately? Involved in pub stock going out of the back door?' I demanded to know, not bothering to lower my voice. There had to be some reason or other why he looked so shifty.

He looked really taken aback at this and for a moment I thought he was about to run from the room, but he just stood there, hands clenched by his sides. Perhaps he was wondering if the law would regard as more serious shoving aside someone who worked for the NCA rather than an ordinary cop.

'I'm not on the make,' he got out finally.

'Good. What was it then?'

After a long pause, he said, 'He gave me a tenner. OK, I was angry. I got done for drink-driving a while back. The cops came down on me really hard.'

'Not for the first time?'

'Er, no. Then I had a few beers one night and thought it would be a good idea to rough one up a bit – give him a dose of his own medicine, like.'

'Surely the officers who pulled you over didn't actually knock you about.'

'No. Anyway, a bloke I know – he's a really rough lad – said he knew someone who would.'

'What's his name?'

'I'm not going to drop him in it.'

'We know about him and he's already dropped in it. I just want confirmation.'

Bradley sighed wearily. 'OK, it's Wayne somebody. I don't know his surname. No real friend of mine, though. I don't go around with crooks.'

But he had been quite happy to recruit one in order to seriously hurt someone. I said, 'What does he look like?'

'He's nondescript really.'

'That's not very helpful. Colour of hair and eyes? Height? Thin? Fat?'

'OK, he's got mousey-brown, scruffy hair, like his clothes. Pale blue eyes, about five foot five, skinny. Yeah, nondescript.'

'How old d'you reckon he is?'

Bradley shrugged dismissively. 'Twenty-five, perhaps older. Hard to tell, really. He never looks very well, has a grey sort of face.'

'Was it an educated guess on your part that the man in question was a police officer? Had he a certain manner about him? Authoritative? Perhaps spoke a bit sharply to you, reminding you of your past brush with the law?'

'In a way, but . . .'

'Go on.'

'A woman came asking for him, by name.'

In view of Rolt's position, that had been stupid of her.

111

Bradley went on, 'He was in the guests' lounge – it's more like a big cupboard really – on his own, I think, and I heard her call out, "How's my lovely commander, then?" I think he shushed her but can't be absolutely sure.'

Staggeringly stupid.

'I thought for a moment that he might be a navy bloke – there are lots of those in Bath working at the Ministry of Defence places – but then she went on to say something like when the cat's away the crooks do play. Then one of them must have shut the door as I couldn't hear any more.'

Rolt had said nothing about this encounter. Had he forgotten? His head injury might have affected his memory. Or had he not wanted his lady friend to be involved in any way?

'Where does this Wayne live?' I asked.

'Dunno.'

'You must have some idea.'

'No, really. He's the sort of bloke to live in a squat.'

'No family home, then.'

'I have an idea he got chucked out a while back and that's why he's in this area. He started off in London but pops home sometimes – quite recently, I seem to remember he said. His ma tolerates him for a while as long as he gives her a fistful of money every time he turns up.'

If true, his mother was a liar as well as quite a few other unpleasant things.

'I have cooperated, haven't I?' Bradley then went on to say sullenly.

I didn't put his mind at rest on this and told

him that I would have to report what he had told me and it was not my decision whether matters were taken any further.

It was a relief to leave and I was not at all sure that he had divulged everything he knew. But the lack of real progress was irksome and it was then that I decided to follow him when he left work.

The Lion and the Unicorn was on the left-hand side of the Wells Road, otherwise known as Wellsway, which rose quite sharply from the city centre, having gone beneath the low viaduct over which runs one of the main railway lines from London to Bristol. A short distance beyond the public house, the land fell away into a steep-sided valley. If Bradley had been telling the truth about where he lived, all he had to do when he left work was cross the road and walk down the hill for half a mile or so. There seemed little point in his using a car, even if he still had one after the drink-driving episode, because, as I had already noted, the pub car park was extremely small and the road outside had double yellow lines. I'd had to park in a side road some distance away.

Disinclined for several very good reasons not to hang around in the immediate vicinity but having a longish wait of at least an hour and a half, I left the car where it was and, on foot, took the route that I thought he would take if he was going straight home. Not far from the corner of the road I expected him to turn into, I went into another pub with a ground-floor veranda that, bizarrely, faced the busy road. I bought myself an orange juice and lemonade, sat partly concealed behind a large and on-the-point-of-death potted plant, where I could keep watch, and braced myself to inhale rather a lot of traffic fumes. If he came this way, I would see him.

He didn't.

Eight

I got home at just after eleven thirty, tired, cross and with a headache from the vehicle exhaust. It was perfectly possible that Bradley's route home was via little paths between the houses that I didn't know about or he could have worked late, called in to see someone, done anything. He could also have stopped off to warn Wayne Biddulph, or whatever he liked to be known as, that the police were asking questions about him. It also occurred to me that the owner of the pub might have mentioned to his barman that someone was coming to interview him.

I left a message on Patrick's phone about my meeting with the barman, heard nothing back from him and the next morning, early, phoned James Carrick and gave him exactly the same news. He was obviously very busy and merely said that he would make a note of it.

'Look,' I said, 'if Patrick had been there he would have arrested him. I don't have the power of arrest now, although, as you know, I did when we were with SOCA, and have informed you at the earliest opportunity as I wouldn't bother you at home. He was involved in the attack on Rolt.'

'Right, I'll look into it,' was all the DCI would promise.

There seemed to be nothing else that I could usefully do in connection with the case, so I prepared to go back to being a mother who wrote books when she could find the time.

Bugger everything.

That afternoon, Patrick rang me. 'At last, F9 have sent me a list of places, only three, that Dorney's mob have been known to use for meetings which Dark Horse – Phil – had reported to them. It was a while back so might be such old news that it's useless. Gangs move around. I intend to pay a visit to all three in a very quiet way to try to get an idea if they might still be in use.'

'For God's sake, be careful,' I said.

'I will. A couple are no more than semi-derelict warehouses on a development site – F9 was good enough to tell me where to find them. The other appears to be someone's home address in a block of flats. All have been kept under surveillance at various times but it doesn't seem that Phil was apprised of the dates of meetings and, if you remember, he told us that he wasn't regarded as sufficiently senior to be allowed to attend them. Who knows, they might not have trusted him right from the start.'

I asked him what had happened during his meeting with Rolt.

'Greenway insisted that we meet in his office on the grounds that one of his staff was involved. I gave them the full story, asked if they had any problems with it – they hadn't – and I then told Rolt what the barman had said to you.'

'Ouch.'

'Yes, thanks for that bit of intelligence. Rolt looked a bit sheepish and admitted that he'd deliberately not mentioned his lady friend visiting him as he thought the likelihood of it contributing to what had happened to him was off the scale. Greenway wasn't at all happy about that but everyone managed not to lose their tempers, and then I suggested that we have lunch together. We did.'

Thereby cementing their perception that although he only had the nominal rank of constable to enable him to make arrests, he had in fact once been in a position to command a regiment or battalion. More importantly, there was every chance that he had healed what had threatened to be a rift between the two.

'I have reservations about all this,' Patrick continued. 'From what Rolt said, Dorney has a fixation about him and wants him dead. It seems to be a huge coincidence that he happened to stay at a pub where a barman works who happened to mention to another man with connections to Dorney that a senior policeman was staying there. It's far more likely that either they already knew he was expected or Rolt went there as he was in possession of certain intelligence about the place and isn't telling us.'

The latter of which would figure. 'Too many coincidences,' I agreed.

'Please don't talk to that barman again. It's too risky as he might be in it up to his neck. Carrick can organize that.'

Not wishing to be accused of causing the case to – using Greenway's description again – stagnate, I immediately drove into Bath and called in to see James Carrick.

'Wayne, possibly calling himself Biddulph,' I said after greeting him briefly. 'He appears to be in the Bath area. I think the barman at that pub has a better idea of where he can be found than he admitted and, right now, he might be the key to the whole case.'

The DCI still wasn't up to flying speed and sighed. 'I can ask Lynn to talk to him if you like.'

'I was going to suggest you send a couple of heavyweight CID constables to accost him as he leaves work.'

'Our embedded NCA officer, who would suit the role admirably, appears to be elsewhere,' Carrick observed slightly sarcastically.

'Patrick's undertaking surveillance on some addresses in London that F9 sent him where Matt Dorney's gang has been known to meet – in other words get drunk, take drugs and listen to what the boss has to say while all the cops are filling in risk assessment forms.'

'Would you care for a cup of tea, hen?' he enquired, straight-faced.

I was forced to smile. 'Embedded NCA bloke's other half having a hissy fit, eh?'

We went to a nearby café.

'OK, I'll send a couple of someones to lean on him,' Carrick promised over tea and biscuits.

I said, 'I'd really appreciate that as Patrick has asked me not to speak to him again on safety grounds: mine. And he thinks there are far too many coincidences surrounding these mobsters knowing where Rolt was.'

'That had actually occurred to me. I've had a

suspicion for a while that information might have preceded the commander's visit. We'll see what Bradley says this time.'

But again, Bradley failed to be where expected and, when questioned, John Fielding, the owner of the pub, merely shrugged, said that he hadn't turned up for work and described him as erratic and unreliable. In receipt of his address the two constables duly 'attended' and, having obtained a key from a neighbour, found the first-floor flat in a state that suggested it had been ransacked, with no sign of the owner.

Carrick sent in a scenes-of-crime team, who immediately discovered spots of blood on the living-room wall, which were recent, and more on the carpet in the hallway. It was hoped that forensic testing on further potential evidence that was found – several hairs thought to be human caught in a damaged corner of one of the eye-level kitchen units and a half-smoked cigarette that had been stubbed out in the bathroom wash-basin – would provide clues and DNA evidence. Meanwhile, house-to-house questioning was put into place.

On the Friday evening, two days later and when there was no news concerning Bradley, Patrick returned home. This wasn't a complete surprise as he had rung me to say he had learned practi-cally nothing from his reconnaissance and needed a weekend break. I told him about Bradley's disappearance.

'Does he live on his own?' he asked.

'He appears to. Fielding didn't think he was

married and he'd not mentioned a girlfriend. Not mentioned any friends at all, in fact.'

'Fielding seems very vague about his staff for an employer. No idea if or when they're going to turn up, and nothing about their circumstances.'

'I get the impression he's only really interested in the business side of things.'

'Um. What does he look like?'

'Middle-aged, medium height, brown hair and eyes – quite unremarkable, really. He was edgy, a bit shifty, really, and I felt the same as I did when I spoke to the barman – there was something about both of them that I didn't like. There was a couple of days' stubble on his face, greying. The description could fit thousands of men.'

'I was wondering if it was worth running a check on him, that's all.'

We then had an influx of children, the two eldest on their way to have dinner with their grandparents, then Carrie carrying Mark, who wouldn't settle, then Vicky to say goodnight – Patrick was later than usual – and Justin who had been playing football at school and was tired, curling up on the sofa at his father's side. I offered to give Carrie a chance to have her evening meal by relieving her of Mark and he immediately went to sleep in my arms.

'Was it a complete waste of time you following up the info that F9 sent you?' I enquired in a whisper in case I woke the baby.

'They were very tidy for places that were reputed to be the haunt of criminals. None of the usual filthy mess they leave behind that I don't have to spell out to you. There was just general rubbish, stuff perhaps in connection with what the buildings had originally been used for.'

'You think it could have been false information?'

'I don't know what to think. Whoever owns them might have had a bit of a tidy up with a view to selling.'

'What about the place that sounded like a private address?'

'It may well have been at one time. There's just a large hole in the ground there now with a security fence round it.'

'Did you have to break in to the warehouses?'

'Yes. Got arrested at one of them when I set off some alarm or other.'

I laughed.

'I soon got unarrested, though,' he said with a chuckle. 'Is that a word?'

'You know it isn't.'

'In fact, it meant I could quiz the guys in the area car about what went on round there. They didn't know of any iffy activities other than local youths trying to set fire to the place.'

We had just finished eating when Elizabeth Ashley rang. I took the call in the kitchen.

'I'm really sorry to bother you,' she began, 'but has Piers contacted you at all? He took Commander Rolt back to London and hasn't been in touch except for a quick call to say that they'd arrived safely. I'm getting rather worried.'

I told her that he hadn't called me personally, that she ought to speak to Patrick and took the phone through to him. A couple of minutes later, he brought it back looking worried.

'Why do I have a bad feeling about this?' he said.

It wasn't the kind of question that needed an answer so I merely suggested that he might be looking up old chums in the Met.

'Or old foes. The more involved I get with F9 the more complicated everything gets, but I'm not the man's minder.' He went away again saying things under his breath that he didn't intend me to hear and later told me that he'd contacted Rolt. As we had come to expect, the commander, having thanked Patrick, was non-committal.

Further news was not helpful either. That same evening a DI from the Met rang to tell Patrick that there was no 'worthwhile' evidence which would point to the identity of the killer in the Hackney house where Phil and the other man, named as Harry Wainwright, had been found murdered. In his view, it had been the work of a professional hitman or men, those who endeavoured to leave no forensic traces in their wake.

Patrick continued, 'Both victims had been shot several times in the chest from point-blank range before they were strung up. That suggests they may have been unconscious on the floor when it happened as there were heavy bloodstains on the living-room carpet in the ground-floor flat. We'll know more when the detailed PM results are published.'

'A lone killer, do you think?'

'In this case, possibly not. If you kill someone

outdoors of course you aren't in the position of having to gain entry to a building, which would further suggest that the killer had an assistant to help overpower them first.'

'That could have been Dorney himself. Piers Ashley said that he doesn't trust anyone and keeps a close watch on what he regards as big jobs.'

'You may well be right. He might have kept these killings in-house and has given up on hiring hitmen from abroad. We've already thought that he might have been in on the other hangings.'

Even though James Carrick had asked for the DNA results on Paul Bradley's flat to be given priority, it was three days before they came through, the lab apparently being 'busy'. Samples, including a tiny fragment of human skin taken from the damaged corner of the eye-level kitchen unit, were found to match hairs on a comb in the bathroom which it seemed sensible to assume until proved otherwise were Bradley's. DNA in the spots of blood found in the hallway and elsewhere also matched. Carrick had already thought that it was fairly safe to conclude that the stubbed-out cigarette was not as a result of any action by the owner of the property as the flat was otherwise clean and tidy and there was no evidence there to suggest that Bradley smoked. He was probably right: DNA in traces of saliva on the cigarette end were not thought to be from the same source, but it was such a tiny sample that was the best present technology could achieve.

'Evidence suggests that he was knocked about in several parts of the flat,' the DCI continued after giving us this information when we called in on Monday morning to see if there were any updates. 'One can surmise that it was either punishment or to subdue him. My money's on the latter as the man's obviously not there, so I reckon they took him with them.'

I had an awful picture in my mind's eye of a man kicked and punched by several others, sometimes managing to break away but relentlessly pursued until he was virtually unconscious.

Patrick said, 'Unless he got away and did a runner. Did the neighbours see or hear anything?'

Carrick shook his head gloomily. 'No, they all seem to be the kind of people who lock and bolt their doors, close the curtains and would be deaf and blind even if mass murder was going on nearby.'

'Motive, though?' I queried. 'Because the police spoke to him? And who knew about that except possibly his boss at the pub, John Fielding? He'd hardly have been broadcasting it to all and sundry.'

'I think we ought to concentrate on finding out where this man is, dead or alive,' Patrick said soberly. 'If he's alive he might be in great danger.'

'*Someone* at the pub must have an idea where he'd go if he was free to do so,' I said. 'Surely people working together mention family, relatives, friends . . .'

'I agree,' Patrick said. 'Shall we talk to them?' This question had been addressed to the DCI.

'Anything that results in progress,' he replied.

The cleaners were busy at The Lion and the Unicorn and, despite apologizing for having to tread on it, we got black looks from the man swabbing down the tiled entrance porch with a mop. A woman with a vacuum cleaner switched it off when she saw us and in response to the enquiry told us that Fielding was in his office.

When he caught sight of me, the man got to his feet with every sign of weary resignation. Sticking to our working practice, I introduced Patrick as my senior colleague and we both sat down on a couple of chairs at the side of the room without being invited to.

Patrick began by saying, 'Paul Bradley, your barman, is missing and evidence at his flat points to his having been seriously assaulted. Has he contacted anyone here?'

Fielding shook his head. 'God knows.'

'You don't seem to be too concerned.'

'Staff come, staff go – mostly go. I'm not a social worker. It takes all my time running this business and organizing the chef to get the food right.'

'We shall have to question whoever turns up for work.'

'As long as you don't stop them working.'

Patrick leaned forward and spoke quietly and venomously. 'Mr Fielding, this man is not only implicated in a serious attack on a senior police officer who was staying here but right now might be *dead*.'

Fielding made no reply to this and Patrick pressed on with: 'He talks to a man by the name of Wayne – we're not sure which surname he uses – who drinks here. Do you know the person I mean?'

125

'I've thousands of customers,' Fielding stated flatly.

'He's around five foot five, has pale blue eyes, mousey-brown hair, is of thin build and has an unhealthy-looking complexion,' I snapped. 'A criminal who appears to be welcome here.'

'I seem to welcome senior cops, though,' Fielding said with a superior smile. He still hadn't had a recent shave.

Patrick shot to his feet. 'Right, we'll continue this conversation down at the nick.'

'Whoa!' exclaimed Fielding. 'I didn't say I wouldn't answer the question.'

'Then answer it!' Patrick shouted at him without sitting down again.

'Yes, I do know who you mean,' Fielding admitted. 'And I suppose he could be described as a regular. But I don't know his surname. You tend not to unless they take part in quizzes and things like that. I have to say I've never liked the look of him but can't afford to be fussy unless people cause trouble.'

'Can you tell us anything else about him?' I asked, Patrick prowling around the room like something that ought to be in a cage but wasn't.

'I have an idea that he's a window cleaner by trade.'

'Does he work for a company or is he freelance?'

'On his own, I think. More of an odd-job man really, I suppose.'

'Does he clean the windows here?'

'No, people like that are usually unreliable. I have a contract with a Bristol outfit.'

Patrick sat down again and said, 'Do you have any idea where he lives?'

'Not a clue. But somewhere a bit basic, I should think.'

No one seemed to have yet turned up for work, so we had to postpone interviewing any other members of staff and left.

'Bradley thought Wayne might live in a squat,' I recalled as we headed to where we had left the car. 'And now this man says it's probably somewhere basic. There can't be too many places like that in Bath now.'

'It might be worth investigating those that there are,' Patrick conceded.

I have become known for what my dear father used to call my 'cat's whiskers' – a certain intuition and, when my hand was on the passenger-door handle, it leapt in with a big idea.

Patrick, now in the driving seat, opened the window on my side. 'Are you going to try something different by travelling on the roof?'

I got in the car. 'Why did Rolt come to *that* pub? He must be quite wealthy, is cultured, the kind of man to enjoy the good things in life and there are any number of beautiful country house hotels in this area as well as upmarket places in the city itself. OK, the food's good but not exactly haute cuisine.'

'We didn't ask him but guessed he'd looked up somewhere to stay on the Internet.'

'It still isn't logical. If the tiny car park's full you can't even park anywhere nearby and he has a Jag – prime material to be stolen.'

'OK, we'll ask him.'

I persisted with, 'Is he sufficiently married to the job to combine a few days off with having a sniff round an area where undercover people have suggested certain mobsters might be moving their zone of operations? If you're going to do that you wouldn't necessarily stay at an exclusive hotel.'

'If that is the case and he's not been straight with us I shall give him hell,' Patrick grimly promised.

Nine

There was no immediate opportunity to confront the commander, however, as Patrick realized, possibly reluctantly, that he ought to give priority to helping Bath CID find Paul Bradley and locate Wayne. The latter, from a pragmatic point of view, was the more pressing.

Carrick's team was still engaged in house-to-house enquiries but completed what were regarded as all possibly fruitful addresses that same day and Patrick cajoled James Carrick into getting them to check derelict, boarded-up and otherwise seemingly empty properties within a fairly small radius of the city centre. There were far more of them than anyone thought. Two days later, all the search had netted were several illegal immigrants, one needing urgent hospital treatment, more than a few dropouts – two of whom were arrested as they closely fitted descriptions of people wanted in connection with crime – and a starving cat with kittens, the RSPCA duly informed.

Patrick paid a visit to the city's planning office with a view to getting any insider knowledge on other properties due to be demolished, redeveloped or known to harbour unwanted guests, and got nowhere. It seemed unreasonable to take up any more valuable police time in searching wider afield and, more tellingly, Carrick had gone off the idea.

'Try the Salvation Army,' I suggested during a phone call while I was in the process of preparing a chicken and pasta bake for the younger children's tea. Unless it's Friday, Matthew and Katie usually eat with us so I was actually making two – one medium-sized one and another larger one to finish cooking later. I prefer to call this meal 'dinner' but they think 'tea' sounds much better as then they'll definitely get something along the lines of chocolate cake or ice cream for 'afters'. Not necessarily.

'Really?' queried a tired-sounding husband.

'They tend to know where people are living rough.'

'Any idea where they can be found?'

'Try Google,' I said, leaping to move a boiling saucepan on the Rayburn before it erupted all over the hob. 'Sorry, I must go.'

I heard nothing more from him and he didn't come home at the expected time. Feeling a bit guilty and thinking that I had given him what amounted to a brush-off, I supervised the younger ones' meal and then rang his mobile. I just got voicemail and could think of no valid reason to leave a message. Matthew and Katie were hanging around hungrily by this time, even though they had had bread and butter with strawberry jam when they got home from school, so I gave them their dinner as well before it was spoilt.

'Dad said he'd help me with my history homework tonight,' Matthew said. 'It's about the Battle of Lansdown.'

'But it's not as if he was *there*,' Katie pointed

out in superior fashion. 'You can look it up somewhere.'

'I know he wasn't, stupid! It was hundreds of years ago. He just said that he would.'

'You always want help with things,' his sister snapped back.

Before everything got a lot more heated – it does sometimes – I told them that if they carried on quarrelling I might not feel so kindly towards giving them ice cream for dessert and, anyway, they'd get indigestion. It went quiet.

An hour later, Patrick had still not turned up, nor was he accessible by phone. I contacted James Carrick, who by now, of course, was at home. He had not spoken to him that day either face-to-face or over the phone. He made me promise to contact him again if Patrick failed to appear.

Clearing away, I had a few mouthfuls of my meal but wasn't hungry. Another ten leaden minutes went by and by this time my partner was breaking our working rules, which was not like him at all, except in an emergency. I switched on my iPad and discovered that the Salvation Army had a hostel on the London Road in Bath. Staff would presumably be on the premises and might have spoken to him. I thought it a faint chance but borrowed Elspeth's car – Patrick had the Range Rover – and drove to the city, a matter of six miles away.

The hostel proved almost impossible to find. When I did finally arrive, having parked the car on double yellow lines, I found the premises locked, with a sign on the door saying that the hostel was now temporarily transferred to Paulton,

131

some miles away, while this place was fully refurbished. An address was given but there seemed to be no point in going there.

Having moved the car to somewhere a bit more legal, I tried Patrick's number again but, as before, just got voicemail. On the off-chance that there was something wrong with it, I rang our home number in case he was there wondering where the hell *I'd* got to. Carrie answered and told me that he wasn't.

Staring straight ahead through the windscreen, not knowing what to do next, I said a few things that I probably shouldn't. There seemed to be nothing for it but to go home, so I did. I had been there for about ten minutes when my mobile rang. It was James Carrick.

'In view of who had gone missing I put out an alert,' he said tersely. 'A passing patrol car found the Range Rover in a country lane not far from the old Boys' High School in Sion Hill. Patrick's in it and he's hurt.'

'How hurt?' I think I shouted.

'He's been shot.'

I sat down very hard on the nearest chair without having intended to.

'Are you there, hen?' James's voice said.

'Yes,' I said.

'Paramedics are already there and an ambulance is on its way. All I can tell you is that he's alive. I won't tell you where as he'll have been taken to A and E by the time you arrive. Don't drive yourself to the hospital. Get your father-in-law to take you.'

In hindsight, I think I rang off without saying

132

anything else and have no memory of walking through the house and into the annexe, only that I went in without knocking.

John and Elspeth were watching a nature programme on the television and for some reason I vividly remember what was on the screen – a killer whale lunging at young sea lions in the shallows of a beach, the attack turning the surf red with blood.

'Oh, do switch it off, John,' Elspeth exclaimed. 'It's just too horrible for words and I think we've seen it before.' She turned to me. 'Whatever's wrong, Ingrid?'

'Something even more horrible,' I managed to get out.

The DCI had arrived before us at the A&E department and was waiting just inside the entrance.

'He's been taken straight in,' he told us. 'We'll just have to wait.'

'Where was he hit?' I asked him.

'All I know so far is that there was a lot of blood on his shirt, leading the paramedics to think that he had been shot at least twice in the chest.'

'But he was found in the car. Was the windscreen shot out?'

'Apparently not.'

'He *can't* die,' I said as Carrick steered me to a vacant chair.

'He won't,' John declared, holding my other arm. 'You can be quite sure about *that*.'

Carrick's mobile rang and he went outside to answer it as the reception wasn't very good.

When he returned, he said, 'As you must have realized, I put in a full sweep of the surrounding area. They've found Paul Bradley. He was bound and gagged in a semi-derelict cricket pavilion at the old school, had been severely knocked about, which we knew already, and is being brought here. Someone had obviously been living rough there but there's no sign of them now.'

'Wayne!' I spat out. 'Why the hell wasn't he and Bradley found when the derelict places were searched?'

'It was outside the area we looked in,' Carrick said humbly.

'Sorry,' I muttered, but furious with him all the same. For, as Patrick had said, 'he had gone off the idea' of searching farther afield.

'So was Patrick shot at this pavilion?'

'There were bloodstains on the floor there but until some tests have been done . . .' He broke off and shrugged sadly.

'How far away was the car from this place?'

'I don't yet know, Ingrid. Look, I must go. I've a manhunt and scenes-of-crime people to oversee. Please keep me posted.' When he was a short distance away, he turned and came back. 'Was he armed?' he asked quietly.

'Didn't the cops in the patrol car discover that pretty quickly?' I replied.

'No, they wouldn't have touched him because of his potential injuries, and anyway, he was sitting slumped in the vehicle.'

I told him that I would have expected Patrick to carry his Glock in the circumstances but couldn't say for sure and had no idea why he

134

should have decided to go to that area himself. Otherwise, the weapon would be in the secure cubbybox in the car.

I don't know how long John and I sat there. I was in a kind of numbed daze, hating myself for not being able to think clearly, nor being able to pray for him as I knew he was, despising that woman who was me behaving like any old duck and not the resilient person I had imagined myself to be. Here you are, I thought, hunched over, on the verge of tears, completely useless to your husband when he needs you most.

At some point, a man in a white coat approached us. 'He's been taken to theatre,' he said, having introduced himself and established that I was the casualty's wife.

'Can you tell me nothing more?' I whispered, his name having gone in one ear and out of the other.

'Sorry, not now. As soon as there's news you'll be the first to hear.'

John took my hand and said in my ear, 'He'll be all right. I know he will.'

A little while later, I became aware of those around me, surprised that I had not noticed before that the waiting area was crowded. Details emerged: a man, a workman probably as he was wearing cement-spattered overalls, was clutching a blooded and dirty rag wrapped around his right hand; a young child cried quietly, hugging herself because her cross-looking mother wasn't; another woman wearing what looked like pyjamas just sat there like a dummy in a shop window, staring straight ahead, pale as death, her lips moving

135

soundlessly. How long had they been waiting? The staff padded around silently.

Time stood still but then surprised me by a clock on the wall suddenly showing it was just before midnight. The man with the injured hand and the child and her mother had disappeared and as I registered the time someone came and spoke to the woman in pyjamas and then led her away.

John had gone, too, another surprise, but he came back shortly afterwards with a tray holding two mugs of tea and a couple of iced buns.

'Patrick likes those,' I said, and then burst into tears.

'He takes after me,' he said, giving me one of the mugs. 'And you must have something. Otherwise you'll be weeping all over him and that won't cheer him up at all.'

I gazed at him with blurry eyes. 'John, no one can survive being shot twice in the chest.'

'People have,' this one-time Royal Naval Reserve officer replied, and then asked if he could borrow my phone to ring Elspeth as in the hurry he had left his behind. I was forced to smile then when he looked at it a bit blankly and admitted that it was a lot smarter than his somewhat basic one, so I rang the number for him.

The tea was only warm but I felt better for drinking it even though John had put sugar in it, which I don't normally take. The business of iced buns though goes back a long time, almost a joke now. I remember at one army establishment where Patrick and I were offered refreshments – our reason for being there defeats my memory now – it proved to be tea and iced buns with two cherries on the top. Crisply, Patrick had asked if officers got two cherries and other ranks one, and was told by a rigidly-to-attention orderly that he thought it was the chef's birthday. I never knew how I managed to keep a straight face and we had both exploded with laughter when he had gone.

For you then but for the last time, I now thought, taking a bite. *I will never eat another if you die.*

'I know it sounds a really boring cliché,' John said later, 'but no news is good news.'

At that very moment, the time on the wall clock – three minutes to three – indelibly seared into my mind, the man in the white coat returned.

We were shown into a room, this doctor's office by the look of it, temporarily or otherwise, a family photo on the back of the desk. My gaze lingered on it. John had come in with me at my request and we seated ourselves in the two vacant chairs. The doctor was accessing a computer on the desk, busy with passwords and so forth, and I began to feel faint.

'Your husband was carrying a gun,' said the doctor whose name I had forgotten.

Was. He was dead then. *Was*. A filthy word. I wasn't ready for 'was'.

'He's a police officer and has permission to,' I said, my voice sounding strange in my ears, sort of hollow and echoing.

'Yes, I know, the policemen who found him had already established that from his ID.'

I suddenly realized that the man was smiling.

137

'Unless there are complications, he's going to be fine, but right now we're treating him for traumatic pneumothorax.'

I probably gaped at him and can remember grabbing John's hand. Treating him for *what*?

'The bullet hit the weapon in the shoulder holster, probably at an angle, which deflected it, and the impact broke three ribs, one of which punctured his left lung, before skimming off across his chest, causing a surface wound which is not particularly serious but caused him to lose rather a lot of blood. We've repaired the damage, removed air from his chest cavity and inserted a tube to draw out any more, which will stay in place for two to three days. He's on oxygen and painkillers and having blood transfusions. A drain's been inserted to draw out any blood from the lung but the damage isn't massive and we're hoping it'll heal itself as he appears to be strong and healthy. We'll have to keep him here for about ten days but he can then recover at home. There will be extensive bruising, of course.'

I said, or rather gasped, 'Please can I see him?'

'Yes, but he probably won't be responsive yet.'

He gave me the name of the high-dependency ward and how to get there but, again, I instantly forgot what was said. John remembered.

'Only one visitor,' said a nurse when we arrived. 'And, please, just stay for a few minutes.'

'I should like a brief moment with him after my daughter-in-law,' John said. 'I'm his father and a priest. I shall pray for him.'

He was assured that that was perfectly all right.

It was a shock to see the tube down Patrick's

138

throat, the oxygen mask, the lines into his arms and his pallor. Monitors bleeped softly. It was then I realized that if, as evidence suggested, he had been shot in the cricket pavilion and had been found in the Range Rover, he somehow must have walked back to it after the attack. That fact and the weapon in its American hand-tooled leather fast-draw shoulder holster had saved his life.

His eyes were closed but he didn't look deeply asleep as his eyelids flickered when I drew up a chair and took the hand nearest to me. Both were connected to medical hardware so I was very careful not to move it much and hurt him. When I leaned over and kissed his cheek he took a deep breath, raggedly, and turned his head towards me.

I said a whole load of soppy things: that I loved him to bits and he was going to be fine, how we all loved him and the kittens were missing him already, that he'd soon be home and Elspeth would make him one of her famous steak-and-kidney puddings and I didn't care a damn if he never wanted to work again as I'd get a job filling shelves in a supermarket to help make ends meet. At this final remark, his eyes flew open and he gave me one of his stock-in-trade, piercing stares.

'OK, delete that last bit,' I said and kissed him again.

On the way home, at three forty-five, I rang James Carrick, knowing that he would want news whatever time it was. He answered immediately and, after expressing immense relief at what I had just said, told me that the Range Rover and Patrick's

Glock, which, obviously, was damaged, would be sent to a lab for testing, the latter to see if it had been fired. He thought not and initial questioning of residents in the locality had borne this out. No one had heard any shots, not even one. This wasn't particularly strange as the playing fields, now used by another school, were extensive and the old pavilion in question was near one of the farthest boundaries on the edge of open countryside. He went on to say that there was no doubt someone had been living rough there and he was hoping to be able to speak to Paul Bradley shortly but had been told that the man was quite poorly. Carrick did not say so but obviously he would also want to speak to Patrick as soon as this was possible to discover what had actually happened. Meanwhile, his every available officer was hunting for Wayne Biddulph, or whatever the little scumbag was calling himself – his words.

'Oh, and Ingrid . . .?'

'Yes?' I said.

'Promise me you won't go after this man yourself.'

I promised, and meant it. One of us had to be a hundred per cent for the children's sake. Not only that, if I succeeded in finding him I would probably kill him in cold blood.

Ten

The police had not only appropriated the damaged weapon and holster but also Patrick's clothes for testing, as there was a faint chance that the DNA of whoever had shot him was on them if his attacker had touched him. I had been given his valuables at the hospital – his wallet, watch and phone, the latter which could be returned to him when he was sufficiently recovered to be able to use it. This was extremely useful to me as Commander Rolt's mobile number was in the memory. Later that morning, but still early by most people's reckoning – I had slept for two hours in an armchair – I rang him.

'Wayne's a full brother to Steve Biddulph who, with his half-brother, Kyle, was found hanged,' Rolt continued musingly, reminding himself after his shocked reaction to what had happened to Patrick. 'But, otherwise, I know little about any of them. There's a possibility that he's bolted for home – the flat over the dry cleaners in Bethnal Green rented to his mother. I'll get the Met to raid the place. They have suspicions that she and her daughter have stolen goods on the premises anyway.'

'There's something I must ask you,' I said. 'Patrick was going to but, right now, he can't. Did you put us completely in the picture or did you choose to stay at that pub because you had intelligence that associates of Matt Dorney were in this area and might be assessing whether it was worth Dorney expanding, or even moving, his criminal activities to Bath?'

'Were that trio capable of assessing anything other than drink and drugs?' Rolt lightly queried.

'Please answer the question.'

He must have recollected that I, too, work for the NCA, for he said, 'I have to confess that it did cross my mind that I could mix business with pleasure as, yes, there was a rumour that Dorney was ambitious in a south-westerly direction. I gather he was overheard saying that as Bath's nick had been sold off and the cops dispersed all over the place, his doing jobs there would be like taking sweets from a baby. You and I know, of course, that it's nonsense as the situation's only temporary until a new station's built.'

'Sharing that information would have been helpful,' was the most polite thing I could think of saying.

'But it was only gossip.'

'That pub in particular, though?'

'John Fielding, the new owner, isn't squeaky clean. He's only very recently changed his name from Burgess so it might not yet have appeared on all the relevant police websites. He's originally from London and we know he had associations with several mobsters, as although he was thought to organize crime on an independent basis he was a successful fence, running a restaurant as a front, but always seemed to avoid arrest and slip through the Met's grasp. We knew he'd changed his name because he'd done it officially, through deed poll, but the man could have any number of false identities. Using what one must suppose was a large stash of ill-gotten gains, he then bought the pub. We're not silly enough to imagine he's gone straight but he has kept his head down. And I have to add that none of this provided any basis for informing other law agencies as it was little more than a series of emails between various individuals.'

Privately, I disagreed with him, but we had to keep the man on side. Hoping that I didn't sound sarcastic, I asked him if there was anything else that he felt he could now tell us.

'Not at the moment,' he replied after a pause. 'But if anything comes up that might be useful to you and DCI Carrick I'll pass it on. I apologize if I've been reticent.'

The following day, Paul Bradley was deemed fit enough to be interviewed but was being kept in hospital for observation as he had severely bruised kidneys and other possible internal injuries from the beating he had received.

James Carrick had contacted me to ask if I would like to be present while he talked to him and finished by saying, 'Bradley might be the key to finding this man but I can't really put the screws on him as he's so unwell. A member of the NCA tagging along as well, though . . .' He left the rest unsaid.

Fine, I told him. As I'd planned to visit Patrick, I would see him at the hospital. After I'd visited Patrick.

First impressions were that he looked a lot

143

happier now the tube had gone from down his throat, removed a few minutes previously, apparently. Oxygen was handy should he need it. I had also been told that he was still on a lot of pain relief as it was very important he didn't take shallow breaths. They were hoping to get him out of bed shortly.

'Has Elspeth been to see you yet?' I asked, having kissed him and knowing full well that she had. Just checking.

'Yesterday,' he replied huskily. 'Sorry . . . I can't talk much yet.'

'Then don't. I'm not going to start badgering you with questions either but will tell you that I'm going to be there when James speaks to Paul Bradley shortly. He was found bound and gagged in that pavilion.'

Patrick took a big gasping breath. 'What pavilion?'

Ye gods, he'd forgotten. Amnesia. I said, 'The cricket pavilion in the playing fields of the old school where you were shot and then found nearby in the car.'

'Ingrid, I wasn't shot in any . . . effin' pavilion.'

'There was blood on the floor of it.'

He just looked at me.

'Shall I go away?' I asked gently.

'Someone riding pillion on a motorbike . . . shot me with what must have been a . . . silenced weapon just as I'd got out of the car. But he screwed up as he left it a bit late and the bike . . . for some reason . . . was forced to swerve.'

Bloody hell, he hadn't forgotten. 'Tell me the rest tomorrow,' I said, but agog to know more details of what had happened. 'Or the next day. When you feel strong enough.'

'Kids all right?' He was very tired.

'Fine. They can't wait until you get home.'

'What have you . . . told them?'

'That you've been in a car prang – a police car, not ours.'

I sat with him for a while longer, suddenly remembered and gave him the bar of his favourite plain chocolate that Matthew had bought for him in the village shop. There was also a present from Katie – her lucky mascot, a tiny silver pony on a key ring. This was a real treasure of hers and, to my knowledge, until now she hadn't gone anywhere without it. When I left Patrick was holding it, smiling.

From what I could see of his face between the bandaging on his head, Paul Bradley looked more poorly than Patrick, but I told myself that he probably hadn't been too healthy to start with. Carrick was already by his bedside, in a general ward, which meant I had no opportunity before-hand to tell him what Commander Rolt had said about John Fielding. But it appeared from his first remark that the DCI had no delusions about The Lion and the Unicorn.

'Your place of work looks all right but, in reality, is a rats' nest of all the local villains,' he began by saying.

'Then why haven't you arrested them?' Bradley retorted.

Good point, I thought.

Carrick spoke more quietly. 'I'm not allowed

to question you for long this first time, but the quicker you tell me who grabbed you in your flat, beat you up and left you to die in a cricket pavilion, the quicker I can go away and arrest them.'

'Is that what that shack was? God knows who they were. They had hoods over their heads.'

'No voices you recognized?'

'No.'

'I think you're lying. Was it this Wayne character?'

'As I've just told you, I don't know who they were.'

I said, 'Who may or may not, but most likely are, involved in the shooting of an NCA officer, my colleague.'

'Sod off,' said Bradley.

'That evening I spoke to you, you didn't go straight home but stopped off somewhere. Where was that?'

'You've been snooping on me, then.'

'It's what cops do,' Carrick snapped. 'Answer the lady's question.'

'I went shopping.'

'What for?'

'Food, of course. For dinner.'

I said, 'There aren't any grocery shops between the pub and where you live.'

This was a bit of a shot in the dark as I hadn't a clue where his flat actually was in the Oldfield Park area.

'OK, I walked down the hill and had a drink in a pub there. I don't drink at work. From there I had to go home a different way.'

'The place that has a street-level veranda that faces the road?' I asked.

'Yeah.'

'You're still lying. That's where I was and I didn't see you.'

Carrick was looking a bit surprised. OK, it was a bit spit and sawdust.

'Perhaps you need to get your eyes tested,' Bradley sneered.

'Doesn't it worry you a little that those who did this to you might find you and carry on when you're discharged from here?' Carrick said.

'No.'

From his subsequent expression, I could tell that he hadn't thought of this and yes, it did.

'Where will you go?' I said.

The man shrugged, and then winced.

'You *will* be given police protection if you supply us with sufficient information to enable us to get hold of Wayne,' the DCI told him.

When Bradley made no reply to this, I said, 'Why did they tie you up and leave you there? Were they going to return later and finish the job?'

After a little thought, Bradley said, 'Dunno. I was out of it really but someone's phone rang. There was some muttering and then they went off.'

'What was all this about, though?' Carrick said. 'You mentioned to Wayne that a police officer was staying at the pub as you wanted revenge for being nabbed for drink-driving. Did they threaten to grass on you or was it because you'd been interviewed by the police?'

There was quite a long silence, and then the barman said, 'They wanted to know what I'd said to the cops.'

'About what?'

'Not what, who. Fielding. If I'd told a bunch of lies to implicate him.' And to me, 'I didn't say anything about Fielding, did I?'

'You didn't,' I agreed. 'But go on.'

'Is it on the line, that I'll get protection?'

'You will,' Carrick assured him, 'but I'm not using it as a bargaining point, just saying that you'll get it if I feel you're in danger.'

'OK, for some reason I believe you. Fielding's connected with some London mobster. Wayne's one of his eyes and ears, looking out potential places for the boss to start an offshoot of his London operation. God knows how he got the job – he's about as clever as a dead rhino. He was living rough in that hut because he'd been chucked out of all his digs, probably for not paying the rent and behaving like the filthy little bastard that he is. Fielding wanted me to disappear after they put the screws on me so they left me there as none of them had the bottle to finish me off. And then your lot found me.'

'They? How many?'

'Three.'

'How do you know all this about Fielding?' I asked.

'I just do. If I knew any more I'd tell you – he doesn't pay very well. Perhaps someone ought to arrange for him to be knocked on the head.'

'Don't think about it,' Carrick warned. 'And

148

you'd have saved yourself a lot of trouble and pain if you'd told us this in the first place.'

'Fielding was questioned by me and my colleague,' I chipped in, seeing that a nurse was approaching, no doubt to terminate the interview. 'Is that the reason he was shot?'

Bradley shook his head. 'I know nothing about shootings.'

'Does Fielding have a motorbike?'

'Yes, a Harley.'

'Don't leave Bath,' Carrick said as we left.

'I don't reckon I'm going anywhere,' the man retorted.

'Motorbikes?' Carrick queried as we made our way out.

'Patrick was shot near the Range Rover, not in the pavilion, by someone riding pillion on a motorbike. That's all I know until he can tell us more. And Rolt had already told me this morning that Fielding's iffy.'

But how had they known where Patrick was going to be?

Carrick noticed the way I was looking at him. 'Something other than the obvious bothering you right now?'

'Sorry, I've just had a nasty thought. Patrick checks over the Range Rover on a regular basis to see if any unwanted devices have been planted on it and did so quite recently. But if there's anything there like a tracker it might have only been in place for a couple of days.'

Later that day, Carrick rang me to say that a tracking device had been discovered under one of the wheel arches. This could only mean that someone had seen Patrick behind the wheel of the vehicle in the vicinity of The Lion and the Unicorn when we had questioned Fielding, perhaps followed us to where we had left it in the same side road as I had and duly reported back.

At this juncture, and presumably having previously kept his anger over what had happened to Patrick well in check, Carrick must have hit boiling point, for he organized a heavy-handed raid on the pub at ten fifty-five that night. The team not only found drugs with a street value of over a quarter of a million pounds and a miscellany of valuable property that looked as though it might rightfully belong to people other than the current landlord, but also came upon a man who answered Wayne's description hiding in an upstairs cupboard. He was armed with a handgun but too slow to use it.

Carrick, who had gone along even though DCIs aren't usually so hands-on, took great pleasure in ordering everyone on the premises to be arrested, it being after closing time, and netted another couple of local villains who were wanted to help with enquiries in connection with other cases.

It had been, he told me the next morning, a good night's work.

Patrick was sitting in a chair alongside the bed when I went to see him later that same morning and was now only connected to one drip apparatus. By this time he was in a different ward, not the same one as Paul Bradley, I was relieved to discover. Before he saw me he put down put the magazine he had been reading with a gesture of extreme frustration.

I gave him a very, very gentle hug, fetched a chair and sat down. 'Are you eating?'

'Sort of. But the food's awful.'

'What I really meant was are you allowed to eat proper food?'

'Yes, it's great. I had a couple of tablespoons of porridge for breakfast made from wallpaper paste and washing-up water. Proper food.' He eyed the small parcel I was carrying. 'What's that?'

'A fruit cake,' I said, handing it over. 'I cut it into slices for you.'

'Mother's?'

'No, I made it.'

He unwrapped the cake, which I had made in a loaf tin for ease of handling, took out a slice and took a large bite. 'I didn't know you could,' he mumbled through his mouthful.

'Liar.' It was obvious that he was still having trouble breathing, something that I guessed would continue for quite a while.

'Has Carrick got hold of Wayne Shitface yet?'

'He has – last night.'

'I'm impressed. What happened?'

I told him what had taken place, and then said, 'Someone had bugged the car with a GPS tracker.'

He swore, but quietly as there were others within earshot. For obvious reasons, he would blame himself for this.

'Why did you go to that area?' I asked him.

'I called in to see Carrick but he wasn't there

and someone told me that an elderly and nervous-sounding woman – she said she was in her eighties – had phoned in to say that a man was behaving furtively on those playing fields. She was worried he would attack the children as it's still used. I thought I'd take a look round there as there was a faint chance it was our man.'

'You didn't tell anyone where you were going?'

'No. Forgot to charge my phone, too.'

Which reminded me and I returned it to him, fully charged. I made light of the lapses, adding, 'James said he'd come along later, but only if you're well enough. Do you think it was Wayne who shot you?'

'Impossible to tell as the person was wearing a helmet with a visor. They both were. But he was shorter and of lighter build than the guy on the driving seat. I think it was a Harley, by the way.'

'Fielding has one and, as I've just said, he was one of those arrested.'

Patrick started on another slice of cake. 'I just want to be there at the nick right now and wring their bloody necks.'

'You'll have to postpone doing things like that for a while,' I said, making a joke of it. 'Do you think it would be all right for Katie to have a ride on George?'

'If you took her out on a leading rein for the first few times. She's a better rider than you anyway and won't let him play the fool.'

I did not mind that judgement as he happened to be correct and, having successfully steered the conversation away from dangerous subjects, we carried on chatting about the family and then I left. But I had felt uneasy about the look in his eyes when he had mentioned those we were assuming were his attackers, and reckoned that it was just as well they were in police custody.

I didn't fancy Matt Dorney's chances at all now, though.

The DCI found himself unable to question Patrick that day due to the pressure of interviewing all the relevant suspects. Also, he told me in a phone call during the evening, he had wanted to get the best possible picture of the crime, or crimes, from anything they said to him and his team first so he could bring the victim of the shooting right up to date.

Meanwhile, and after I had mentioned to her a possible nourishment problem, Elspeth had gone to the hospital bearing sliced roast chicken and boiled new potatoes, still warm, together with fresh fruit salad, all most gratefully received, I gathered. I offered to take a turn the following day but she would have none of it, saying it would give her something to do; this from someone who seems to spend just about every day of the week working for charity or the local community. Her dedication was rewarded when, four days later, Patrick was discharged and placed under the care of his GP and family.

Before he came home, the DCI had visited him in hospital to say that, in his opinion, out of those arrested, six men and two women, only Fielding and Wayne, who was using the same surname as his late brother, Steve Biddulph, 'out

153

of admiration for a great guy' apparently, were directly connected with the case. The latter was adamant that he had had nothing to do with the shooting and had not been hiding out in the cricket pavilion. When it was pointed out to him that his fingerprints had been found in the building and DNA collected from hair and blood on the floor – he had cut his hand on a piece of broken glass – matched his, the suspect then had a sudden surge of recollection and admitted 'hanging out there for a bit'. He would confess to nothing more.

Fielding was an old hand at police interviews and insisted a solicitor be present even though he hadn't been charged with anything yet. This was done and a young woman turned up who demanded that her client be released pending further enquiries. Carrick, also no novice, had pointed out to her that he was investigating an attempted murder in which a Harley-Davidson motorbike had been used in a drive-by shooting, one of which was in Fielding's possession. They were such cult acquisitions, the DCI had cunningly pointed out, that even if the bike at the scene of the crime hadn't been Fielding's, it was possible that he knew of a villain in the district to whom it might belong. He had then escorted her to the interview room and, together with Lynn Outhwaite, started the questioning.

Unfortunately, they got precisely nowhere until Carrick received a phone call from the main witness, the victim. Patrick had remembered that both of the helmets his attackers had worn were gold in colour and had a silver skull and crossbones on the back. After the call, the DCI had immediately asked Fielding where his bike and helmets were kept and was told they were in a lock-up garage not far from the pub. When this was accessed, the keys having been handed over, a couple of constables sent out to investigate discovered the bike concealed behind a lot of old furniture and rubbish, together with two gold helmets each with a silver skull and crossbones on the back. When told of this a little later, Fielding lost his temper and tried to escape, punching a constable. All Carrick could do was charge him with assaulting a police officer and harbouring someone carrying a firearm.

A little later, Wayne Biddulph was told about the bike and helmets, promptly folded up like cardboard in the rain and confessed to firing the shot – he was forced to, he bleated, by Fielding and, he guessed, *his* boss in London, name and whereabouts not known. This fitted in with the findings of a newly delivered report on the silenced weapon he had been waving ineffectively around when arrested; it had been fired fairly recently.

Interviewed again, Fielding apologized for losing his head but still denied having had anything to do with the shooting, insisting that Wayne Biddulph was a liar as well as being a well-known local thug and trouble-maker.

The morning after Patrick came home, Commander Michael Greenway turned up at the rectory. Having introduced himself, he apologized profusely for the intrusion to Elspeth, who had been in to see her son in our living room and had met him as she exited the house via the front door to go to the post office. He told her that he was on his way into Bath to check on the investigation as an NCA officer was involved and thought he would drop by.

This was interesting as he lives in North Ascot and Hinton Littlemore represents more than a slight detour if one is driving to Bath. I wondered if there was another reason for his visit other than checking on Patrick's recovery progress. This proved to be even more interesting, for when I returned with coffee and biscuits he was in the process of handing over not only a bottle of whisky but also a new Glock 17 together with a replacement holster identical to the one that had been damaged beyond repair. The latter are not general issue, which meant that he must have bought it himself.

My husband was not looking particularly devastated by any of these developments and I didn't know whether to be glad, angry or extremely worried.

Eleven

Although he didn't mention the word 'stagnating', it immediately became apparent that the commander was under the impression that Carrick had not made much progress, and it was gratifying to be able to correct this. I did most of the talking because Patrick had slightly reduced the dose of his painkillers. They made him feel woozy and he was paying the price.

'Is this Fielding character aware that you're man and wife?' Greenway demanded to know.

'Of course not,' I replied. 'We're officially just colleagues and always have been when working together.'

'I'd like you to be there when he's questioned again.'

'Carrick might say that I'm an interested party,' was my reaction to this. 'It's against the rules.'

'Bugger the rules. You leave Carrick to me.'

Police protocols have never been a strong point with him.

'Rolt's back at work,' he went on, something we knew already. 'I understand that he's put into place a review of security and working practices after the attack on him and the subsequent murders of two of his personnel.'

Patrick said, 'He put his head into the lion's mouth by staying at that pub. He knew there were rumours about the place before he went and it just

157

happened to coincide with the barman's need of revenge after being picked up for drink-driving.'

'But how did they know he was a cop?' Greenway wondered. 'Surely he didn't tell them.'

'Pass,' Patrick said. 'But he does look like one. Or an overheard phone call from work, perhaps.'

We had already agreed that we would not mention the business of Rolt's girlfriend arriving and as good as trumpeting his profession from the rooftops as there was no point in providing Greenway with any more fuel for his resentment. The conversation veered to the subject of the sick leave Patrick would need – I said at least two months – but was overruled by both of them and a month was agreed upon, this to be reviewed in the event of any setbacks. I was assured by the commander that he would only be given 'light duties' to begin with.

Yeah, right.

They reviewed the case together before Greenway left. Patrick then made his way, slowly, to his parents' annexe to give his father the whisky as he was not allowed to drink anything alcoholic at the moment and didn't want to, a measure of how unwell he was feeling.

A couple of hours later, James Carrick contacted me. 'I ken you'd like to be in on my further questioning of John Fielding.'

Yes, delighted.

'Oh, and Paul Bradley's discharged himself from hospital. Don't worry, I'll find him.'

There were no obvious signs, in that the DCI's ears weren't still visibly burning, of any input of

Greenway's that had resulted in my presence in the interview room; in fact, he seemed to be in buoyant mood. As might have been expected, Fielding wasn't and gave me a look that promised injury and worse, much worse. For a few seconds, my skin crawled.

'I could have done with Patrick being here,' Carrick had said before we entered, then immediately corrected himself by saying, 'No offence, Ingrid, it's just that he seems to be able to get inside the criminal mind.'

This had been put more bluntly during our spy-hunting days by someone in MI5 – I've forgotten exactly who – saying he put it down to the fact that Patrick 'scared the shit out of them'.

I reckoned that the only person Fielding was scared of was Matt Dorney. He did not appear to feel he was in much danger right now either, as when asked if he wanted his solicitor to be present he had just shrugged and said that she was useless.

After the suspect's previous attempt to escape, Carrick was taking no chances, and a constable who looked as though he might engage in mud wrestling with water buffalo in his spare time stood just inside the door.

The DCI formally opened the interview, and then said, 'You've already been charged with assault when you tried to escape, and harbouring Wayne Biddulph, who has admitted riding pillion on your motorbike and firing a shot at a police officer.'

'It wasn't me and it wasn't my bike,' Fielding snarled.

159

'It was your bike, your helmets, your orders to him following orders from Matt Dorney. I take it you admit you've heard of him.'

'I have heard of him. All of London and the south of England has heard of him. He makes rings around all you idiots. But I've never met or spoken to him.'

'The handgun no doubt came from Dorney too,' Carrick continued. 'We think Dorney was behind the attack a few weeks ago on the senior police officer who stayed at your pub, the subsequent murder of the men who were responsible for that and the murders of another police officer and a retired one who were watching the area in London where he operates. Dorney gets a real kick out of killing and rids himself of those who may grass on him or he deems to have failed in what he ordered them to do. I'd be very, very nervous if I was in your shoes. Still, at least Biddulph will be in prison – he's confessed to the shooting, by the way – and out of harm's way. Until he comes out, that is.'

There wasn't a scrap of real evidence for nearly all of this, I thought, but hey ho.

'Wayne's a right little louse,' Fielding muttered. 'And, as I've said several times, a liar. A lying little louse.' He smiled and then chuckled at what he obviously thought was funny.

My notepad isn't for writing down what transpires word for word, although I can if I want to. My shorthand is still quite good and also secure as not many people can read it these days. If necessary, I can probably repeat practically word for word short to medium exchanges as I have a good memory, so I use my notepad to jot down my reactions to the suspect's answers, a lead to be followed up or a possible line of questioning of my own. Carrick hadn't actually mentioned my saying anything so I would have to act appropriately or risk hazarding his concentration.

Yes, it was a real shame Patrick wasn't here, I thought. I don't have to worry in similar situations about thus treading on *his* toes as we seem to work instinctively as a team. He knows that if he engineers leaving me on my own with an accused for a short while – but not unprotected, he and others are always very close by – I sometimes get results. This is probably because professional writers are good with words – mightier than the sword and all that.

'So,' Carrick was saying, 'it wasn't your bike, you didn't give Biddulph the weapon and didn't take him to where the shooting victim was attacked. That right?'

'You've no evidence for any of that so stop playing around with me,' the man said, meeting his gaze.

'There was a tracking device on the victim's vehicle that had been placed there after he questioned you at the pub. I think you reported to Dorney that you were under suspicion and he reacted as might be expected – he's mentally unbalanced, to say the least – by telling you to take out the officer in question. He either sent you the tracker, perhaps one that can be used in conjunction with a mobile phone or computer, or you already had one in your possession.'

'No comment,' said Fielding.

'There appears to be a tracker installation on the computer at the pub.'

'You had no right . . .' Fielding began, and then his mouth shut like a trap.

'Search warrants permit in-depth poking around,' he was blithely informed. 'And we have some people who are really clever at defeating passwords.'

'Clever shit, aren't you? It was Wayne, I keep telling you. He acts stupid but isn't. Anyone can go in the office.'

I caught Carrick's eye and said, 'What's the going rate for killing a cop these days?'

This shook Fielding out of his sullen stupor for a moment and he said in surprise, 'God knows.'

'You wouldn't have got London weighting as he'd regard it as a job in the sticks. London mobsters regard anything that goes on outside London as mostly beneath their notice, unless there's money to be made in it.'

'You don't say,' he drawled sarcastically.

'Dorney regards you as a jobsworth in the sticks, someone to be used and then discarded. You may not realize it but your life's not worth anything to him. You might be used to fence some more stolen property if he decides to move part of his operation down here but that's all.'

Angrily, Fielding said, 'Look, it's Wayne's word against mine. He was with another bloke on another bike.'

'With identical helmets?' Carrick suggested.

'With identical helmets,' the other man agreed.

'Well, no, actually,' Carrick said smoothly. 'DNA found in one of the helmets, extracted from

162

a few greasy hairs, matches yours, which we got from a sample of saliva found on a half-eaten chocolate bar in the office. Your helmets.'

'Then Wayne must have borrowed them for the job. And the bike. It was his chocolate bar.'

'Where are the keys to the lock-up and the bike normally kept?'

'On a hook in my office. They're on the same keyring.'

'But you had them in your pocket when you were arrested.'

'That was because I'd been to the lock-up an hour or so previously to get something. I keep other stuff in there too.'

I said, 'And we haven't even touched on the business of Paul Bradley, your barman. Badly beaten, abducted from his flat to the cricket pavilion in the old school grounds, kicked and beaten some more and then tied up and left to die. He's still in hospital – under police guard.'

A crafty look came over Fielding's face. 'Wayne told me about that. It was something between them, he said, a private matter. Money. He bragged that Bradley wouldn't have known who it was as they'd worn masks.'

'They?' Carrick queried.

'Wayne took a couple of chums with him.'

'Bradley said he was beaten up to make him talk as you wanted to know what he'd said to the police.'

'Then he's lying again, isn't he?'

'Everyone's lying but you,' I said.

There was no reply to my remark. There was something wrong with this. We were getting nowhere but my cat's whiskers were screaming stinking fish.

Carrick said, 'It's true then that Dorney hopes to extend his empire to the West Country?'

'No idea,' Fielding replied.

'But you used to fence stolen goods and knock around with London criminals. You must still hear gossip from various sources.'

'I've left all that behind me now.'

'All I want you to do is tell us how we can get hold of Dorney. It matters little to you now, surely – you've been charged and I think those charges will stick. It's in your interest to help us find him as, ultimately, he's responsible for just about everything we've been talking about. D'you want this man to get away, laughing at you?'

But he just smiled and nodded his head, mocking us. Despite what Carrick had said, I very much doubted whether he would be found guilty, if indeed there was enough evidence to bring him to court in the first place. Yet again, little or no progress had been made.

The next morning, and despite taking the antibiotics he had been given, Patrick had a high temperature. Following a visit from our doctor, he was taken back into hospital, where he was found to have a serious infection. I hope I don't use clichés in my novels but to say that my world fell apart describes exactly how I felt. He had looked ghastly, the wonderful grey eyes dead and dulled, and I had an inner terror of a future without him or to have him alive but as

164

a husk of his former self, old before his time, nothing to live for.

Matthew and Katie were intelligent enough to be able to see through the forced optimism and cheeriness with which I felt obliged to face everyone and, that afternoon, bought me a bunch of flowers from the village shop, a detour on their short journey across the village green from where the school bus sets them down. They were not commercially produced flowers but from a local garden, bronze and white spray chrysanthemums, the proceeds, I already knew, going into a charity box.

'The smell of autumn,' I said to myself, having thanked them and given them each a hug.

'Are you going to see Dad?' Katie asked hesitantly, as though I might be about to give them terrible news.

'Grandma and Grandad left for the hospital a short while ago,' I told them. 'I'll go later as he can't have too many visitors at once.'

'He's going to be all right, though?'

'Of course he'll be all right!' Mattthew declared. 'Anyway, I thought you'd given him your pony thing.'

'I did,' she replied. She glared at her brother. 'It's not a pony *thing.*'

I gave them a snack to keep them going until they had their dinner, while a garbled version of a ghastly old jingle went round and round in my head: *Ingrid Langley took and axe, and gave Matt Dorney forty whacks. When she saw what she had done, she gave John Fielding forty-one.*

Patrick's bouts of incandescent bad temper, rare

these days, had at one time scared and repelled me. Now I could understand it.

For three ghastly days, he was very ill, unable to eat. I had been to see him every morning and he had been mostly inert, back on drips, his hands horribly bruised where various needles had gone in and lying in bed with such miserable resignation that tears pricked my eyes. On morning four there was a slight improvement.

'Any news?' he asked weakly.

'Everyone's absolutely fine,' I replied.

'No, I mean work.'

'Not good, I'm afraid,' I said. 'James has been ordered by the super to drop the charges relating to the attack on you against John Fielding.'

'He's been released!'

'On police bail. He punched a constable when he tried to get away the first time he was interviewed and has been charged with assault and harbouring someone carrying a firearm.'

Patrick's lips moved in a silent and no doubt pithy reaction to this.

'He's insisting that Wayne took the bike and helmets without permission, that there had never been a firearm on his premises before and that he had absolutely nothing to do with it. Frankly, there's no proof. Carrick's been given permission to try to find more evidence against him as there's a certain sympathy from the super given Fielding's past record.'

'And Wayne Biddulph's still sticking to his story that Fielding made him do it on the orders of Dorney?'

'Not quite. He said he doesn't know the name

of the London mobster who issued the order to Fielding, even if there is one – it's all hearsay.'

'So who rode the bike?'

'Biddulph refuses to say.'

'But why? He'll get a longer sentence.'

'In my view, he's too frightened to say anything else.'

'You were there when Fielding was questioned. What did you make of him?'

'I think he drove the bike.' I thought it best not to mention the look he had given me. There was then a silence, which I broke by saying, 'What are the medics saying about *you*?'

'That the infection was probably caused by fibres from my clothing driven into me by the bullet skating across my chest. They've cleaned the wound out again and I have to stay here for another couple of days to be monitored while I'm on these stronger antibiotics. I'll be fine – after all, I do have Katie's good-luck charm.'

'I'll take her out on George.'

'I asked Mum to bring me something to eat. I can't stand boiled tripe and that's what's on the menu for lunch – intravenously if I refuse to eat it.'

'Oh, for goodness' sake!' I exclaimed, having to laugh.

He just smiled wanly and then, still smiling, said, 'What else is on your mind?'

'Nothing, just the general situation.'

Still, he smiled. 'Never mind, then.'

'You're using one of your interrogation methods on me,' I said. 'Charm, retreat and then pounce.'

'I'm hardly going to shout at you, Ingrid.'

'No, you're just lying there like a horse with a broken leg waiting to be put down, which is even worse,' I managed to get out before bursting into tears.

A remarkably strong and comforting grip claimed my hand, which was resting on the bedcover. 'Please tell me.'

I took a deep breath. 'It's pure cat's whiskers. Probably utter fantasy brought on by my mind being unbalanced because of worrying about you.'

'Codswallop. Tell me.'

'I think John Fielding is Matt Dorney.'

Patrick was silent for a moment, his eyes slitted, thinking, and then said, 'Have you shared this with Carrick?'

'No, it seemed too far-fetched.'

'Perhaps you should. There are no mugshots of Dorney that I know of.'

I felt a sudden urgency to do this but promised that I would bring him something to eat to save his mother another journey.

Twelve

James Carrick was having either a late breakfast or early lunch in his office, the temporary accommodation Bath CID was using not boasting a canteen, only a machine for coffee, tea and soft drinks.

'You shouldn't be eating sausage rolls,' I scolded. 'Death on a plate.'

'I was in a hurry and it was all I could find,' he said and rammed the last piece into his mouth.

I aired my theory and, for a moment, feared that he might choke.

'It's right off the wall,' I admitted. 'But I would like you to organize armed protection for Patrick. Please.'

The DCI dealt with his mouthful, and then said, 'I'll try but can't promise anything. The lack of evidence won't help.'

'When will you know?'

'I'll try and fix up something this afternoon. But—'

I carved him up with, 'Tight budgets, shortage of manpower, the chief constable's official car falling apart at the seams, a heavy tax on soap and toilet paper for the various nicks' loos and God knows what else have to be taken into consideration.'

'Ingrid, I'll do my *best*.'

'You promised Paul Bradley police protection and he's a suspect!'

'I really will do my best.'

'Your bloody force let bloody Fielding go!' I raged at him.

'OK!'

He tried his best there and then, and the answer was no. As we had feared, higher authority's view was that there wasn't sufficient evidence against him. Furthermore, a man who had been arrested had confessed to firing the shot.

I thanked James, really meaning it, asked him as I left how he could work in a room painted in such a cat-sick shade of greenish-yellow, went home, found something civilized for my husband's lunch, removed my Smith & Wesson from the wall safe in the living room where the weapons reside when they're not in the Range Rover or in use and drove back to the hospital, breaking all the speed limits. There, I rang Michael Greenway. He answered briefly to tell me that he was in a meeting but would phone me back as soon as possible.

Patrick, still looking dreadful, was nevertheless making slow inroads into potato salad, some cold ham and a small piece of pork pie. There were a couple of yoghurts to follow, which was all the fridge had had to offer of a practical nature, and he was looking at me in slight puzzlement.

'While Fielding's on the loose, you're in danger,' I explained. 'I'll ride shotgun until you're given armed protection.' I patted my bag. 'I've been given permission to stay.'

It was typical of our relationship – or come

to think of it, perhaps it was the drugs he was on – that he didn't react with horror, merely saying, 'You could leave it with me, or fetch the Glock.'

'You have to sleep, and besides, I can't see the hospital authorities being too pleased about that. Nor am I, not while you're dosed up to the eyebrows. You'll end up by killing the tea lady.'

'I did see a unicorn in here last night,' he murmured.

Fine. The happy juice he was on was either making him flippant or hallucinate, or both.

Perhaps I needed some.

'Ingrid . . .'

'What?' I snapped.

'I was joking and you're freaking out. Relax.'

I tried to take this on board but failed, looking around me to try to think of something other than impending rampant blood poisoning. There were six beds in the light, bright ward, one of which was unoccupied.

'He died,' Patrick said matter-of-factly, seeing where my gaze was directed.

'Oh,' I said. Great.

Ten interminable minutes later, Mike Greenway rang me back and I outlined the problem. There followed a rather long silence at his end of the line.

'I'll hound the Met to see if they've a better photo of Dorney and get back to you,' he assured me at last.

I said, 'According to Piers Ashley, there's only a blurred one of him leaving a strip club in F9's records. That's probably the same one that's in

171

every department's records. He said it was useless for identification purposes.'

'Do we know which strip club it was?'

'Only that it was in Barking.'

'Leave it with me, Ingrid.'

'Give me the gun,' Patrick said when he saw by my face that I hadn't yet got anywhere. 'You need to be at home. Writing.'

I told him that I would wait until Mike rang me again, which he did, after an hour and twenty minutes had elapsed.

'Sorry, it's a bit frantic here,' he began by saying. 'No luck with a decent photo, I'm afraid, only the blurred one you mentioned. But I will organize something and it'll probably be in place later today.'

Although I felt like screaming, I nevertheless managed to thank him. Patrick had been dozing but the phone ringing had woken him.

'Later today,' I said. 'Probably.'

'Then go home.'

I shook my head.

He went back to sleep.

Periodically, nursing staff came to look at him, adjusted this and that, took his temperature, checked his blood pressure and then went away. He mostly slept through this and I did not like to ask questions as that would have woken him again. The afternoon wore on. Someone gave me a cup of tea, then a doctor – a different one again – came to look at Patrick, walked away but then returned.

'Your husband was tired before this happened to him,' he said very quietly. 'Exhausted. It's the reason he's taking a while to get over it.'

'Will he completely recover, though?' I whispered.

'Yes. I'm fairly sure of that.'

When he had gone, I thought about it. The lapses – Patrick had not informed anyone where he was going when he had investigated following the report of the man behaving suspiciously in the playing fields area, he had forgotten to recharge his phone, he had failed to do his usual check of the Range Rover for planted bugs . . . And occurrences at home: a tendency to fall asleep in an armchair after dinner, turning down a recent invitation from James Carrick to have a drink in the Ring o' Bells by saying he had work to do but again falling asleep in a chair, forgetting a promise to take his mother into Bath the previous Saturday as her car was being serviced.

Exhausted.

I didn't like the 'fairly sure' either.

At eight forty-five, after I had had one lightning break when I'd dashed to the toilet, a burly man wearing jeans, a faded denim jacket and a baseball hat that he suddenly remembered to remove came through the double doors into the ward and approached me.

'Your ID, please,' I requested.

'I might be someone who's come to kill this man here,' he said with a broad smile.

I was too tired and edgy to smile back, saying, 'In my experience, plainclothes armed protection officers – male, that is – tend to look like plainclothes armed protection officers. Perhaps it's your good teeth and neat hair. And hitmen don't normally take their hats off. Your ID.'

173

He produced it and observed, 'It's much easier if whoever's being guarded is in a small ward on their own.'

I stood up, noticed that Patrick was awake and said, 'There's no specific threat other than what's already happened but we are talking about a London mobster who might like to shift his operations down here. Is someone taking over from you later?'

He said that there was.

I kissed Patrick on the forehead – there was nothing else to say – and went home.

Nothing happened, absolutely nothing. Then word came through from Greenway that an informer had said that Matt Dorney had a scar on the right side of his face. Did John Fielding? No.

End of story.

A couple of days later, Patrick was discharged from hospital, thin and weak despite Elspeth's and my efforts and still having to take medication, which made him feel worse, a long way from recovery. Feeling small and guilty that I had cost the Met a lot of money, I gave this information to the commander and he volunteered to notify David Rolt. Also, someone else would have to be assigned to the case as, clearly, Patrick was unable to work. I was content with this; the oracle had almost certainly failed and from now on I would keep quiet about my suspicions. Keep quiet full stop, actually.

I went somewhere private and had a little weep.

The family threw themselves into getting

Patrick better. I didn't mind at all when Elspeth offered to cook his main evening meal for him. This was practical and she had more time to prepare light recipes than I did right now as Carrie was on leave. On trips to Bath with their grandparents, Matthew and Katie trawled through charity shops looking for books Patrick might like to read and, during the day, Vicky surrounded him with her favourite teddy bears and dolls to keep him company when he was sitting or lying on the sofa. Justin's contribution was to bring him a large toad he had found in the garden, forcing his mother to exclaim, 'Go and put that back where you found it! Gently!'

'He's doing his best,' my husband protested.

'They're poisonous, aren't they?'

'We weren't about to eat it.'

Joanna and James called in at weekends, the former bringing Patrick little presents, including a miniature bottle of whisky with a fluff-covered toffee stuck to it that she had found in a kitchen drawer, the amusement this engendered better than the gift, her husband bringing him up to date with all relevant case information. There wasn't much to report. A witness to the shooting, an elderly man living opposite to the scene of the crime, had been located but there was nothing he had to say that incriminated anyone. He had seen a motorbike, registration number not noticed, swerve around a Range Rover and then had to swerve again as a car came from the other direction. He had heard no shots fired – Patrick had already said that the weapon was silenced – and had then observed a man who had seemingly

175

been knocked over, he thought by the bike, picking himself up, with difficulty, afterwards. Nothing really to worry about then, he had thought.

A date when Patrick might return to work – if he ever did – was, rightly, not mentioned during these visits.

A week and a half after Patrick came home for the second time, there was a distinct improvement. He had finished his medication and one evening he found the energy to meet James Carrick in the Ring o' Bells for a drink, which, at the moment, would have to be orange juice or something similar. I was finding it extremely difficult to smother my worries about any further action Fielding – no, not him, stupid, Dorney – might order if he knew where we lived, which I had to admit was doubtful as we are not in the phonebook. Even more difficult was preventing myself from bringing up the subject with Patrick of what he intended to do when fully fit. But, seeing him make his way across the village green that evening, taking his time, I knew that right now the subject had to be postponed. My main concern was that he wasn't really communicating. Too tired to talk? James Carrick told me afterwards that he had hardly said a word when they met.

The next morning, when I was clearing away the children's breakfast things after they had left for school and Patrick was still in bed, my mobile rang.

'Hi, Ingrid, it's Piers.'

For a moment, my mind floundered, and then

I gathered my wits to say, 'The last I heard was that you'd taken Commander Rolt back to London.'

'Yes, I stayed for a bit, catching up with friends, and then, of course, had to return home. Mother was worried. She worries about me too much, really.'

'She almost lost you.'

'I know.'

'I almost lost—' I began, and then, to my utter shame, wept again.

Eventually, I managed to explain. He then asked if it would be of benefit to Patrick if he came to see us.

Why not?

I had apologized to Piers that, due to the size of the family and despite a lot of work having been done to extend the rectory's accommodation, we no longer had a spare room for visitors. Ashley said that he had already decided he would stay at a hotel in Bath as he was sure I had more than enough to do already and insisted that it would give him pleasure to take us out for a meal. To save the patient a journey he would come out to Hinton Littlemore as he had been impressed by our local pub.

As on the previous occasion, he was there before us and seated on a bench on the green. And again, the evening was fine, if a little cooler, after a day of heavy rain. I had the sudden bizarre and unsettling thought of being in some kind of loop, trapped into doing the same thing over and over again until we were old and frail. If Patrick lived that long.

As before, Ashley rose to greet us and we exchanged a few pleasantries. 'This is serious,' he then said, eyeing us both.

'Oh, yes,' Patrick replied softly. 'Literally bloody serious.'

There was no further conversation until we were seated at our table and had drinks in front of us. The place was quiet, a few locals in the public bar, the holiday season over with just a few dedicated ramblers to be seen in the local lanes, a couple who fitted that description seated at a nearby table to ours. Their Labrador came over to sit hopefully by us and I stroked its silky ears. Odd, really, I thought, when I had hardly dared touch my own husband for weeks in case I hurt him.

'Thea's in London,' Ashley broke the silence by saying. 'She's gone to see Rolt – staying with him, I *think*. One can't ask, of course.'

'Not even brothers may ask that kind of question,' I commented.

'Sorry to be so blunt, but it's obvious to me that the pair of you are on your knees, physically and mentally.'

Patrick stirred restlessly. He was still in pain but determined not to keep dosing himself during the day unless it was necessary. 'I've discovered that being on the wrong side of forty is no help when one is blasted into the road.'

'I discovered that stopping a bullet was no fun when I was on the wrong side of twenty,' Ashley said with a grimace. 'I ended up having what was practically open-heart surgery to remove it. Mother had the hots for the surgeon, who was a family friend, and it turned out he was black-mailing her. He'd actually hired the local arsehole to take a pot shot at me to frighten me into leaving the area as he had his eyes on Mother's jewellery on account of gambling debts. Trouble was I moved and the arsehole was a lousy shot anyway. I'll tell you about it one day.' He got to his feet. 'I'll get some menus.'

When he had gone, Patrick and I exchanged glances.

'A breath of fresh air for us?' I hazarded. 'Or a kick in the pants?'

'He's a member of the minor aristocracy,' Patrick said. 'And as we know, they think big and live in a different world. Richard Daws did.'

Who had been Patrick's late boss and whose death he had avenged, the perpetrators having either been arrested or ending up very dead. It occurred to me that that episode, which had culminated in something I have no hesitation in describing as a small war, was probably the cause of his present exhaustion.

We ordered our meal and Ashley, following a query from me, told us about the family estate. It had been decided that although the house would remain closed to the public on an everyday basis, they were setting up a scheme where historical societies and garden clubs would be able to book to visit Ashleigh and/or the gardens, which were in the process of being restored. A cream tea would be included in the price. This arrangement would be less intrusive and hopefully guarantee a more peaceful solution for his mother, who had become exasperated with people who let their children run wild in her home and made a fuss, if not a scene, when there were no chips and burgers to be had in the tea room.

'I know that sounds like pure snobbery,' Ashley finished by saying, 'but it was awful.'

Having had to cope with Justin during some of his more difficult moments, I could sympathize.

'I didn't just look up old colleagues while I was in town,' Ashley revealed while we were eating and he was halfway through his T-bone steak. 'For God's sake, don't tell anyone but I'm trying to track down Matt Dorney.'

'Have you ever met him?' I asked eagerly. 'When you were working for his father, I mean.'

'Not that I'm aware of. They'd had a big row and Len had told him he'd kill him if he didn't go somewhere else.'

'There are no mugshots of him.'

'Tell me about it,' the other man responded with feeling.

'Ingrid has a theory,' Patrick said.

'Which has been proved to be rubbish,' I quickly put in.

'What, though?' Ashley asked.

'That he's using the name John Fielding and running The Lion and the Unicorn pub in Bath,' I told him. 'Fielding's under suspicion in connection with the attack on Patrick but there's no proper evidence, even though the man who fired the shot has implicated him. Not only that, the barman at the pub was beaten up and left in a derelict building to die after he'd spoken to the police.'

'It's not impossible,' Ashley said thoughtfully.

180

'But apparently Matt Dorney has a scar on the right side of his face. Fielding doesn't,' I added.

'Isn't that the pub where Rolt was staying?'

'Plenty of circumstantial evidence,' Patrick observed dryly.

He had previously offered no opinion and I realized with a shock that he might actually believe me.

'He's on police bail?'

'Yup.'

'You'll never see him again – not here, anyway.'

'He does own the pub,' Patrick pointed out.

We carried on with our meal, our companion silent and obviously in deep thought.

'You really shouldn't get involved in this,' Patrick said gently over coffee.

'I know,' Ashley morosely agreed. 'But it beats supervising fencing and filling in forms any day.'

'I thought you were getting married soon,' I said.

'No, she decided she'd be better off in the States living with the son of an oil baron she met at a party. No nasty English weather, no mud on her Gucci shoes and, most importantly, no lack of cash.'

One could hardly say so but he was well-shot of the gold-digging little cow.

'And she thought it would be a good idea if my mother went into a home so she herself could be lady of the manor,' Ashley added.

This really left me speechless.

'I think I might go and have a drink in that pub,' was his parting remark.

'Be very careful,' Patrick said in his lieutenant colonel voice.

'Yes, sir,' Ashley replied with one of his big grins.

'And please don't go off the map as far as we're concerned.'

'OK.'

'Bloody hell,' Patrick muttered on our way back across the green.

'Is that a general comment or are you worried about him?' I wondered.

'Right now, I'm worried about everything.'

Thirteen

The next morning, I thought it best to inform David Rolt that we had made contact with Piers Ashley in the event of the latter still indulging in his one-time department's secrecy. But it appeared that the commander was now fully aware of his previous assistant's movements and, slightly oddly, did not seem surprised when I told him of his previous evening's intention to have a drink at The Lion and the Unicorn. Still wearing my NCA hat, I went on to say that I hoped he would dissuade Ashley from doing any more private investigating but, as usual, he would not be drawn.

As soon as that call had ended, James Carrick rang me.

'I'm going to question Wayne Biddulph again,' he began. 'I think he knows a hell of a lot more than he's saying. I know I should have spoken to Patrick directly but thought I'd check with you first to see if you think he's well enough just to sit in. We might get somewhere if he's present.'

'Is the crime victim permitted to attend as an observer?' I queried.

'Biddulph's confessed to having fired the shot and been charged with attempted murder. I only want to talk to him about Fielding and who he's in the pay of. I've already trotted it past the super and he's OK with it.'

Yes, if the Avon and Somerset force could catch Matt Dorney right under F9's nose . . . I said, 'Patrick probably isn't strong enough but phone and ask him anyway.'

I said nothing about the call to Patrick, but when he was having his breakfast he asked me to drive him into Bath and explained the reason. 'Purely as an observer,' he added.

This state of affairs was mirrored in the interview room as two chairs had been placed well to one side so the pair of us were not directly in front of the man being questioned. I had been adamant about being present on the grounds that I needed to monitor the observer. If Patrick passed out it would probably have a more terrifying effect on Biddulph than if he'd threatened to wring his head off.

When he was brought in the DCI carefully explained to Biddulph that the interview was being recorded but at present he was not being charged with anything else. All the police were interested in was finding and arresting the 'big boys'. Personnel from the National Crime Agency, whom he not did introduce, were present only because they had cases involving the same suspects.

Biddulph turned his head; his gaze flicked over us and then, dismissively, away. We were already in possession of a description of him – this author immediately ransacked her mental word-hoard and came up with the word 'runtish'. The man had obviously been malnourished since the day he was born. An idea went through my mind: if mothers fed their children properly would fewer of them turn into criminals, or, as our friends across the pond put it, losers?

Then I had a truly amazing thought. He had been wearing a helmet with a visor during the attack, this no doubt not perfectly clean, and simply wasn't sophisticated or clever enough to hide his feelings. There was every chance that he had no idea Patrick was the one he had shot.

A quick glance in that direction told me that if Patrick had come to this same conclusion he was keeping it to himself, an expression of acute boredom on his face. There's nothing like looking bored to guarantee annoying the opposition.

Carrick said, 'Are you aware that Fielding's been known to the Metropolitan Police for years?'

'No,' said Biddulph.

'He's an associate of several mobsters, has fenced stolen goods for them but has always managed to avoid prosecution.'

'I reckon that makes him a bit of a hero, then.'

Carrick remained unruffled. 'Trouble is it's the poor sods working for him who get caught. Like now. There's no real evidence against him but you're taking the entire rap for attempted murder. And yet you say he organized it, gave you the gun, it was his bike, he was at the controls of it and he pointed out who you were to shoot.'

'Well, perhaps I made a mistake about that.'

'Do you want to make another statement?'

Biddulph swore at him. 'I don't want to do anything.'

'How much did he pay you?'

'Can't remember.'

During this exchange, Biddulph had been

glancing in Patrick's direction, something that I've noticed before during interviews, even when he says, and does, absolutely nothing. Perhaps it's a bit like having a loaded shotgun propped in one corner of a room for which nobody offers an explanation.

Carrick sighed. 'It must be a hell of a lot of cash he gave you that you've stashed away for when you're released from prison. I hope it's somewhere safe.'

Biddulph stared at nothing and said nothing.

'On the other hand, he might not have paid you in advance, which means you won't get it at all – ever.'

There was no reaction to this either.

'Why are you protecting Fielding?'

'I'm not. I lied. It wasn't anything to do with him.'

If you look up words for 'anger, war, fighting' and 'aggression' in *The Scots Thesauras* there are pages of them, those for 'peace, calmness' and 'patience' in very short supply indeed.

'*Why* did you lie?' the DCI barked, reflecting the above.

'He refused to pay me the last time I cleaned the windows at the pub – said I hadn't done a good enough job. I thought I'd make him sweat.'

'He doesn't clean them,' Patrick said in little more than a whisper. 'A firm in Bristol does.'

'Who asked you?' Biddulph bawled at him.

For this, he received a sunny smile.

'Fielding said you were a lying little louse,' Patrick went on to say helpfully.

'You think that's funny, don't you?' the other yelled.

Patrick laughed uproariously. 'So did Fielding. And you've just proved it by telling us you lied.'

Biddulph banged both fists down on the table. 'I'll kill the bastard!'

'You're in the slammer,' he was reminded. 'The last lot, your brother and half-brother, got paid by being hanged rather untidily by the neck until dead so I don't fancy your chances of getting Fielding when you come out of prison either.'

The observer then went into stuffed owl mode and there was rather a long silence.

'Oh, God,' Biddulph moaned.

'Don't you want to avenge Kyle and Steve's deaths?' Carrick said, in my view ruining Patrick's initiative.

'No, I hated their guts.'

The wretched little man hated everyone, didn't he?

After another silence, Biddulph continued, 'They were both stupid. Kyle rang me, bragging how he and Steve had attacked a cop in the sticks somewhere on orders from the boss. He went along as well. It was the big-time for them, he crowed, they'd arrived, were a force to be reckoned with and would soon have so much money they wouldn't know what to do with it. Yeah, they got paid all right. As I said, stupid.'

'And now you've attacked a cop on orders from the boss,' Carrick remarked silkily.

'I needed the money.'

'Which makes you just about as stupid as they were!' the DCI shouted and Biddulph started violently.

'On the other hand,' Patrick said, again quietly,

187

'get out of the hole you've dug for yourself by sticking to your original story. That's the intelligent thing to do.'

'But you haven't any evidence against Fielding,' Biddulph said, giving Patrick a scornful look and clearly not having thought through this suggestion. 'He's just said so.' A grubby-looking thumb was jerked in the DCI's direction.

'Then give us some. Think positive. Despite what this senior cop says' – a much cleaner thumb was jerked in Carrick's direction – 'I can tell that you're brainier than both your brothers put together.'

'Really?'

'Um.'

Yet again, there was another very long silence during which, this time, judging from the expression that flitted across the senior cop's face, Patrick fired a look at him that would have felled an ox to stop him from saying anything.

Finally, Biddulph breathed out noisily and said, 'All I know is that Fielding might not be his real name. The barmaid, Stella, told me that a couple of times someone's rung up and asked to speak to Matt. He laughed it off and said certain friends called him that – it was an old nickname of his after Matt Dillon in the telly cowboy show. But Steve used to go on about a Matt before we had a bust-up over money.'

'The same man?'

'God knows.'

'But d'you reckon your brother was working for this man called Matt when he first told you about him?'

'Could have been.'

'I know you're only a customer at the pub but are there times when Fielding isn't around?'

'According to some of my mates there, he's not around quite a lot.'

'Was anyone else in the know about the planned attack?'

'No idea.'

'Where did he get the weapon from?'

'He said he had contacts.'

'Come on – who?'

'Just some bloke he said was reliable and could get anything he wanted – at a price.'

'Locally or on the Internet from abroad?'

'Dunno.'

'What I mean is, had Fielding gone to meet someone to get it or had it arrived by, say, courier?'

'How the hell should I know?' Biddulph said angrily. 'No, wait a minute, I remember now. He had to serve behind the bar one evening as Bradley was late turning up and gave me a wink. He'd just come in from somewhere, was soaking wet and said some bitch had driven through a puddle and drenched him, done it on purpose but he didn't care as she'd given him what he wanted. I thought as he seemed so happy that he meant they'd had a quick one on the back seat but . . .' He broke off with a shrug.

Patrick sat back in his chair and I noticed that he was shaking slightly.

Carrick said, 'Are you sure your original statement is correct?'

'Yeah, it's the truth.'

189

'Do you want to retract or add anything to it other than what you've just said?'

'Only that he said I'd get five K for doing the job.'

The DCI made a few notes.

'And Fielding provided the weapon and drove the bike – no one else did?' Patrick persevered.

'He never lets anyone else have a go on it.' Having said that, Biddulph brightened. 'Just as well the bloke didn't die or I'd have been up for murder.'

I longed to scream at him that he was an unprincipled bastard.

'Coffee in my office,' Carrick declared when Biddulph had been escorted away.

'Five K?' Patrick lamented. 'Is that all I'm worth?'

'Your weight in gold to that lady there and your children. Thanks for observing.'

It was felt vital to have a debriefing in the Ring o' Bells that evening.

'Any female arms dealers round here?' Patrick asked Carrick.

'No, but I know of someone who's married to one. They live in Bristol – sometimes.'

I said, 'But otherwise are to be found on their luxury yacht anchored off one of the Greek islands?'

'Something like that. I've contacted Bristol CID but there's still not a shred of evidence that means I can apply for a warrant for Fielding's arrest. It's just one man's word against another's. And how many Matts are there in the UK?'

190

'Can't he be tailed when he goes off some-where?' As soon as I had spoken, I knew it had been a silly question.

Patrick said, 'I don't think there are the funds available to authorize watching someone just in case.' Although still weak, he had recovered quickly after a hot drink that had been followed not long afterwards by lunch in a nearby bistro.

Joanna had come along as well and was sipping wine while gazing appreciatively at the blazing log fire. She was soon to complete her initial training and hoped to be stationed not too far away from home. I knew that her husband shares his cases with her and values what she has to say.

With this in mind, I asked her what she thought about it.

'Are we quite sure about this girlfriend of Rolt's?' she replied after briefly thinking.

'He said that she's a lawyer,' Carrick said.

'Does that mean she's a barrister or a solicitor?'

'No idea.'

'Well, for someone connected with the law, she behaved in a pretty stupid fashion when she visited him at that pub by broadcasting his profession to all and sundry.'

'Perhaps she's involved with company law and wouldn't be that aware of the need for security,' her husband offered.

'I prefer to say she's either thick and probably therefore not a lawyer, or dodgy. Or, come to think of it, has a drink problem and was half canned when she arrived.'

I had to admit that this last possibility had a lot going for it, bearing in mind what Paul Bradley, the barman, had said were her actual words.

'Can't you question Fielding again?' Joanna continued. 'Put a bit more pressure on him. I mean, for goodness' sake, there he is as bold as brass just a few miles away.'

'I have no new evidence and the one able to put on the real pressure can't do so because he was the victim of the crime,' Carrick answered heavily. 'You know that.'

I wondered if that was official recognition of Patrick's interrogation skills.

'And, sadly, thumbscrews are illegal,' Patrick said under his breath.

'What would you have done in your MI5 days?' she went on to ask him.

'I had carte blanche.' Seeing that she was still curious, he added, 'Taken him away and pasted all hell out of him. But I'm a cop now – I think.'

He was, I knew, depressed and feeling utterly useless.

Carrick's mobile rang and he went outside to talk to whoever it was. He was back very quickly.

'Got to go. A serious fire's broken out at The Lion and the Unicorn. There might be fatalities.'

'I'd like to come with you,' Patrick said, half on his feet.

'You're not well enough.'

'I'm fine.'

'No. I don't care what the hell goes on in the NCA and shall pull rank on you if you persist.'

Patrick sat down again and I gave James a big smile.

'OK, Ingrid, but you'll probably have to make your own way home.'

As we walked away, Joanna offered to buy Patrick another drink but he just shook his head.

Wellsway had been closed off, only police and emergency vehicles permitted to enter. It was almost dark by this time but even in the dim light I could see the thick pall of black smoke rolling across the road and up the hill, a backdrop to the flashing blue lights of the fire appliances and ambulances. Carrick showed his ID to the patrolman stationed on the barricade and we drove closer. Despite the showers of sparks, people had come out of their houses on both sides of the road to watch.

The building was well alight, the ground floor an inferno, flames emerging from the first-floor windows and starting to lick through the roof tiles and around the chimneys. The DCI parked his car where it wouldn't be in the way and we both got out. I had never been so close to a large fire before and the roaring crackle of it, the heat, the threat to destroy everything in its path, was frightening.

Standing by one of the fire appliances, Carrick spoke to, or rather shouted with a firefighter directing the two hoses being utilized at ground level, one being used to cool down the house next door. He was also in contact by radio with those on an aerial ladder to direct water on to the upper storey and roof.

'It went up like a torch,' he reported when he came back and we had moved a little farther away as a gust of wind caused smoke to billow in our direction, the acrid fumes making us cough. 'The fire chief thinks there's a possibility of arson but he can't tell until the fire's out. Old buildings often burn like this as the timbers are so dry, he said. There was no chance of any of his crews going inside to look for anyone as the building was too dangerous by the time they arrived, even though they got here in minutes. The roof will probably go.'

Carrick then organized bystanders to be questioned at a safe distance.

We stayed while this was done and a few of the customers at the time were located. We discovered that those inside had heard someone, a man whose voice they didn't recognize, shout that smoke was coming from a storeroom and to leave the place immediately. According to one man, the barmaid, Stella, had been seen leaving and the kitchen staff had been hurried off the premises by the chef, but no one knew of Fielding's whereabouts. He had been due to help with the cooking that night but seemingly hadn't turned up, the chef having made no secret of his anger about it.

'Dead in his office?' I suggested.

'There's always hope,' Carrick said darkly. 'No, forget I said that.'

Involuntarily, I grabbed him as the roof collapsed with a massive roar, the firefighters running back just before masonry, burning beams and tiles crashed down into the road where they had been standing. Refuelled, the fire raged ever brighter and they tackled it again with an intensity that seemed to me like revenge. Another fire engine arrived.

'Sorry,' I said, dropping my arms. 'Autopilot.'

A large black smut on the end of his nose, Carrick gave me a grin. 'Anytime.'

He was approached by a constable. 'Sir, there's a man who wants to speak to someone senior.'

'Did you get his name?'

'No, sir, he's rather distressed and a bit incoherent.'

'I suppose I'd better talk to him then.'

I went with him and it was Paul Bradley. He was very out of breath and dishevelled – he had obviously been running.

'Thank God it's you!' he burst out as soon as he saw Carrick. 'Look, it wasn't me! I swear I didn't do it!'

'Please calm down,' said Carrick.

'My neighbour's just knocked at the door and said the pub's on fire. I didn't believe him, thought he was having me on but—' He broke off for a moment, gazing wildly at the scene, wringing his hands, and then said, 'I knew you'd think it was me after what I said about Fielding.'

'I haven't had a chance to think about it at all,' the DCI told him. 'I ken you shouldn't have discharged yourself from hospital. Please calm yourself, go home and come and see me tomorrow morning if you have anything you want to add to what you've already told us. No one's accusing you of anything and it might have been a complete accident. I won't know any more until I get the fire department's investigation team's report.'

Shoulders drooping, the man walked off downhill through the smoke.

'So was that genuine or a good piece of theatre?' Carrick asked me.

'I wouldn't have thought him capable of acting as convincingly as that,' I answered.

'Nor me. But you never know. I might pull him in and question him again anyway.'

I prepared to leave. 'Let me know if there's anything I can do.'

'I'll arrange a lift for you.'

'It's all right. I'll walk down to the railway station and get a taxi.'

'Not with him wandering around apparently half off his head, you won't.'

We compromised and I was given a lift to the station.

Fourteen

It was well into the next day before the site of the blaze had cooled sufficiently to allow anyone to investigate the cause and the work, including literally sifting through the finer material of what remained, took another two. In a telephone conversation to James Carrick while this was taking place, the 'hardboiled' – according to the DCI – chief fire officer pointed out to him that although no human remains had yet been found the missing owner of the premises might have already been dead or unconscious somewhere before it started. The cellar was another matter and it would take quite a while to remove the debris from that. He had finished by saying that the findings so far were that arson couldn't be ruled out, and he would send a detailed written report in due course.

Carrick had phoned to tell me this the morning after he received the call and went on to say that, as we already knew, people who had been in the building at the time had reported that the initial warning had been given by someone who had shouted that smoke was coming from a store-room. Apparently there had been three of these, like the rest of the interior now little more than piles of charcoal, ash and blackened bricks within the shell of the building. The 'someone' had yet to be identified.

Recognizing that all chief fire officers have no choice but be hardboiled – and if Carrick didn't he ought to – I related these developments to Patrick as we set off for the hospital so he could have the latest in a series of check-ups and an X-ray.

'It could have been Bradley,' he murmured. 'It's not unknown for people to rush to a crime scene and protest their innocence, assuming for a moment that it *was* arson. A bit like the parents of children they've murdered who have ostensibly gone missing going on TV shedding copious tears and offering rewards for information.'

'Before he rang off, James said he hadn't heard from Paul Bradley and was going to talk to him again. I get the impression he didn't believe what the man said the other night.'

'Did you?'

'I don't know.'

'Come on – switch on the cat's whiskers.'

'As I said to James at the time, I wouldn't have thought him capable of acting so convincingly.'

Later, back in the car, preparing to drive home, I suggested having a light lunch out.

'Wouldn't you prefer to be working at your desk?' Patrick enquired.

'We still have to eat.'

'After that session I'm happy to have something at home.'

I gazed at him. He had been rather pulled about to assess possible muscle damage – there wasn't anything lasting – and to assess his upper body mobility. This, together with a physiotherapist making sure he could do the exercises he had

198

been given, had not been pleasant for him. No complaints, just a man going pale under his fading tan.

'You're going to say diddums,' he complained now, staring back.

'I was about to offer to buy you a pint of something restorative followed by beef and horseradish sandwiches, actually.'

After the merest hesitation: 'OK.'

It was eventually confirmed that there were no human remains in what was left of The Lion and the Unicorn, not even charred bone fragments. Fielding had, it appeared, lived in what amounted to a flat on the first floor, rudimentary with a very basic bathroom, according to Stella, who had not wanted to reveal how she knew. Lynn Outhwaite, who was probably more, yes, hardboiled with regard to her own sex than her boss would have realized, had an answer to that. But Stella was adamant that she knew nothing about him other than that he regularly caught the train to London, where he stayed for two to three days, phoning for a taxi to take him to the station. She said she didn't think he had a vehicle of his own in Bath, which was understandable as the traffic was so bad and parking difficult.

I reckoned it was good of everyone to keep Patrick and me abreast of developments, either Carrick or Lynn phoning us most days. There seemed little point in my going into Bath to do anything in connection with the case, or rather cases if one regarded the attack on Commander Rolt as something different.

199

Patrick, whose thoughts over breakfast on this bright autumn morning must have reflected my own, suddenly said, 'Despite what someone said, no one appears to have turned up to take over from me on the Rolt case.'

'Perhaps they assume you're working from home,' was the only thing I could think of saying.

'I've done absolutely nothing,' he responded wretchedly.

'No, but your consultant has been standing in for you. That's what you can say if anyone asks.'

'I don't want to have to cover up for myself, to hide behind you.'

'Patrick, you're being so—'

He carved me up by angrily saying, 'Where is this bloody man Fielding anyway?'

Katie and Matthew came in, ready for school. This was unusual – the fact that they were together, that is – and it looked more like a deputation than a coincidence.

'Dad . . .' Katie began.

'I am he,' Patrick said, never miserable in front of the children. 'And an honorary one, which is even better, of course.'

With a bright smile, she embarked on what I guessed had been carefully rehearsed. 'Mum's been taking me out on George. He's been really good. But she said I mustn't canter as she doesn't want to let me off the leading rein and she can't run that fast.'

All right, a deputation of one.

Patrick said, 'I think you're already aware that

he won't play up when he's a bit fresh *until* he's let off the leading rein and asked to go a bit faster.'

Undeterred, Katie went on, 'Padraig said he's asked the lady who owns Haggis if you could ride him and come out with me and she said yes.'

'Ingrid can come out with you on Haggis.'

'But he ran off with her.'

I hadn't said a word about this to anyone, *anyone*.

'I've already told you that Dad's not yet fit enough to ride,' Matthew said to her.

'I have thought of that. There's a Plan B.'

'Which is?' Patrick asked, all seriousness.

'Padraig said that if Mum hasn't the time he'll gallop George around the field a few times and then he'll be a bit tired and not silly.'

The one whose ribs were mending beautifully rested his chin on his hands and stared out of the window, giving it thought. Inwardly, I was pleading with him to see sense.

'Tell you what,' he said finally, 'ask Padraig to gallop Haggis around the field a few times first and I'll come with you. But you're staying on the leading rein.'

Well-schooled not to give him big hugs at the moment, she ran over and kissed him.

Ye gods.

Or was this highly observant child also a genius?

'I've had another update from the Fire Brigade,' James Carrick said as he pressed buttons on the coffee machine that had been in his office at the nick in Manvers Street and was now putting in an appearance here. 'It *was* arson.'

I had called in to see him the following day as I had to go into the city anyway.

'They're still digging out the cellar so can't yet provide a final report,' he continued. 'But it looks as though the fire, or rather fires, were started in all three storerooms. No burned-out petrol cans or similar containers have been found so far and the floors in that area are concrete so evidence like that hasn't ended up buried in the cellar below. The rest of the place, but for the toilets and kitchen, had wooden floors. The storeroom floors have damage that indicates the intensity of the fire and that some kind of accelerant was used. Perhaps he, or she, took away the cans or whatever it was in, out through the back.'

'One assumes that the rooms were full of junk and inflammable stuff,' I said.

'I ended up having to phone Paul Bradley about that. He was a bit twitchy to start with but calmed down as we spoke. He told me that there had been all kinds of things in them and he'd actually mentioned to Fielding that it was a fire hazard. One room, the smallest, was primarily used for plastic containers of cooking oil, new and used, and there were also a couple of fridges. Cleaning materials were stored in another room together with disposables like toilet rolls and paper napkins. The third contained mostly rubbish that Fielding kept saying he was going to take to the tip, a few old tables, broken chairs and sacks of junk mail, old newspapers, cardboard boxes and so forth that were in the place when he bought it.'

'Was he saving it all up for a lovely bonfire?' I ventured.

'You think he might have burned down his own pub and run?' Carrick said in amazement.

'It has to be considered, surely. Think of the potential insurance payout.'

He gave me my coffee. 'I have to confess I hadn't thought of that. But I still think it could have been Bradley. I'll pull him in and question him about his movements that evening.'

'And Wayne Biddulph's in custody.'

'Yes, otherwise *he'd* be the prime suspect. How's Patrick getting on?'

'He's gone horse-riding with Katie.'

'You're kidding!'

'I dropped them off at the stables but couldn't bear to stay and watch. I'm convinced he'll really hurt himself one way or another. Padraig's going to give them a lift home – or take Patrick to A and E,' I added grimly.

'Who's Porrick?'

I spelt it for him, explaining, 'He's Irish and the owner of the livery stable.'

As I was leaving a little later, Michael Greenway rang me, mostly to ask after Patrick. Then he said, 'If you're wondering why no one else seems to have been given the job of investigating the attack on Rolt, it's because no one has. He's asked for it to be given a lower priority.'

'Any idea why?' I asked.

'As usual, he didn't say a lot when he spoke to me yesterday but hinted at a staff shortage and the fact that what happened to him is quite likely connected with other cases that they have to concentrate on.'

'We already knew that.'

'But he did tell me he'd heard about the fire that gutted the pub where he stayed. As you're aware, Fielding's on their radar because of his connections with Matt Dorney, his father and other mobsters who are now dead, still alive and/ or in any number of slammers. Tell Patrick not to rush things,' he ended his call by saying.

Like going out on a horse he'd never ridden before, for example?

When I got home with a carload of household shopping, having seen no ambulances with flashing blue lights on the way, Carrie helped me to unload it all.

'He's having a rest,' she whispered. 'Didn't say anything when he came in.'

I tore indoors to find the joy of my life lying flat on his back on the bed.

'I knew it was you hammering up the stairs. I didn't fall off, Katie got her canter, she didn't fall off and I've taken painkillers,' Patrick reported without opening his eyes.

I went away.

When I put my head around the door about an hour later to check that he wasn't in a coma as a result of having taken too many of the afore-mentioned pills, Patrick had put on his new Glock gun harness and was practising drawing the weapon.

'It was arson,' I said.

'Bradley? It's all right, it's not loaded.'

'James thinks there's every chance he did it. And the man does seem to be a bit unbalanced after what happened to him.'

'For which he's hardly to be blamed. But if you get involved with what I'll call the rough element . . . Who then, if it wasn't Fielding himself for the insurance money?'

'Anyone with a grudge against him or even someone investigating the case, hoping to make things happen.'

'You mean a *cop*?'

'Not necessarily. But it was something you might have done at one time.'

'I don't think I've ever burnt down a pub,' Patrick said, sounding a bit offended. Beyond the call of duty, perhaps.

'No, but you did once shoot a mobster.'

'Putting him in hospital under police guard prevented him from being actually killed by another mobster,' Patrick reminded me. '*And* he proceeded to sing like a canary.'

Another name came into my mind, but I said nothing.

Commander Greenway was still keen that his own NCA department arrested whoever was behind the attack on David Rolt. I was in no doubt about this as he had told me so himself later that same day. But, wary because of the high cost in murdered personnel suffered by F9 already, not to mention the attempt on Patrick's life, he proceeded with caution and decided to seek advice. This entailed again visiting the latter of these, bringing with him a more work-orientated mindset than on the previous occasion.

'I'm not here,' he began by saying when we had seated ourselves in the living room. 'You haven't seen me and today, to your certain knowledge, I'm in Harrogate for a conference.'

'That's a hell of a long way to go for a G and T,' Patrick said.

Unusually for him, Greenway wasn't amused, just eyed the speaker with what I can only call a clinical gaze.

'I'm a lot better,' Patrick told him peaceably.

'I need your help.'

'I can't—'

'No, I don't mean anything strenuous,' the commander interposed hurriedly. 'I need to know what you would have done when you worked for MI5.'

'You're not the first person to ask me that.'

'Nevertheless . . .'

'I take it we're talking about Matt Dorney.'

'Yes.'

'If he was a serious criminal who was also compromising national security – selling state secrets he'd somehow got hold of to a hostile nation, for example – I would have probably been ordered to arrange a little accident to befall him. And before you ask, I'm not doing things like that these days.'

'But how would you have found him?'

'You know the answer to that already – I'd have gone undercover. And I do have to point out that there's nothing against this man right now that would stand up in a court of law,

206

just some circumstantial evidence and other people's testimonies – and most of those are criminals as well.'

'It seems likely that he was ultimately responsible for the attack on Rolt and possibly on you, seeing that these same criminals are saying a mobster in London is behind it all.'

'How many mobsters in London are there?'

'You're playing the devil's advocate.'

'Perhaps I'm a bit more level-headed than I used to be.'

'Before you got this job you were my adviser,' Greenway said. 'I think I'm a bit desperate for ideas here.'

'Mike, you have any number of people, experts in many fields, at your fingertips. You don't need *me*.'

'I do. You have contacts that I'm not supposed to know about; for example, you know exactly where to buy illegal firearms in London because you've done it, you're an expert in silent killing and there are all kinds of oddball characters that you've knocked around with, including that mad-as-a-box-of-frogs one-time Royal Tank Regiment brigadier.'

'Who, Shandy?'

'He's now set himself up as some kind of maverick investigator – in his spare time, one imagines – and is chumming up with people who make a serious amount of money from crime.'

'Yes, and if he carries on like that he'll be found in the Thames tied up in a sack with a couple of concrete blocks for company.'

'You knew?'

'I met him quite recently. I agree – the man's right off the wall. I told him to forget it and go home to his wife and family, and then we both got drunk.'

'Did you mention Matt Dorney to him?'

'I may have done.'

'He's trying to track him down and has had a degree of success. Did you know that he reports to the Met?'

Patrick shook his head. 'He's a damned fool. No.'

'That's how I know. Apparently someone told him that Dorney bought a pub in Bath under an assumed name with a view to using it as a West Country HQ so he could launder money through the business. But he then changed his mind. That's what Shandy's saying, although he doesn't know if the place has been put up for sale.'

'He's probably partly correct – as you know, The Lion and the Unicorn on the Wells Road has burnt down. Ingrid has a theory that he and John Fielding are the same man.'

Greenway's eyebrows shot up. 'Why haven't you mentioned this to me before?'

'For the good reason that Dorney has a scar on the right side of his face and Fielding hasn't,' I said, sticking to the facts. 'So, more correctly, I *had* a theory. Although, I have to mention in mitigation that Wayne Biddulph said he knew that people had phoned Fielding's pub and asked to speak to Matt.'

'Was Fielding clean-shaven when you questioned him and were you present when Carrick did?' he asked me.

'No, but—'

'If it was a small or faint scar, stubble would hide it. He may also use stage make-up. We must also bear in mind that scars tend to fade as people get older.' He pondered. 'So if true and this man, who comparatively recently changed his name from Burgess to Fielding, has a duel identity, or even others for that matter, and is Len Dorney's son, it wouldn't be the first time a mobster's had multiple personas. The question is does he still have the same house he owned when he was calling himself Burgess?'

'I very much doubt it,' Patrick said, even though Greenway had probably been thinking aloud.

'I shall organize a raid.' And with just the briefest of goodbyes, and having refused coffee, the commander departed, saying he would call in to see Carrick in Bath.

'Are you concerned about Tim Shandy?' I asked Patrick.

'Slightly, but when you've been involved in hand-to-hand fighting against the Serbs in Bosnia after you've retired from commanding tanks, you tend to be able to look after yourself. He went off and was a mercenary for a while, if you remember, ending up being seriously wounded and blinded in one eye. But I feel responsible for what he's doing now. I shouldn't have said a word.'

'Blame the whisky.'

'I wish I could.'

'The worst thing is having had Fielding in custody.'

'I'd rather not be reminded of that as well, thank you.'

Greenway's raid on a house in Ealing in the early hours of the following morning discovered nothing but a pair of extremely frightened tenants who thought they were bailiffs come to evict them for being behind with the rent. Enquiries that started at the letting agency soon proved without a doubt that the couple involved had absolutely no connection with John Fielding, Matt Dorney or crime generally, and that the owner of the property was a woman by the name of Lucy McCallum. Mrs McCallum had had no brushes with the law, either.

Feeling a lot stronger the following day, Patrick spent most of the morning at the premises that Bath CID were temporarily using and I gathered that for most of that time he brainstormed with James Carrick. They went through the complicated case, or rather mixture of cases, right back to when Commander Rolt had been clubbed down on The Monks' Way. Despite these efforts, nothing in the way of useful ideas emerged. Then, when Patrick had been back home for about twenty minutes, he received a phone call on his mobile.

'You've done *what*?' I heard my husband shout, and went into the conservatory to investigate.

'Now, you listen to me—'

By the time I got there, he'd broken off to hear what was being said.

Then, 'No, Tim, emphatically not. I have no wish to get involved with anything like that. Besides, you don't know the whole story.'

The argument went on for a while, and then Patrick furiously hung up on him.

'So is it cheese and pickle sandwiches or are you going to start chewing on that fern over there?' I gently enquired.

'D'you know what that idiot Shandy's done? After nosing and asking around, he's, as he put it, "bumped into" Matt Dorney at a strip club. Apparently the barman, on request, pointed him out. Shandy, pretending to be half-canned and in the know, told Dorney that one of the investigators trying to build a case against him was shot by a local mobster in Bath and is now having to resign due to his injuries. This investigator is so bitter and twisted about the lack of official support he's received he's ready to sell his soul to the enemy. Dorney said he'd quite like to meet him, at the club, which he apparently owns, so it's probably the same one he was photographed leaving. All *I* have to do is turn up – it's called Lanny's – with suitable back-up and arrest him.'

'Shandy doesn't know about Fielding though and that he and Dorney might be the same person?'

'No.'

'And that you've already spoken to him on more than one occasion so he'll put two and two together, know whom to expect and will act accordingly, turning up with a hit squad of his own to make a better job of killing you this time.'

'Riveting, isn't it?'

Fifteen

'The NCA isn't the NCIS,' Patrick said thought-fully later that day, clearly wishing that it was.

'You're not seriously thinking about Shandy's proposal!' I said in alarm.

'There *is* an opportunity here.'

'Look, Special Agent Gibbs, as you said your-self, he's right off the wall. I like Tim but his thinking processes are not normal and sense of self-preservation when started on something non-existent. *And* he's obsessed with explosives.'

'He did a wonderful job of blowing up that old slate mine cavern in Wales that a rogue cop had been using for a school for terrorists. The place was lethal and likely to collapse at any moment and he saved the park authorities a mint of money in demolition fees.'

Seeming to forget for a moment that he hadn't been a witness to that epic explosion and I had, Patrick chuckled wistfully and then went into a reverie, brainstorming again.

Whatever this entailed regarding any proposals or plans, it had to be put on hold when he was told by the medics to continue to rest, further blood tests indicating that there was a lingering infection in his wound. He was given yet more pills, different ones.

I then had to reassure Katie that this further but minor setback was nothing whatsoever to do

212

with his having gone riding with her and an arrangement was made to enable her to ride George soon in the outdoor ménage at the livery stable with her 'honorary Dad' watching, on foot, offering advice if necessary.

The next morning, the TV news was on when we were having breakfast and there was a report of a fire at what was described as a nightclub at Barking, east London. The club, one gathered, had at one time lost its licence and been closed down due to non-adherence to fire regulations and after illegal immigrants – trafficked women – had been found on the premises, forced to work as prostitutes. It had, however, since reopened, ostensibly under new management. It did not appear that anyone had been killed or injured in the fire as it had occurred just before six a.m. The fire brigade had successfully prevented the blaze from spreading to adjacent properties and were still on-site, damping down what was left of the building. Judging by what was on the TV screen, the place had been as good as gutted and instantly brought to my mind another similar occurrence.

I caught Patrick's eye and he shook his head.

'Even assuming that it's the same club, I haven't contacted Shandy for *any* reason,' he assured me, carrying on thickly spreading marmalade on a slice of toast.

'Perhaps as you turned him down flat he decided to go about things his own way.'

'Give the man some credit. He has no axe to grind over this. He doesn't owe me any favours either and wouldn't regard reducing Dorney to

213

cinders as any solution to the problem of bringing him to justice – if it even was his club.'

'Another thought then – add it to what happened at the pub in Bath and you might have someone intent on driving a mobster out of all his hideaways.'

'Rolt?'

'Surely not.'

'I wouldn't actually put money on his not being involved after what happened to him and the murder of a couple of members of his team.'

I switched off the TV when my mobile, on the table before me – I never seemed to be able to get away from it these days – rang and it was Greenway.

'Didn't want to get Patrick out of bed,' he began. 'Have you seen the news?'

'Patrick's right here and yes, we have,' I replied. 'But is it the same club that Dorney was photographed leaving?'

'It is and I only know that because the Met have been keeping an eye on the place since it reopened due to a suspicion that despite what was said it's under the same management. Although the place doesn't seem to be run as a brothel this time, there's a rumour illegal activities are going on there.'

'But they made no connection with Dorney?' I asked incredulously.

'I'm told that there was never a suspected connection with mobsters. He was once spotted, and photographed, leaving the premises. End of story.'

'And he hasn't been noticed there since? Surely that's downright incompetent of them.'

'Plenty of people go in and out after dark . . .' Greenway muttered, and left it at that.

I handed the phone to Patrick. 'You'll have to tell the boss what Shandy said to you.'

'I already have.'

Patrick's criticisms of the Met were put more forcibly and I gathered from the following conversation that the commander had viewed Shandy's efforts as a sleuth not worth acting upon.

After the call, Patrick sadly laid my phone back on the table and said, 'Everything is going to rats.'

And he could do absolutely nothing himself, of course.

But Shandy was not a man to give up easily. That evening, late, and when Patrick had gone to bed, Tim rang his mobile, which I had with me.

'We haven't spoken for such a long time,' he began by saying a little shyly when I had explained the situation. 'What an adventure it was in that damned cavern, eh?'

'I'm really glad it isn't there any more,' I said.

'It would still be and so would I, mouldering bones, if you hadn't got me out. Ingrid, old friend, I have to tell you – and risking the ire of Patrick by stirring it up again – that Dorney didn't go up in flames with his confounded club last night. He phoned me – I'd given him my number – and was livid. Someone's out to get him, he raved,

215

some petty crook is out to force him, *him*, out of business. First Bath, he howled, and now London.'

I said, 'Tim, how are you playing this and why is he so chummy towards you?'

He chuckled. 'I'm playing myself, an old fool whose brains have been addled by warfare and booze. For some reason, he seems to be able to relate to that and I yarn away about fighting with tanks, the sort of thing most men like to hear. Anyway, he's still interested in meeting a disenchanted cop – to see what info he can get out of him, obviously. He might even offer him a job.'

'Where does he want to meet him?'

'Apparently that's the next thing to be discussed.'

'I'm not sure that Patrick's well enough for anything like that,' I said cautiously to buy time while I thought about it, all the while furious with him.

'I did mention that he was still recovering.'

'Tim, there's something you don't know. We're fairly convinced that he's changed his name to John Fielding and was almost certainly involved with Patrick being shot. Plus, we've both interviewed him. He must already know who you're talking about and won't believe it because Patrick doesn't come across as a man who'd get all bitter and twisted and assist criminals. Not only that, Dorney must have a suspicion that Patrick's aware of who was responsible for the shooting. It would be terribly dangerous and have a high risk of failure.'

'I have to agree with you there. But—'

'This isn't a game of chess!' I yelled.

'Please put it to him,' was his humble parting remark.

Which I did, the next morning.

Patrick heard me out, and then said, 'The oracle's been quiet of late. What do you think?'

'My opinion is that you should place it before Greenway again with the firm recommendation that it be handed over to the Met. I wasn't aware that the NCA carried out major armed raids, covert or otherwise, anyway.'

'I know what he'll say – Mike has no time at all for amateurs.'

'Besides, as I pointed out to Tim, you don't give the impression that you're a man who could be all bitter and twisted.'

He looked a bit surprised and then put on a horrible expression, instantly a man who was seriously bitter and twisted.

'What, then?' I snapped, unnerved. 'We can't just do nothing.'

'Shall we go and talk to Rolt about it?'

'*I'll* go and talk to Rolt.'

'Ingrid, I'm perfectly well enough now to sit on a train and in a taxi.'

As we had half expected, Commander Rolt preferred us not to visit him at the Woodford HQ, saying that New Scotland Yard would be better as far as he was concerned because he wanted to talk to someone else there face-to-face and it would be easier for us too. A time was agreed for the next day and he said he would meet us in the visitors' entrance lobby.

When I first glimpsed the commander, my immediate thought was that here was a man at roughly the same stage of recovery from serious injury as the one by my side. The scar, still livid on the side of his forehead, was surrounded by a hint of faded bruising, and the impression I got as he came towards us was of overall weakness.

We exchanged greetings and then he led the way to a large room on the third floor that was lined with portraits, paintings and photographs of one-time unsmiling law enforcers and was obviously normally used for formal meetings. A long boardroom sort of table was in the centre with chairs around it, a smaller number of armchairs arranged at the sides. The decor could only be described as mind-numbingly boring, in the old Great Western Railway livery colours of brown and cream. In a corner was a built-in unit with a coffee machine and Rolt provided us with some, apologizing for the apparent lack of biscuits. No, not someone with the patience or inclination to rummage in cupboards.

Rolt seated himself, surprisingly laughed softly and said, 'A victims' support session, anybody?'

'I have my support,' Patrick said with a smile, clapping a hand on my shoulder.

'You're very fortunate,' Rolt murmured. Becoming businesslike, he then asked what was on our minds.

Patrick told him while I pondered on what might have happened to the loud-mouthed female with a possible drink problem who had turned up in Bath. I rather hoped that she had been given

218

notice to quit. And Piers thought he was seeing Thea, didn't he?

'Greenway won't touch it,' Patrick finished by saying.

'I'm not surprised,' the other remarked dryly. 'This Shandy – is he on the line?'

'Absolutely.'

'Can you rely on him, though?'

'Yes, but it has to be borne in mind, as Ingrid says, that his sense of self-preservation once he's started something is nigh-on zero.'

'There would be no need for you to be involved personally,' the commander said, reading the reason behind Patrick's statement quite wrongly.

'How's that?'

'I'm sure you could find a police officer who would be a good enough lookalike if the meeting place was sufficiently dim – another club, perhaps.'

'No, that's simply not ethical.'

'It's been done before.'

'Not by me, it hasn't.'

Well, OK, I thought, but in our MI5 days a colleague, Terry Meadows and I had once 'borrowed' John, Patrick's father, who had been very enthusiastic, to take his place in a non-hazardous situation without Patrick's knowledge. He had been furious with us.

Rolt said, 'Am I to understand then that you want my support for this scheme? I can't see that Greenway will be too pleased.'

'I've been upsetting higher authority for as long as I can remember,' Patrick countered. 'What I'm doing here is trotting it past you in the same way

219

I have Greenway. If your reaction is negative as well, I shall have to think again.'

'Whatever happens, you'll need armed back-up and that means involving units from the Met or Avon and Somerset forces and I can't see your chief constable agreeing to *that*. My department tends not to get involved with armed intervention as I simply don't have the staff and have to request support from the Met.'

'I'm not planning on having any kind of shoot-out but the possibility of it has to be factored in.'

Rolt sat back in his chair and regarded us soberly. 'Any ideas as to who started the fire at the strip club?'

'Not one,' Patrick said. 'Shandy might be in the frame for it as people in adjacent properties reported that there was a bit of a bang before the fire started.'

'Shandy's into bangs?' asked the commander.

'Yes, I forgot to mention that he's an explosives expert. But you don't have to be an expert in anything to start a fire – and I would like to point out that no one has yet said this recent one was arson.'

'But before that there was a fire at The Lion and the Unicorn, which was.' He took a deep breath. 'I'm sorry but I don't think I can be helpful here. Naturally, it's in everyone's interest to get hold of Dorney but—' He broke off with a shrug, and then added, 'Keep me in the picture. If anything more concrete comes up, for example, if we can really find out where this man spends most of his time, then please get in touch again.'

Outside in the roar of traffic and gloom of an

overcast sky, Patrick took my arm and said, 'It's a bit early for a drink, isn't it?'

'Not as long as it's just more coffee,' I told him.

'Neither of those career cops wants to risk his pension,' Patrick said bitterly a little later, savagely cutting his Danish pastry into four.

'That's not quite fair,' I said. 'The fact that they're career cops makes them professionally cautious. Unlike you, they weren't trained to blow people's heads off and *then* ask questions.'

As I had predicted, this made him laugh.

'Is the oracle back in working order?' Patrick went on to ask.

'No. But it's beavering away, churning out all kinds of rubbish. I'm ignoring it.'

'Look, you may be perfectly correct about Fielding being Dorney.'

'There's no evidence.'

'Ingrid, nobody expects you to be right all the time.'

'You know how I feel: that you're not strong enough yet to bring this man to justice. I only came with you today to keep you company and I really wish you'd wait until you've fully recovered. The Met can arrest Dorney.'

'But I was assigned to the case and they haven't given the job to anyone else. He'll be in South America by the time everyone gets their act together.'

'Bugger Dorney. You're far more important.'

'So you're not going to tell me your latest hunch.'

'No.'

Instead of staying the night as we had planned, we went home, my husband a very unhappy man. A phone call from Tim Shandy while we were on the train did not improve matters. Patrick spoke to him and told me afterwards that he had sounded extremely worried. He had apologized awkwardly, saying that he was leaving London immediately, having been warned off, but didn't go into any more details. For his family's sake, he had to abandon what he had started.

'At least he's seen sense,' Patrick sighed afterwards.

I soon realized that I'd done the wrong thing in not sharing my thoughts with him as Patrick's misery and frustration caused him to throw himself into what I regarded as wildly unwise activities. The morning after we got home he went out on George, returning in pain and exhausted. After taking a couple of painkillers and sitting down for a while waiting for them to take effect, he set off for a walk, not asking if I wanted to go with him. After lunch, he cut the grass, even though a man is employed to help in the garden. I wasn't reading into this any attempt to pay me back for refusing to reveal my ideas – it was just male stubbornness. To try to improve his mood I offered to treat him to a meal at the pub that evening and, gloomily, he agreed.

We were early and, as it was an unseasonably warm evening, we sat in the twilight on a seat on the edge of the village green where we were in the light cast from the pub windows and through the open doorway. Across the green, owls hooted from the trees surrounding the churchyard.

'George behaved himself this morning,' Patrick broke our silence by saying.

'Just as well,' I commented.

'Greenway rang me while I was out for my walk. He wondered if I knew that the strip club fire was arson too. Same sort of method as at the pub in Bath; fires started in several locations in the utility areas where what amounted to rubbish was stored until it could be disposed of. Some kind of accelerant had been used, which the fire brigade did not think was petrol. Mike thinks another mobster's either out to get Dorney or destroy his assets.'

'Or both.'

'Um. D'you think—'

He stopped speaking as, in the distance, a woman started shouting. The shouts turned to screams and then, full tilt, she came running across the green, shouting for help. I noticed that she was quite young, her feet were bare, her dress appeared to have been half torn off her and then, when she had almost reached the pub and safety, two men caught up with her, the first tackling her and slamming her face down on to the grass. He got up, wrenched her to her feet, spun her round as he shook her and then slapped her face hard.

Any second blow didn't land, her assailant's arm caught and twisted by Patrick, thus lining himself up for a clip to the jaw, a carbon copy of the one that had dealt with Dorney's henchman at Hackney. His friend lashed out and then endeavoured to kick away the arrival but both efforts missed and he got roughly the same treatment, joining his companion on the ground.

'Call the cops,' Patrick gasped, bending over, hands on knees, when I had arrived, having jumped up as soon as he did. I had caught the woman as she overbalanced and clutched her to me.

No one seated at the tables or on the benches had moved and still sat there as though frozen. I took the girl over to the seat we had just left and it seemed to shake them out of their torpor, a woman coming over to offer her jacket as the muddied assault victim was shivering violently. Through tears, her voice shaking, she told me that she had gone to the churchyard to lay flowers on her mother's grave and had stayed for a while, thinking about her. The men, she now realized, had been there already, drinking, as one of them, laughing, had thrown a bottle at her and called out that she was hanging around hoping to have sex with them.

Remarkably quickly, the police came, one of whom recognized Patrick and invited him to make the arrests, which he did, the men sitting on the grass, scowling. An ambulance arrived and took the girl to hospital for a check-up. Statements were made and I heard mutterings about an illegal travellers' camp, and someone else – a woman – complaining in a loud voice that excessive force had been used in the arrests.

At last, everything calmed down and the village returned to its autumn evening peacefulness. We went inside the inn where I ordered a bottle of a rather good red wine, night-flying insects having sampled and then drowned in our unfinished drinks outside.

'You know I'm not allowed to have any of that because of the bloody pills,' Patrick said when it was brought to our table together with two glasses.

'You can with the new ones. I double-checked at the chemist's. In moderation, though.'

He had said nothing other than what was necessary to the police and I hadn't wanted to enquire after his welfare and thereby possibly embarrass him with others around, but now, having ordered our meal, I gazed across the table at him. Our eyes met and I saw that although he was still in pain the glitter was back in those wonderful grey eyes.

'Your health, battleaxe,' he said, raising his glass.

Sixteen

The following morning, Elspeth told us John had declared that the lychgate entrance to the churchyard would in future be locked at dusk, and a couple of parishioners, one a retired police sergeant, had volunteered to take it in turns to keep an eye on it during the day. A little later, James Carrick rang me with the news that one of the arrested 'suspects' – both were members of the travellers' community mentioned – had been wearing a Rolex watch that had been stolen the previous week in the latest of a series of local burglaries. The travellers had packed up and disappeared overnight but were being sought as he had an idea other stolen items might be found in their vehicles. The DCI had finished by saying that someone had made a complaint about the brutal way the two men had been apprehended. Did I have any thoughts on that?

I told him that I had an idea who had made the complaint as she had been loudly proclaiming to that effect at the time. She was known in the village as an eccentric troublemaker who held the legalization of gay marriage against the rector personally and on those grounds, and others – fabricated – had tried to get Elspeth ousted from the WI. And yes, Patrick had floored each of the semi-inebriated men seemingly intent on mindless violence and rape with, for him, great restraint.

'In that case, I hope he's going to turn up for work on Monday,' Carrick had replied glumly, for ever a Scot.

Patrick, who appeared to have suffered no lasting damage, did indeed set off on Monday, in a taxi as he was driving only for short distances, with a view to working mornings only throughout the week. Relieved and yet anxious at the same time, I was able to give time to writing, finding that I had to read my latest novel right through from the beginning as it had been such a long time since I had done any real work on it.

On the Wednesday, my mobile rang for the fourth time that morning and I almost hurled it into the wastepaper basket.

'Hi, it's Piers,' said a familiar voice. 'I tried to get hold of Patrick but he's not answering his phone.'

'I think he's in court today,' I said. 'He'd have had to switch it off for most of the time.'

'Is he recovering well?'

I mentioned the patient's stubbornness, gave him a few other details and then asked if he wanted me to give Patrick a message.

'Well, you can if you like. It's just that I've run down Matt Dorney and thought I'd let you know.'

I promised that I would pass on the message as soon as Patrick got home and that one of us would contact him. Then I added, 'How good are you at starting fires?'

I distinctly heard him draw in his breath through his teeth before he said, 'I'm good at bonfires on

227

November the fifth and barbecues.' Then he laughed and rang off.

'It's real progress,' Patrick said. 'I'd like to know how he got the information.'

He'd had a late lunch at work and we were walking in the garden. I was holding Mark and Patrick. Vicky, who'd been to playgroup that morning, tripped on the way home and grazed both hands and her chin. Only being carried around by Daddy seemed to help the situation, and Daddy was being very stoical about it.

I had already passed on Ashley's message and now said, 'Dorney raged to Shandy that he thought someone was trying to drive him out and/or put him out of business. First the pub in Bath, then the club in Barking. Now Piers is saying that he's tracked him down. To his HQ? Home? Business number three? He didn't go into details, obviously preferring to talk to you about it. And, while we're on the subject, what I didn't feel I ought to bother you with is that my instincts tell me that Ashley started both fires.'

'The oracle's out of its bottle then.'

'Only on licence.'

'It's quite a good theory. He's been to Bath, he knew where the pub was and might have seen something that aroused his suspicions while he was there. Then he tracked down Dorney's strip club and did the same.'

'You don't just burn down places on suspicion,' I argued.

'No, and if he did he appears to be the kind of guy who would have to have very good reasons.'

228

We strolled for a little longer and then, both offspring having nodded off, went back indoors and filed them appropriately, Mark in his cot and Vicky on one of the sofas, her favourite.

Patrick then gave me what I can only call an armed smile, which I hoped meant that he had no intention of committing himself to any rash enterprises, and rang Piers Ashley. Or tried to – his number was unobtainable and remained so for the rest of the day.

And the next.

This slightly alarming news was given to me when Patrick came home that evening having ended up working all day. He went off to have a shower and to say hello to everyone, came back with Vicky who was clutching a couple of teddy bears and still in need of cuddles, poured himself a tot and seated himself, his little daughter and her friends on his lap. The kittens, finding no room to curl up, perched on a shoulder each.

'That's it,' he said. 'From now on I refuse to have my conduct in this case dictated to by cops, ex-cops, barmy ex-army officers and a mobster who thinks he's above the law.'

'Piers might be in danger,' I pointed out.

'Everyone who goes near Dorney is in danger. But let's put this in perspective. A man who must now be regarded as a member of the public, as Shandy is, is messing around with serious criminals. The police can't be expected to go running to their aid without any indication of where they actually are.'

Which, of course, made me feel dreadful for

not having asked Ashley for more details at the time.

In the early hours of the following morning, a wine bar not far from the Roman baths in the city was raided by several masked men who had driven down the pedestrianized street in a stolen 4x4, a Shogun, and rammed it into the building, smashing through the windows and door. The place was closed and not their main target, for they then used powerful drills to make holes in a party wall, set charges and blew a large hole through it into the jewellers next door, the front of which was protected by steel shutters. By this time, at least two intruder alarms were going off but they coolly grabbed everything they could lay their hands on in both premises, including cases of spirits and a small safe. All this was manhandled outside where, by this time, a getaway van was waiting.

A woman looking out of a window in a second-floor flat over a shop opposite had been awakened by the noise and had already dialled 999. She could only watch, horrified, as a man who seemed to be the leader of the gang appeared on the pavement shouting and swearing at the others and then shot two people who were running towards the scene, one of whom was later found to be an off-duty community support officer. Later, both he and the other man died.

'And that wasn't the end of it,' James Carrick said grimly. 'On their way out of the city, on the London Road, they deliberately knocked a nurse off her bike. She was cycling home from her shift at The Royal United Hospital. She's back where she works with multiple injuries that she *might* not die from. The van was then aimed at a couple of people on a zebra crossing who managed to jump out of the way, and then the bastards fired several shots at a man sleeping rough in a shop doorway, all of which, miraculously, missed. The van has subsequently been found burnt out near Chippenham. This has all the hallmarks of someone we've heard of before, hasn't it?'

Together with quite a few other people, we were in the general office of the temporary police station where, later that same morning but early by most people's standards, the DCI was partway through holding a briefing. I rather got the impression that he hadn't noticed we were present, which was fine by me as I love being a sort of fly on the wall.

Carrick continued, 'A witness living in a flat opposite reported seeing four men load boxes and other stuff into a white Transit van that turned up a few minutes later. She thought the driver stayed behind the wheel of the vehicle while this was going on, although in the confusion she can't be sure. I think one can safely assume that those same four were inside the Shogun when it rammed the wine bar premises and, rightly, the witness pointed out that she couldn't see what was happening as the vehicle was mostly inside the building and blocked her view. One wonders why they didn't reverse it out a bit to make getting past it with the stuff they'd stolen easier. It doesn't appear there was any inside help – that is, no one had stayed behind in either premises to assist.

Both proprietors and their staff will be inter-viewed as soon as we've finished here.'

Lynn Outhwaite entered the room in some haste and apologized for being late.

'Any developments?' Carrick asked her.

She said, 'Well, as everyone will know, the badly damaged Shogun has been taken away for forensic examination. The vehicle was very dirty. The inside appears to be filthy too and, at a guess, regularly carried around several dogs. There is hay and straw on the floor, so farming or what I shall call rural pursuits might be involved. In short, there's every chance that the fingerprints and DNA of half the population of Somerset are in, and on, it.'

'Do we know who the owners are?' someone wanted to know.

'Not yet. Both registration plates had been removed.'

I wondered if whoever it belonged to had been involved in, or connected to, the raid and just happened to have a fairly worthless vehicle they wanted to get rid of.

'There were a couple of other witnesses,' the acting DI resumed. 'They dived into shop door-ways when the shots were fired, and after the van drove off went to the aid of the men who had been hit. Luckily, they stayed around until the ambulances and an area car arrived and left their names and addresses with the crews. I thought I would talk to them when I leave here and get any more details they might be able to give me.'

'Then go,' her boss said, making shooing gestures.

'Or would you rather I gave priority to interviewing the owners of the businesses?' she queried.

'No, it's OK Lynn, I'll get someone else to do that.'

'I'll do it if you like,' Patrick offered.

No, the DCI hadn't noticed us standing at the back. 'Something's cropped up that I need to see you about first,' he called.

Lynn departed and the DCI carried on with the rest of what he had to say, for a couple of minutes outlining why he regarded Matt Dorney as the main suspect.

Carrick caught up with us as everyone filed out. 'By the way, I contacted that woman who complained about your hardline tactics and told her that you were officially on sick leave, having been shot and wounded, so I could only think that she was exaggerating.'

Patrick blew a kiss to him.

'Just don't go over the top with Dorney as we really, really need him alive after what's just happened,' the DCI said, and led the way to his office. When we arrived, he invited us to be seated and dropped into the chair behind his desk in the manner of someone who was extremely weary.

'I got a call from Rolt, *very* early this morning,' he began. 'Apparently a man by the name of Piers Ashley, who he said used to be his assistant, appears to have gone missing. The name seems familiar and I might have seen it on the restricted access F9 website. Do you know anything about him?'

Patrick gave me an 'over to you' look and I

233

told James the whole story right from when I had gone to Ashleigh Hall to talk to him on Rolt's suggestion, mentioning that we had been unable to return a call from him.

'What kind of man is he?' Carrick asked me when I had finished.

'Think of a young, upper-class ex-policeman recently crossed in love whose much respected one-time boss was violently attacked,' I said. 'Add hot-blooded ancestors in armour who thundered off on horses referred to as destriers, sprinkle in a bright sword, a couple of lances and a shield and stir gently. His sister appears to be Rolt's new girlfriend and that's the connection with Piers now.'

Carrick put his head in his hands. 'God. What have I done to deserve this?' There was then a fairly long silence which he broke himself by saying, 'I'm not sure Rolt wanted me to do anything about it. Perhaps he was just keeping me in the picture.'

'He wouldn't feel that he was in a position to give you orders,' Patrick observed. 'He's a greater stickler for protocols than Mike Greenway.'

'So we have to ask ourselves if the *apparent* disappearance of Ashley is closely connected with the case of Rolt's attempted murder.'

'Given that he's said he's located Dorney, it is,' Patrick said. After a pause, he added, 'I know what you want to say – say it.'

The DCI met his gaze. 'Are you well enough?'

'Yes.'

He wasn't.

'OK, go and find him. See what he has to say.

He might provide the golden shortcut to getting hold of this bloody mobster.'

Now, of course, I had my huge problem again – the old dilemma. Leaving Patrick out of it for a moment, there was no escaping the fact that I'm responsible for five children. Our working rules have always insisted that if one partner went away, engaged on a dangerous mission, the other remained at home or, at least, within easy reach. As previously stated, I've broken that rule on several occasions when I felt the situation demanded it. I supposed that if I resigned altogether from the NCA instead of working part-time they would have to find him an assistant. But would they? Not in the time available with regard to this assignment, that was for sure.

If I'm honest and admit that my first loyalty has always been to my husband, not the children, it probably makes me a freak among women, someone to be despised. We had met at school and, at fifteen, I had instantly fallen in love with him. Other girls had been put off by his somewhat lofty manner and it was only much later that I realized – he was gifted in assuming various personas, even then – that he displayed this chilly reserve with females whose motives he thought were iffy. Initially, my only motive as far as he was concerned was the fact that he had been sent round to our house – our fathers were friends – to help me with my physics homework. Soon we had become involved, not with physics but chemistry.

Now, quite a few years later, I had a good idea

235

what would happen as it wasn't the first time the situation had arisen recently, but this time were we not talking about going to London merely to gather evidence. There was every chance that when I told him I intended to accompany him to search for Piers Ashley he would say no. He would then instantly recollect that under such circumstances I usually follow him. On the other hand, he was certain to say, after a few moments' thought, it was better to have me right under his nose than God knows where. There would then follow a short period of the above mentioned chilly reserve while he thought about it some more.

We were seated in the conservatory at home when I brought up the subject. He had just brought Katie back from the livery stable where they had checked on the well-being of George and Fudge. Matthew was at a friend's house in the village, the two youngest were in bed and Justin was kicking a football around the lawn, gently, with John, the pair under the watchful eye of Elspeth as she dead-headed the last of the roses.

I stated my case. This resulted in Patrick fixing himself a tot of whisky – a bit like Sherlock Holmes' three pipe problem, perhaps – and reseating himself at my side to pensively stare at nothing. Then, after about half a minute, he turned to gaze at me with a hint of a smile and I saw that it had been a sham.

'Subject to the usual terms and conditions,' he said.

I removed the whisky glass from his grasp,

took a sip and gave it back. I tend to do this at New Year and in what I regard as emergencies.

'Remember Kenneth Mackie?' he said.

'One of the three names on that list of mobsters being investigated by both the NCA and F9?'

'That's him. I found out today from someone in the Met that he's the one trying to take over Matt Dorney's manor. Dorney was blaming Dark Horse, Phil, for the failed raid on the off-licence, if you remember, thinking he was in the pay of a rival who hoped to get him arrested. Well, we know it was poor Phil who alerted his colleagues but that's unimportant now. And as we also know, it's Mackie's policy to have a rapid turnover of what he refers to as staff in order to stay ahead of the game and confuse the cops.'

'Rolt thought that Dorney might assume you were from an outfit like that when you almost chucked his thugs into the canal.'

'Yes. So if I improve on what must have turned into a fairly strong rumour doing the rounds among the criminal low life by going to work for Mackie, I shall be in a position to hear all the gossip and hopefully discover where Dorney is. If, in the process, I find Ashley, so much the better.'

'That's if he's still alive.'

'It's important to remain positive. What I suggest we do is go back to Hackney, find you somewhere low-key to stay and play it like we did when we met Phil in The Barge. I'll contact you, we can meet for a drink and you can pass on any useful intelligence I give you to relevant parties.'

'Patrick, this Mackie character might not want you to work for him,' I protested. And then the full meaning of what he had said hit me. 'Not only that, I don't think you're strong enough yet.'

But, looking at him, I knew that particular argument was a non-starter. 'You'll have to prove yourself. Commit crimes!' I persisted.

He just laughed and then, with a winning smile, asked, 'Do you want to start by helping me write a CV?'

It occurred to me years ago that it was no good professing to be a writer of fiction if I bleated when asked to use my imagination. Pushing to the back of my mind the problem of what I was going to do all day long in Hackney in between lurking around The Barge waiting for him to put in an appearance, I set my mind to creating a persona, a 'history' for him. Appearance-wise, there was no point in straying too far from how he had looked during the episode in that pub, so that could be regarded as done.

This CV, of course, was not going to be handed over to anyone, merely memorized by Patrick in order to appear convincing. He had not done this before – not for any length of time, that is – and I was hoping he was going to abandon wearing the leather belt with a brass buckle in the shape of a skull that has red glass eyes. He says it brings him luck. In the past, this has usually been teamed with black jeans, a matching silk shirt and leather jacket, smarmed-down hair and a nasty scowl. This was effective and ghastly.

I felt it was important that the prospective hireling hadn't committed any serious crimes in the past or he might be asked to repeat them. Perhaps he ought not to appear too intelligent and be capable only of beating up other mobsters' honchos, acting as a scout while others carried out whatever crime was planned or . . .

I broke off from making notes, ideas having fizzled out. 'Patrick, where are you going to draw the line? You'll have previous convictions for what? How can I do this so you don't end up breaking the law?'

Patrick looked up from reading, saw that Justin was still playing in the garden, glanced at his watch, realized that it was past his bedtime and got to his feet. 'Don't worry about it.'

'You asked me to write a CV.'

'Sorry, I've had a rethink. I'm going to be a one-time special operations soldier who's killed quite a few people. I can easily do that because it's true. So, yes, a killer.'

Seventeen

A killer. This opened up such a potential can of worms that I found myself unable to think sensibly about it for a moment. All that was going through my head as Patrick supervised Justin going to bed was the realization that his need to do his job and catch Dorney had overridden the after-effects of being forced to shoot Martin Grindley before he succeeded in killing me. But no, common sense insisted. Just because he was about to portray himself as a hitman for hire it didn't mean that he was going out to slay all and sundry on demand.

Revisiting this after a surprisingly good night's sleep, I saw that what after-effects had occurred following Grindley's shooting had mostly been mine as a result of having had such a close brush with death. My retired lieutenant colonel husband had been understandably very upset by what had happened and subsequently not himself, and this had continued for some time. But in the real world he had saved my life, full stop. Looking at it as cold-bloodedly as I was able, I had to admit that if he couldn't outmanoeuvre the likes of Matt Dorney then he shouldn't be in the job.

'Have you told Greenway what you're going to do?' I queried as we gave the three eldest children their breakfast, porridge with a choice of various kinds of dried fruit. They're not allowed to have sugar- and chocolate-loaded cereals and their fitness and teeth have benefitted.

Patrick was making milky coffee for Katie and Justin, and tea for the rest of us. 'I haven't because he'll say the same as last time.'

'So you're going to be naughty, Daddy?' Justin piped up.

Patrick gave me a look. No, I shouldn't have mentioned it. Then, to his son, he said, 'You know when we lived in Devon and you were told not to climb the tree that hung over the river and you did, the branch you were on broke and you fell in and gashed your head on a rock?'

Justin nodded, not remotely sheepishly. 'Carrie had to rescue me. But I could swim a bit and she didn't have to come in very far.'

He could easily have been killed but seemed to have inherited the nine-plus lives of his father.

Patrick said, 'I'm going to do something like that. But it's not a tree with branches that might break and there's no river underneath so I'll be all right.'

Justin couldn't work this out but it didn't matter. The elder two exchanged glances, realizing what was going on, but they knew that they mustn't ask questions about Patrick's job as he has previously told them he would not want to have to resort to telling them things that weren't true. He always relates to them anything funny that happens, though.

'You told us you didn't chop down the tree because it wasn't the tree's fault,' Katie said in a faraway voice.

241

'It wasn't,' Patrick said with a smile. 'But I'm going to chop down this one.'

It had been decided that I would play it in a similar fashion to Patrick. That is, be myself, an author visiting a district in order to research her latest novel. I would wait a couple of days to give Patrick time to do some research and surveillance and then get an early afternoon train, find somewhere to stay in Hackney and text him with the address. Then I would carry on acting naturally while waiting for him to contact me. He had already left, again behaving normally, as though travelling up for one of his regular visits to HQ. You never, ever knew who might be watching; even local friends and neighbours might gossip if we told them everything that we were doing. He would leave the Range Rover in the car park at HQ in case we needed it and call me if and when it became necessary for us to meet.

That was the plan.

I reckoned that a fairly well-known author would travel first class and told myself that I could claim it on expenses. This decision did not reflect my usual mindset but as the job ahead promised to be particularly difficult – all right, shitty – I may as well enjoy a little comfort while it was available. The Smith & Wesson was in my bag with, heaven forfend, extra ammunition. Further baggage other than what I would need for a few days consisted of the anxiety that went with what I was doing but I was sternly, if ineffectively, telling myself that I was the one who had been hankering after excitement.

Having arrived at Paddington and unable to face the Tube, I got a taxi and asked to be put down close to a medium-priced hotel in Hackney. This proved to be modern and clean, and I was given a double room overlooking a pleasant square. I reckoned, having quickly consulted my London A to Z, that I was roughly three-quarters of a mile away from the canal-side Barge and its somewhat Dickensian surroundings.

After sending Patrick a text with the relevant information, I unpacked my small case, washed and changed and, in need of exercise and fresh air, went out. It was a fine evening, a cool breeze on my face. Ahead of me, silhouetted against the after-glow of sunset, the stall holders of a street market were packing up for the night. Turning down, with thanks, a free melon as I passed – 'it's just a bit over-ripe, luv' – I carried on walking, heading in what I thought was the direction of the town centre, looking for a restaurant where I could, a little later, have something to eat.

Any warm feelings towards the place had started to wane a few minutes later when I saw how many people were standing huddled in the doorways of boarded-up empty shops that were either offered for sale or to rent. Hooded youths congregated at the entrance to side alleys, smoking and sniggering among themselves. One openly relieved himself against a wall.

I then realized that I was walking in the wrong direction and, mentally calling myself names, I turned. Immediately, behind me, I saw a man I had spotted standing outside the hotel giving every impression that he was using his mobile phone. Not unduly worried, I played safe and crossed the road to make a show of looking in the window of a shop that was still open, a news-agent. In the window were the usual notices about local events and postcards offering services and advertising things for sale but my gaze only skimmed across them. The man had carried on for a short distance in the same direction and stopped, again appearing to make a call.

It seemed impossible that I was being followed, having only just arrived. I still couldn't work out why I had made such a bad mistake but had no choice but to go back the way I had come as this road seemed to lead nowhere I needed to be. Setting off again, I walked quickly without looking round until I had gone about two hundred yards and then sneaked a glance. There were quite a few other people in sight but not him.

'You are old, mother Ingrid, and your nerve is getting weak,' I muttered under my breath, while reasoning that a walk on the wild side was fine when one had one's very own potentially wild man around but not otherwise.

A few minutes later, in brighter lights and less intimidating company, I was beguiled into looking in fashion and shoe shop windows, something I rarely have time to do at home. I had paused and was reading the menu outside an Italian restaurant when my mobile rang.

'Where are you?' asked Patrick without further preamble.

'On the point of going into Antonio's for some-thing to eat,' I replied.

'Which is where?'

'God knows.'

'Ingrid . . .' He sighed.

'Until I see a street sign, all I can tell you is that it's roughly in the direction of The Barge on a main road that has a large building that isn't the town hall.'

'It's probably the museum and art gallery which is round the corner in the next street. Everything all right?'

I told him everything was fine. No point in mentioning my fears as they had been groundless.

Before I could ask him where he was he rang off, saying he would keep in touch.

I entered the restaurant thinking that it would have been nice to have eaten together, but then realized he might be miles away.

The place was quite large but practically empty. There were just a few couples and one or two loners, like me. I was shown to a table, asked for another one in a corner where I could observe the comings and goings at the entrance and studied the menu. Patrick should have been here, I thought. There was one of his favourites: squid cooked with the ink, a black nightmare on a plate that actually makes me feel queasy.

I started thinking about Piers Ashley. It seemed quite the wrong thing to ring his home number in case I made his mother worry without any reason if he was perfectly all right somewhere else and hadn't told her. But that seemed to be out of character and, on a whim, I rang his mobile number. There was still only the messaging service.

A waiter came for my order and I ordered chicken cacciatore and a small glass of house white wine. I then went back to thinking, rapidly coming to the conclusion that I ought to get an update, if there was one, from Rolt.

But he had nothing to tell me and was obviously worried.

The chicken was tasty but I only really noticed this when I had almost finished it. I was angry. Nothing was being achieved; the case had descended into nothing more than endless travel, phone calls and going round in circles while a mobster got away, literally, with murder.

OK, another phone call. Pushing my plate away, I rang Tim Shandy, hoping that he would answer his mobile. He didn't always and hadn't given us his home number.

'Sorry, I really don't want to be involved any more,' was his reply when I had explained the bare bones of what we were doing.

'Tim, I don't want to involve you,' I assured him. 'I just need you to tell me if it was decided where you would meet Dorney, with Patrick, before you were warned off.'

'I'm afraid arrangements didn't get that far.'

'Please tell me where you were warned off.'

'Oh, some bruiser cornered me as I was coming out of a pub. The bastard slammed me up against a wall and said the boss had ordered him to get rid of me. He didn't explain how but I got the message it would be curtains if I persevered.'

'Had you seen him before?'

'Once, when I met Dorney in his strip club that went up in flames, serve the bugger right. This

246

character was hanging around outside – couldn't miss him actually. No, wait a minute, I'd seen him before on another occasion. Inside the club. He's some kind of bodyguard wallah, I expect. Dorney must have changed his mind about offering Patrick a job.'

'What did this man look like?'

'Oh, tall, fair-haired, quite big built but not like someone who pumps iron, or whatever that ridiculous activity's called. I could imagine women finding him attractive, which rather proves that gangsters don't all look like orcs. I did rather enjoy *The Lord of the Rings*. Sorry, Ingrid, I'm wittering.'

'Did he hurt you?'

'Not really. Is Patrick there? Is he still speaking to me?'

I told him no, he wasn't and yes, he was. Then I added, 'He's looking for someone called Kenneth Mackie.'

'I think Dorney mentioned someone with that name,' Shandy said after a short pause. 'He's going to kill him.'

'Any idea where he can be found?'

'These scum are usually in some low dive or other, aren't they? No, wait a minute . . . let the dotard have a think . . . there *was* something he said . . .'

I waited.

'Yes, that was it,' Shandy suddenly said. 'Dorney had somehow got wind of a raid – through a mole or whatever, I expect – that Mackie planned to carry out in the provinces, take the cops unaware kind of thing and shake off any surveillance on his own doorstep. Naive, these mobsters, aren't they? Dorney thought it would be amusing to beat him to it. It was a jewellers with a wine bar next door. I seem to remember reading about something like that in the papers recently.'

'Bath?'

'That's it. That's why he wanted to do it – the fact that he knew the place quite well. And there was something else in the pipeline planned in that area but I'm damned if I can remember what it was . . .'

'Please try,' I begged.

'Sorry, I'll have to put on my thinking cap and ring you back,' he said apologetically after what had seemed like a long silence. 'My wife's saying that dinner's ready and it's guinea fowl with thirty cloves of garlic.' He rang off.

I realized that I was staring at the phone. *Thirty* cloves of . . .

Tim finally contacted me again when I had returned to the hotel.

'I simply can't remember the details,' he began, 'but it's to do with something that's really valuable. According to the same source of inside information, this Mackie character has a contract to pinch whatever it is for a foreign collector or some bod like that. Sorry to be so vague – the old brain's not what it was. Dorney's planning to do the same thing as last time – get there first. But the whole thing might be a load of hot air as he was always bragging.'

'Have you remembered where Mackie might be found?'

'Sorry, I don't think he ever mentioned that.'

I thanked him but omitted to add that I didn't think he had anything to worry about with regard to the warning-off he had received. One-time operatives of F9 didn't like amateur detectives either, not even when they could be described as doing the same thing themselves.

I sent Patrick a text to tell him that I had information for him as that method of communication seemed safer than a call he might find awkward to answer. I heard nothing until the evening of the next day. Earlier I had spent time in a couple of modern art galleries, had a look round the shops and had been wondering where an author could now take herself as she had decided that she didn't want to set any part of her novel in those particular venues.

'We're in The Dog and Duck. Coming?' he said roughly when he called, again without hellos. Well in character, perhaps.

'How do you want me to be?'

A dirty chuckle.

'Like that?' I said, having translated.

'Yes. See ya. Half an hour.'

Ye gods.

Absolutely the last thing I want on these escapades is to be recognized as who I really am. Without make-up and wearing my hair scraped back into a stumpy ponytail, a few bits of hair trailing, I think I present an unremarkable figure – definitely not Ingrid Langley, anyway. This time, though, it appeared to call for something completely different to the thicko of my previous visit, so I decided on presenting myself as a posh tart. I then realized with a pang that I would be a no-spring-chicken posh tart.

Not all that long afterwards and definitely going to be late, I left the hotel and was lucky to get a taxi – very important as I had no idea where the pub was. The driver didn't glance twice at my make-up – heavy for me – micro-skirt and cropped top only just covering the teddy-style bra, the absence of reaction encouraging as it suggested my appearance was 'normal' by local standards. The bra, which does quite amazing things with my modest bust, is a subject of contention between Patrick and I as he says it spoils his concentration on the job. I didn't care about that right now. Perhaps I had sex on the brain as, for obvious reasons, it had been in short supply of late – frankly, practically non-existent. In all fairness, you can't expect a man who has recently been shot to be a ball of fire in bed.

The Dog and Duck didn't appear to be too far from The Barge, as I saw a sign directing the way to a new canal-side development we had seen the last time. The building was thumping with music and busy insofar as from the outside it appeared to be literally jammed to the doors. But when I had penetrated this outer layer, with difficulty and only treading on a few toes, I found that within things were better if one ignored the tatty decor and general need of a good clean. At least it was possible to move around. In fact, in the saloon bar, which entailed a short walk to find it, there was a narrow but significant cordon sanitaire around a group in a corner, some of whom were seated by a small table, the rest standing. Tim probably would have said that most of them looked like orcs. They did rather.

Patrick, one side of his face shadowed with bruises, was sitting next to a man with a red, blotchy complexion that clashed horribly with his greasy ginger hair. When my husband saw me he rose with a smile on his face – the smile of an arrogant bastard, that is – and, still smiling, heaved the man who had been seated next to him out of his chair by the collar of his denim jacket and thrust him out of the way. The man with ginger hair laughed loudly but the others remained silent, watching Patrick warily.

I seated myself in the newly vacated chair. I felt fairly safe here as my right shoulder was almost touching the bar and Patrick had reseated himself and was between me and the man with ginger hair, who I had an idea was Kenneth Mackie, the mobster Patrick had come here to look for. He looked a lot older than I had imagined – raddled, actually. Dyed ginger, then. The henchmen, three black men and two white, or rather dirty grey, and not counting the ejected one who had walked out, stared at me as though I was a hot steak pie on a plate with gravy and mash.

'Your woman?' Ginger enquired, rather unnecessarily, I thought.

'What d'ya think?' Patrick snapped in the voice of someone who hadn't spent too much time at school. Then, to me, 'This is Ken. He runs everything round here.'

251

'Congratulations,' I simpered during a short pause in the music.

'I've taken him on to replace Robbie,' Mackie told me in a strong Glaswegian accent. 'Just because Robbie was one of my countrymen doesn't mean that he was God. He'd started to play God, though, and I don't like being told what to do by someone who's stoned for most of the time. And I like to have a high turnover of staff – it breaks any links to me that the cops might think they have.'

'He was your right-hand man?' I queried tentatively.

'He thought he was. Jethro here sacked him for me. But, hey, I don't usually allow women at meetings. What are you doing here?'

'I wasn't aware of your rules,' I countered.

'You didn't tell her?' Mackie said to Patrick.

'You were here when I asked her to pop in. We'll have a meal together later,' Patrick replied heavily, and loudly, as the music had started up again.

'OK, she can stay – just this once.' A hard stare in my direction. 'It's your round. And get them to turn down that bloody racket!'

On the receiving end of a wink and the merest nod from Patrick, I took some notes from my bag and, without getting up, waved them over the top of the counter next to me. Service arrived instantly, the drinks were organized and I didn't have to repeat the request about the music.

Mackie leaned around Patrick, fixed me with his black, unsettling eyes and whispered, 'You don't breathe a word of anything you hear

252

tonight to anyone or you're as good as maggots. Got it?'

I nodded and he stared a little longer, only at my bosom, and then continued, to the others and now able to speak more quietly, 'To recap what was decided a few days ago, the exhibition of all this stuff starts next week, Tuesday, and goes on for three days. It's at the Abbey Street Gallery in Bath. Security will be tight but a friend of mine' – here he smiled to himself – 'has got himself a job as one of the security guards. He has no form and owes me as it's because of me that he's clean. You might say that I regard him as an investment. Any questions so far?'

Patrick said, 'Are you going to lead this or do you want me to?'

'You are. But I'll be around – watching.'

'Which day?' someone on the other side of Mackie asked.

'That's what must be decided now. I reckon day three. Everyone in charge will have relaxed by then and my helper will have really got all the routines in his mind and can report to me accordingly. We'll go in while it's open as I'm damned if I'm getting involved with security systems at night. That should be in our favour as cops in the sticks are probably useless.'

'Don't be too sure,' Patrick said quietly when the obligatory chuckles had died down.

'Is that you being a smart-arse?' Mackie demanded to know.

'London crime lords always underestimate provincial police forces,' Patrick said with a shrug. 'Known fact.'

'Day three then?' Mackie said bullishly, and no one was prepared to argue.

'Shooters?' one of the black men asked into the silence that followed.

'How the hell else do we persuade people to lie down on the floor and keep quiet?' Mackie grated.

'I've never shot no one,' the man muttered.

Mackie nudged Patrick in the ribs, hard, and I winced for him. 'That's what I've hired *him* for. It's what he does.'

'Yup,' Patrick said proudly.

'And when I find out who the bastard was who leaked my plans to Dorney . . .' Mackie left the rest to everyone's imagination. 'You're not drinking,' he said accusingly to Patrick, looking at his empty glass. He hadn't had anything when I'd paid for the last round. I could have done with a glass of wine but just had orange juice.

'Make up your bloody mind!' Patrick said. 'You asked me to get rid of the other bloke because he was hardly ever sober, and now——'

'OK, OK,' Mackie interrupted. 'Keep your hair on.'

A few arrangements were made for the raid. Travel, who would drive, where they would meet, where they would disperse to afterwards, who would fetch the weapons from a lock-up garage, all of which I hoped I would remember. Finally, after around another hour, during which all but two of those present drank far too much and Mackie kept repeating himself, it ended.

Mackie grabbed me as we left. 'Don't forget what I said or you're finished,' he almost spat at me.

254

Patrick removed his hand from my arm without saying anything.

'Your face,' I agonized as we walked, Patrick occasionally turning to check if we were being followed. He said nothing so I took it that we weren't.

'Robbie was like the side of a barn and I'm not fit. I'm sorry, Ingrid, I shouldn't have asked you to come over. I didn't like the way they were looking at you, but it's partly your fault for wearing that damned bra.'

'I rather got the impression you wanted me to look like this.'

He nibbled my ear. 'You don't need it to turn me on, though.'

'Jethro isn't *quite* you,' I murmured, savouring the moment.

'You were the one who called me Special Agent Gibbs.'

'D'you know what's being exhibited?'

'Only that it's old and very valuable. Mackie didn't say and I haven't had time to check up on it. Have you eaten?'

'No.'

'Neither have I. There's a place I know of just down here.'

It turned out to be a kind of cellar bar run by Czechs where they served just one dish of the day – take it or leave it – in this case what I can only describe as a spicy mutton stew with dumplings, which was delicious. We sat on wooden benches and drank red wine. It was like being on holiday.

The mood persisted and we were quite

unprepared – or at least, I was – when we came out to see a group of men hanging around outside, Mackie's thugs by the look of them.

'I thought someone was following us,' Patrick said tautly out of the corner of his mouth. 'If I can't handle it go back inside, call a taxi and get yourself out of here.'

I postponed thinking about that and, although I badly wanted to hook an arm through his, didn't do that either.

'You have a problem?' Patrick said as they closed in on us.

'Mackie says we share wimmin,' muttered one of them. 'It's another of his rules.'

There was no argument; Patrick just started to swear at them. When he really gets going like this, in his parade ground voice, utilizing a vocabulary that, fortunately, as far as I was concerned, could be a language from another planet, it tends to blast people right off the pavement. I was aware of passers-by hurrying out of range, throwing horrified glances in our direction. Someone thought to stop and remonstrate but changed his mind.

Quite quickly, the men slunk off.

Eighteen

'It ties in with what Tim told me,' I said over breakfast after relating what he'd said. 'Dorney's going to snatch whatever it is from under Mackie's nose.'

Patrick looked up from his poached eggs, sausages and bacon. He had thrown off his clothes the previous night and flopped on to the bed like a beached flounder to sleep for seven hours. 'I shall have to involve Carrick heavily from now on. Especially as I seem to be chief honcho on this job. Who's the mole, then?'

'Piers Ashley?'

'Whoever it is would have to be involved with both gangs and Mackie didn't mention anyone else. And, having met Ashley, I can only think that he would have been in Robbie's position by now, Mackie's right-hand man. As far as Dorney's lot are concerned, it's not all that long ago that Ashley was working for his father. I can't believe Matt never clapped eyes on him during that time.'

'Didn't someone say that Len threw him out?'

'I still don't think he's the informer, even though Shandy was warned off by someone who fitted his description close to where Dorney was. But fine, if Ashley wants to help catch whoever tried to kill Rolt and is lurking around accordingly, I'm not going to try and stop him.'

257

'Patrick, how the hell did you get accepted into Mackie's gang?'

'I knew what he looked like as there are several mugshots of him in police records taken over the years due to his unfailing enthusiasm for breaking the law. Anyway, I asked a policeman if he knew where I could find him.'

For a moment, I thought he was joking, but no.

Patrick went on, 'The good officer of the law asked me my business with Mackie and I told him – the truth. I was pointed in the direction of The Dog and Duck. He warned me that the Met are hoping to pounce on him soon as a woman he's associated with for years was recently found seriously assaulted in her flat by a neighbour. She's still in hospital and they're going to throw attempted murder at him. It's just a question of persuading her to bring charges. That's why there's a delay.'

'And?' I encouraged when he stopped speaking.

Patrick took a sip of coffee. 'I was lucky as I came upon them all in a side alley near the pub and there was a blazing row going on. It was the shouting that drew my attention. Mackie was trying to get rid of Robbie, the one he said was drunk all the time, and not doing very well. I volunteered as I said I wanted a job.'

'But what about the others? Mackie could have ordered them to do it. It would have been around six to one!'

'They were terrified of Robbie as he'd boasted that he had back-up of his own.'

'That lot are useless to Mackie, surely.'

'A fact that'll come in very handy.' And, in

258

response to a question I hadn't asked him, he added, 'Mackie's on the make. He wants to destroy Dorney and be cock of the rock. The cop I spoke to said the sooner he's behind bars the better. I felt that was pretty obvious.'

'I still don't understand why Mackie didn't suspect you.'

'Cops and similar don't fight as dirty as I do.'

'I'm not going to any more of those meetings.'

'Definitely not. I think you ought to go home. Go to HQ first, report to Greenway and then take the car as I can't use it. I never dreamed events would progress this quickly. Would you then go and see Carrick, put him in the picture?'

I had no problem with any of this. 'The question,' I said, 'is which day of the exhibition will Dorney decide to conduct *his* raid, the first or the second – if he does anything at all and even assuming that the mole will inform him.'

'At least we'd have a chance to catch Mackie in the act. Up until now not enough evidence could be brought against him that would stand up in court.'

It occurred to me a little later that, following Patrick saying that he had identified himself to a police officer, the Met now knew what he was doing. The truth of this manifested itself extremely quickly, for when I had paid the bill at the hotel, Patrick having gone off a while previously, and was making my way across to the exit, a dishevelled individual who had all the right physical attributes of a rugby forward blocked my path.

259

'I must speak to you,' he rumbled in the deepest bass voice I had ever heard.

I'm not the kind of woman to scream, and neither do I gun down someone in such circumstances, but both options crossed my mind. For this, surely, was Robbie, and he had the recent cuts and bruises to prove it.

'Somewhere not so public,' he went on to say, looking around anxiously.

'There's a coffee bar here,' I told him briskly. 'I'm not going anywhere else with you.' I had an idea my fears were without foundation as he looked, and moved, like someone who had been hit by a bus.

Preferring to handle something I was going to drink myself, I fetched two coffees, one black, one white, and placed the black one before him. While I had been thus engaged he had subsided on to a padded bench seat and was flicking through a travel magazine. Wondering where he was going to spend his ill-gotten gains, perhaps?

'Explain,' I ordered when I had seated myself just out of range of being grabbed.

'Relax,' he countered and dug in an inside pocket of his leather jacket to give me a Metropolitan Police warrant card.

'Well, DS Richard Paul Gregory?' I said, handing it back.

'Your husband chucked me out of Mackie's gang.'

'So it would appear. Mackie got fed up with you because you were drunk most of the time.'

'I wasn't. You have to act.'

'You overcooked it. That was bad judgement.'

'I was trying to behave so as not to arouse suspicion. And it was very important that I stayed right where I was.'

'Would you have acted any differently if you'd known then that he worked for the NCA?'

'Of course not, I had a job to do.'

'Well, you can hardly expect me to sympathize!' I bawled at him.

He shot a series of quick glances around the room before saying, 'My boss doesn't like it when this sort of thing happens. She wants you both to back off and—'

I butted in with, 'To hell with your boss. Tell me something: how did you know where I was staying and what I looked like?'

'The Internet. You booked in under your own name – we have access to hotel guest lists – and have a website. The NCA's restricted website had already told us who your husband's married to and that you often work together.'

I wanted to be sarcastic and congratulate him on his detection powers but that seemed petty, so instead I asked, 'Are you the mole who's telling Matt Dorney what Mackie's doing?'

'Surely you don't expect me to give you that kind of information,' he replied stiffly.

'And then I'll tell you which day Mackie's planning on carrying out his raid.'

'You know?' he asked incredulously.

'It was decided last night. I was there.'

After a short mental struggle, Gregory said, 'OK. Yes, I am. I only phone him, though – I said I'm with Mackie but hate his guts and want him six feet under.'

'The latest is that he's going to do it on the last day while the exhibition's actually open,' I told him. 'Now I shall expect you to inform Dorney about that and then tell *me* if he tells you when he's going to act. If he does, that is.'

'I reckon he will. It's an obsession with him. The pair'll end up killing one another.'

I had difficulty finding a downside to that. 'Will you do that?'

'Er, all right.'

'I mean it. This crime's going to take place in Bath – our patch, not yours.'

'Yes, of course. Right, I will.'

I gave him my and James Carrick's work mobile numbers, and then said, 'D'you know someone by the name of Piers Ashley?'

'I don't think so.'

'He's tall, fair-haired and good looking.'

The undercover policeman shook his head. 'No, they're all ugly, like me.'

'What's this exhibition about?'

'No, idea. I forgot to find out. Must be something pretty valuable.' He lumbered to his feet. 'My boss'll kill me for letting the NCA grab my job.'

'The NCA can't be blamed for a breakdown in communication from your lot.'

'She won't see it like that – she's a hard woman.'

On an afterthought, I asked for, and got, his mobile number.

When he had gone I accessed the hotel's wi-fi and looked up Bath's forthcoming attractions. An official website listed an organ recital at the

Catholic church taking place the following evening, a series of lectures on the history of the city at the Sheridan Gallery in a month's time, a book fair in a church hall in Weston the coming Saturday, various charity fundraising events, an exhibition of medieval artefacts taking place for three days at the Abbey Street Gallery starting the following Tuesday . . .

Really?

Something along the lines of historically important jewellery, priceless Chinese porcelain, paintings or antiques I had expected. But medieval artefacts?

I sent Patrick a text with an update about Robbie and took a taxi to the NCA HQ. There, I discovered that Commander Greenway had gone home as his wife Erin had been taken ill. Borrowing someone's computer, I sent him an email with the latest developments and then collected the Range Rover and drove home. The farther I drove west the harder it rained and, by the time I reached Bath, it was of biblical proportions.

'This thing haunts me,' said Carrick when I'd given my third account of recent events, my jacket making small puddles on his office floor.

'What thing?' I asked irritably. I hadn't stopped on the way and, unusually for him, he was yet to ask me if I wanted any refreshments.

'I'd put money on them hoping to steal the Chantbury Pyx,' he said. 'It's been stolen before – from the Sheridan Gallery a few years ago when it was the star attraction at a similar exhibition. This time the insurers are insisting on a

263

more secure venue, necessary as any number of dodgy foreign collectors are queuing up, offering stupid money.'

I said, 'I'm afraid you'll have to tell me what it is.'

'It's an extremely rare item and belongs to the church at the village of Chantbury, around ten miles from here. It's only the front panel of a pyx, which is a reliquary, a box used to hold the Eucharistic host. I seem to remember that it's made of bronze, with gilding, and depicts two angels standing outside the empty tomb. It's thought to date from the twelfth century.'

To me, it was unbelievable that those disgusting and ignorant mobsters wanted to steal something like that, and my expression must have suggested as much, for Carrick added, 'If a secret Internet auction took place it could be worth millions. Easy to hide in transit too – it's only around five inches by three. It's not the only valuable object being exhibited, either. Apparently there's something called the York Triptych and a trio of solid gold chalices studded with jewels – to name but a few.'

'I can't imagine how you're going to police this. Mackie's planning to conduct his raid while it's open to the public – if Dorney hadn't already done it beforehand, say, during the night.'

'In which case we would have already caught Dorney,' Carrick replied, appearing to be unworried.

'Or, on the other hand, as Dorney's sworn to kill him he might time his raid to coincide with Mackie's, aiming to wipe out the lot of them. You'd end up with a war – both gangs carry firearms.'

The DCI looked alarmed. 'You think he might do that?'

'It's a possibility, isn't it?'

'The implications, though. . . .' He stopped speaking, reached for his phone and then stayed his hand. 'I've already asked for extra personnel from HQ. We'll have to have police in the gallery during the day and extra security at night. And you say Mackie has a man inside?'

I nodded. 'Someone with no criminal record.'

'That would figure as no one with form would get a job as a security guard.'

Mike Greenway contacted me as soon as I got home. He told me that Erin had had a miscarriage, horrible for them, of course, but it had happened very early in the pregnancy and he was just grateful that she herself was all right. I offered them both my sympathies. He already has a son from a previous marriage, Benedict, who is slightly older than Matthew.

'I'm still at home but the work stuff is always sent to my computer here,' he went on to say. 'I thought I'd heard everything in my career but you're telling me that Patrick's in charge of this raid Mackie's planning?'

'He had plenty of experience of doing things like that in his service days,' I reminded him, probably, on reflection, unnecessarily. 'James Carrick thinks they might be after the Chantbury Pyx.'

'Is that something I need to Google?'

I explained what it was, adding that it had been stolen before.

'Well, Patrick appears to have got rid of the

265

Met so hopefully the NCA and Avon and Somerset Police will be able to crack this together.' He appeared to have forgiven Patrick for disobeying orders.

'It's going to take a lot of organizing,' I warned, always slightly irritated by the gamesmanship he seems to go in for. 'And we probably won't know until the last minute whether Dorney's going to go for it first or even at the same time. And, don't forget, we're heavily relying on DS Gregory for that information.'

'Yes, I'm forgetting. If it all comes off satisfactorily I'll make sure he gets a commendation.'

I had no choice but to give priority to home matters for the next couple of days but found it difficult to concentrate. Then it was Friday and, with a little shock, I realized that Patrick wouldn't be coming home for the weekend.

It seemed important and, I told myself, would be a distraction from my anxiety, to go and have a look at the Abbey Street Gallery where there was an exhibition of paintings by local artists that finished this evening. I wondered how they would dismantle that and install The Glory of Medieval England, as the next one was called, in two days flat. Work on Sunday, perhaps.

Should I phone Carrick and ask him if he wanted to accompany me? No, let the cops do their own thing.

The gallery was situated on the ground floor of a large Regency terraced house, the upper floors of its four storeys probably converted into flats. A plaque on the wall outside indicated that one Ichabod Hoolity, poet, had lived, and died of cholera, in the premises in the eighteenth century. The good old days, those, I thought as I entered.

The paintings and drawings were all for sale and, going by the few sold tickets on the stands and walls, there were a lot left. My knowledge of art is limited and I'm afraid I judge what I see by asking myself if I would hand over good money for whatever it is and give it house-room. The conclusion I came to in around sixty seconds – but it might just have been my ignorance – was that those unsold were the kind of things I wouldn't inflict on a henhouse. There were also a few exhibits that I believe are referred to as installations. These consisted of a pile of drain-pipes wrapped in wire netting, a propped-up section of a dead tree, the branches draped with what looked like large red, dead worms and three plastic chairs in a row painted black with shop window mannequins seated on them that were stark naked but for upturned flower pots on their heads. No one had volunteered to buy any of these.

This wasn't an official visit – there no reason whatsoever to make it one and frighten the horses – so I had paid the entry fee, which was too much. Squashy black leather sofas were provided to accommodate the weary, so after a perfunctory look at what was on offer, I seated myself. I had been on the go solidly since six and it was pleasantly warm in here. One could easily go to sleep.

It was important, though, for me to look at this

place from both a police and a criminal's point of view. I had already noted that the gallery's offices, including a staffroom, were situated off the imposing entrance lobby. Other than the woman at the reception desk and a security guard – the man Mackie had mentioned? – no other members of staff had been visible. In the large exhibition area in which I was seated, an emergency exit and toilets were signposted and I intended to go and investigate the former in a few minutes' time. Then I would try to discover if there were any other weak points to the rear of the building.

Although I had met several people leaving as I entered, all looking rather glum, there were only three other people in the gallery. A man was seated on another sofa on the far side reading, perhaps one of the catalogues that I had declined to buy, and an elderly couple were wandering around – the very overweight man appearing to be bored. His wife, or whoever, was gazing at each exhibit with deep concentration. A couple of minutes later, Mr Bored uttered a deep sigh and bad-temperedly hurled himself on to the other end of the sofa on which the man was reading. This individual bounced in a most captivating fashion and almost dropped his reading matter. The arrival did not apologize.

I laughed. It sort of burst out of me and was the kind of laugh that probably hadn't ever been heard in these select surroundings, even in the days when it was a private house. The woman turned and shushed me loudly, setting me off again.

'I'll have you thrown out!' she hissed loudly when I had wound down a bit.

'Just try it,' I hissed back, making like Medusa on a bad hair day.

The man who was reading got to his feet and, giving her a bleak smile, came over. Every inch an ex-services officer brought in to keep an eye on security and eject undesirables in his sober suit, white shirt and sober tie, he seated himself at my side. Then, in an undertone, he said, 'This kind of thing always brings out the worst in you, doesn't it?'

'Definitely,' I whispered. 'Posing, precious, a pile of pretentious piffle.'

'Apparently alliteration is a characteristic of English writing.'

'What the hell have you been reading?'

Patrick smiled. 'I don't just soak up police procedure manuals.'

'Er, Mackie?' I said after a short pause.

'I told him I'd come down and case the joint – what else? He can't possibly know I have a connection with the city. I take it that's why you're here.'

I nodded and then said, 'Sorry, I still can't understand why he trusts you.'

'I've done a couple of little jobs for him that seemed to clinch it.'

'What, for God's sake?' I asked, alarmed.

'Oh, he pointed out to me a Latvian drug dealer new on the block who he wanted permanently removed. I reported the next day that I'd knifed him and slung him in the River Lea.'

'But really?'

269

'I arrested him as he was carrying and gave him to the Met. The other job, as you're going to insist on knowing about that too, was to deal with the neighbour who found the woman he'd lived with and half killed. She'd seen him coming out of the apartment shortly beforehand and he'd spotted her. He said she was to be persuaded by any means from giving evidence – *any* means. I persuaded her to accept police protection and then contacted the DI dealing with the case. I'm going to be a bloody wonderful witness for the prosecution when this little shit lands up in court.' Patrick gazed around and added, 'You know, that really is a ghastly painting of Beckford's Tower.'

'Didn't Mackie want proof that you'd done those things?'

'Yes, I flicked my knife under his nose. That seemed to convince him.'

This being his Italian throwing knife, with which he is deadly.

I asked, 'Does the management of this place know about you?'

'Of course. But I'm only here for a couple of hours. The pair of us – the manager's name's Sarah – think we've pinpointed the individual in Mackie's pay. He's still on his month's probation and just about useless. It's his day off. Sarah was all for getting him arrested – as you might imagine, she's concerned about a raid but, at the same time, unwisely in my view, can hardly believe that what I'm telling her will actually take place. I told her we daren't touch him yet as that would jeopardize everything.'

270

'I'm completely superfluous then,' I said. 'You've done all the surveillance.'

'You're not at all superfluous – you're fantastically useful, in fact. I could come home and we could eat at the pub tonight and then . . .' He broke off, one eyebrow raised in a way no woman could fail to recognize.

I was just about to utter a crisp riposte, even though I knew he was winding me up, when the woman yelled across, 'I thought you were supposed to be getting rid of her!'

'Madam, this lady is one of the installations,' Patrick thundered, startling the man on the sofa, who had been dozing. 'And it's a great shame in this world heritage city of ours that the general public cannot recognize pure art when they see it.'

I rose and affected a dignified exit, as though not prepared to remain in the same room with such ignorance.

Nineteen

'With your permission and approval, I'm going to convince Mackie that carrying out the raid on the third day while the gallery's open is a not a good idea and during the early hours of the second morning, Wednesday, is preferable,' Patrick said to James Carrick. 'I'll tell him that I've discovered there's a problem with the rear door, which incidentally doubles as an emergency exit, that can't be fixed properly until around ten thirty a.m. on day two and that temporary padlocks are being fitted. The installation of those padlocks can easily be arranged. That will be the time to strike, I shall say, as they can be removed with bolt-cutters, making access easy.'

'And the owners of the gallery are all right with this arrangement?' Carrick said incredulously, leading the way up the stairs to his office from where we had come upon him in a corridor.

'I've convinced them that there will be such a heavy police presence that even if the wrong criminals cut the bolts off they'll be arrested anyway.'

'Will Mackie fall for it, though?'

'I've taken photos of the area at the rear where staff and the residents of the flats above park their cars. It's also used for deliveries. I'll show them to Mackie to prove my point as actually it's a gift. And if we're going to have any kind

272

of shoot-out it's better to have it there than on the road at the front – the folk in the flats above having been evacuated, of course.'

'So what happens after they cut off the padlocks?' Carrick asked over his shoulder.

'I suggest that we allow them to get through this emergency exit, the door actually left unlocked to give the impression that it's faulty. Inside is a corridor of some twenty yards in length with public toilets, a baby changing room and some kind of storeroom. The door to the actual gallery is at the far end and there are hefty security locks on it. Some, if not all, of Mackie's gang can be bottled up in that corridor and apprehended by armed police personnel concealed in the toilets and others coming from the rear, hiding in parked cars.'

'In the event of a shoot-out the folk in the flats won't like their vehicles left full of holes.'

'No, James, when they're evacuated they'll take their cars with them and, to make everything look normal, you substitute them for a few driveable old bangers from the nearest scrapyard brought in by plainclothes cops. As I've just said, they can be used as cover for more firearms officers.'

'Alarm system?'

'I'll tell Mackie that only the gallery itself is alarmed. It's not true but by the time they find out the whole complex is it'll be too late for them.'

'Where will you be?'

'At the front having wielded the bolt-cutters. They'll be trapped.'

'You might not be able to convince Mackie.'

'I'm sure I can.'

Carrick thought about it as we arrived at his office, and then said, 'Who's going to tell Dorney of a change of plan now the DS calling himself Robbie is out of it?'

'You are.'

Carrick, irritated, possibly because he felt events, and Patrick, were overtaking him, slammed the door. 'The hell I am!'

'Think. He's a Scot too. He has a deep voice. All you need to do is drop yours another octave.'

'I don't happen to have mobsters' phone numbers!'

'I have DS Gregory's number, though,' I said, giving him a look as I thought he ought to calm down. And then, for his benefit, added, 'A Met sergeant who had infiltrated Mackie's gang.'

After a few moments hesitation, Carrick nodded and I called him, handing the phone to Carrick when he answered. Having had the situation explained to him, Gregory said that although he had been taken off the job he would make the call.

There was then a briefing in the room being used as a general office, with just about everyone likely to be involved present. It was more of a pre-briefing really, as the DCI explained that another would take place on the following Monday afternoon after detailed plans had been made. He outlined what had to be achieved and, after speaking for a few minutes, finished by saying that no one knew what the two mobsters might do and he was damned if he was going to refer to these scum as crime lords.

By this time it was after six in the evening and Patrick and I went home, my husband pensive and, I guessed, working on his strategy. Rather a lot rested on his shoulders and he still had to hear from Carrick whether he would give the plan his official blessing. Personally, I couldn't see the DCI coming up with anything better.

Carrick's permission, with reservations that would have to be addressed, was forthcoming in a phone call at a little before eight the next morning. Among a couple of minor points was his concern that Dorney might strike at the same time as Mackie as he had sworn to kill him. Had that been factored in? He thought not.

Patrick conceded that Dorney was a grey area and he could only advise that there was a full alert at all times for the three days of the exhibition. It would be a good idea, he suggested, if there was also a concealed police presence at the front of the building as well, but he didn't need to tell Carrick that.

When the call was over, I said, 'You didn't say to him that sometimes you have to make it up as you go along.'

Patrick kissed the back of my neck as I stood frying bacon on the Rayburn. We were still experiencing an afterglow from the previous night when we had made up for what he had described as 'the famine'.

'No, I've discovered that most cops aren't wired that way. My problem is that I have to leave so I can't provide any more input at this end. I don't know whether it makes it better or worse that the people I'm organizing in London are, by and large, stupid.'

'Not Mackie, though.'

'He's the worst of all as he's going senile, drinks too much and is unpredictable. If you remember, he said he'd be watching. Catching him will have to a flying-by-the-seat-of-your-pants thing, too.'

'Patrick, what do you want me to do in all this?'

'Stay right away, what else?'

'Shall I hide somewhere and keep an eye on him?'

'No!'

I removed the cooked rashers from the pan on to hot plates, put them back in the top oven and started cooking more. The whole family always has a big breakfast at weekends.

Reading rebellion into my silence, Patrick said, 'No, Ingrid. If you want to help, and believe me I have appreciated your presence on various assignments, I—'

'Like saving your life on more than one occasion, you mean?' I interrupted.

'OK, yes, point taken,' he said after a pause, during which he probably ran the wife bit through his personal hard drive again. 'All right. Suppose you surreptitiously keep watch out the front as soon as it gets dark. I'll impress on Mackie the importance of darkness. I don't know what Carrick will organize there but you'll discover that when you attend the briefing on Monday afternoon. I gather he's putting in covert surveillance from first thing, that is, six a.m. on Tuesday, and I don't think you need get involved with that; in fact, you probably ought not to show your face until it gets dark in case any of Mackie's gang members who've seen you before are nosing around. If Dorney doesn't do anything on Tuesday and everything goes according to plan we'll have Mackie's lot under arrest and can go from there.'

'Do my own thing out front, then.'

'Safely!'

Justin ran into the room in his usual hell-for-leather manner and yelled, 'Are you still being naughty, Daddy?'

'No, I'm really well-behaved now,' Patrick said. 'And don't shout.'

Yes, *right* now, perhaps.

There was no reason for my presence until the briefing unless Carrick wanted me there, and I didn't hear from him. This was actually a relief as my mind would only have been filled with details that didn't really concern me. Patrick, to whom I had given an extra hug when I'd dropped him off at the station late on Saturday morning, didn't contact me either. I told myself that this was good news and got on with whatever needed doing at home.

James Carrick appeared to have his thoughts in order and had reassumed his normal air of calm but brisk efficiency. I had arrived in plenty of time for the briefing in the event of his wanting a private word with the NCA's representative, but this did not happen. All those involved, that is, in positions of authority including beat managers, had filed into the room being used, the DCI already there.

'Right,' he began, 'as I've heard nothing to the contrary, yet, from various informer sources concerning this raid, or raids – and I have to tell you that none of them have had wind of it at all – we must assume that Mackie's still going ahead. Each team will be briefed separately by those in charge of them and I've prepared concise written orders. The overall picture is that the gang in question will strike in the early hours of Wednesday and enter at the rear, where there is a long, fairly narrow private car park surrounded by high stone walls. They'll gain access to the gallery through the emergency exit, which will be secured only by two padlocks, the door being specially modified for the occasion. The gang boss, Mackie, has been told that this door is faulty and won't be fixed until later that morning. We're going to bottle them up in the corridor within, the entrance to the actual gallery having been secured, and arrest them. Firearms officers will be concealed in the male and female toilets on the left-hand side of the corridor. The rest of the police presence, back-up, will be out of sight in unmarked cars which will be left in the car park. Any questions so far?'

There were quite a few and someone asked about the existence of security lights.

Carrick said, 'I was asked by an NCA officer working undercover to arrange for them initially to be switched off. There will be one small light over the emergency exit that I understand is independent of the electrical systems. It's powered by a solar panel and for use in emergencies. And if anyone was about to ask, although the gang have been told that that part of the building is not alarmed, it is, so they'll be taken by surprise.'

After dealing with another couple of queries, Carrick continued, 'There *is* a complication. Another mobster that most people know by the name of Matt Dorney may well strike at the same time as he's sworn to put Mackie out of business, preferably by killing him. That will have to be handled separately and I shall try to make sure that there's no confusion. In practice, we'll end up with two teams, one for each threat. That doesn't concern anyone in this room except Lynn Outhwaite and me, so just concentrate on your own orders.'

'What other security arrangements are being made regarding the front of the gallery?' I asked him.

'Thank you for reminding me. Plainclothes personnel will be coming and going, sitting in cars and generally behaving like ordinary members of the public from about six a.m. tomorrow. The exhibition's being opened by the president of the Wansdyke Fine Arts Society, Mrs Blanche Adams, at ten. She'll be accompanied by the mayor, his wife and a few other dignitaries, and we're expecting media interest – local radio, perhaps TV – and quite a few onlookers. In addition to those police I've just mentioned, there will be the usual, and expected, obvious police presence including one or two community support officers, depending on who's available. The plainclothes people will stay, changing over as their shifts end. On all three nights there will be low-key surveillance, both courtesy of the existing security cameras and people on the ground, or in parked vans and cars.'

Was I superfluous after all? Too right.

I could appreciate Patrick's thinking when he had advised me not to appear in Abbey Street before dark as he would not be able to prevent Mackie from sending a member of the gang to reconnoitre and my appearance at The Dog and Duck could hardly have been described as much of a disguise. But I was hanged if I was just going to loaf around pointlessly and would far rather be party to what was going on at the back, because it was far more likely to actually happen.

As the meeting ended, I caught up with Carrick and asked him if he intended to be present.

'Yes, but in the vicinity. Firearms people don't like what they regard as outsiders breathing down their necks on a job.'

'I might not be nearby when Patrick's arrested, or worse,' I pointed out. 'Who'll identify him? He won't be carrying his ID – it's too risky.'

The DCI frowned. 'Good point. I'd already made a note to inform the relevant people of his presence when they're briefed – in other words, tell them not to arrest the tall guy at the front. You could have his ID with you in case it's needed.'

'Do you suggest then that I conceal myself somewhere out the back so I'm nearby?'

'Yes, good idea. But do stay out of danger, Ingrid.'

Sorted.

* * *

At home the following day, I deliberately watched the local news bulletin at lunchtime. There was a short piece on the opening of the exhibition, Mrs Blanche Adams resplendent in a coral-pink outfit and a glorious hat with half a florist's shop on it. Another shot inside the gallery showed her as she inspected the Pyx: a small rectangle, the remaining gold on it glittering as it lay on its blue velvet cushion in the brightly lit cabinet. Such a little thing worth such a lot of money. I then realized that the man standing next to her, whom she appeared to be in conversation with, was Carrick.

Everything appeared to have gone off smoothly.

'Are you going to the exhibition?' Elspeth asked me, having popped her head in the door to ask if I wanted to have lunch with her and John and noticed what I was watching.

'Yes, later,' I said without thinking.

'Mind if I come with you?'

I floundered for a few seconds, not sure what to say.

'It's quite all right if you don't want me to,' she said, preparing to leave.

'Elspeth, please don't be offended,' I hastened to say. 'I'm going tonight – a sort of police exercise after the exhibition closes to the public. Patrick'll be there and hopefully will be able to come home with me afterwards. We can go tomorrow if you're free. And yes, I'd love to have some lunch with you.'

Aware that I sometimes work with Patrick, she asked no more questions.

The day dragged on.

My mobile rang as I was putting the dinner on the table – four hungry children plus Mark to feed. It was Carrie's day off but she would be back well before I went out.

'Hi, it's me, babe,' said a coarse voice I'd heard before. 'I'll be along later. There's a job on. Keep yourself hot for me.' He sniggered.

'And what time shall I expect you, Jethro?' I enquired in stupid ninny fashion in case anyone could overhear at his end.

'Oh, around two, probably.'

He rang off and I discovered that eight eyes were staring at me. No, ten – Mark too.

'Who was *that*?' Katie asked in a hushed voice.

'Your honorary Dad,' I replied. 'Grown-ups do have silly moments, you know.'

Not sure if he was able to phone the DCI, I put my own dinner back in the oven, picked up Mark and his bottle in case he got upset when the others started eating and he was left out, and hurried off to call Carrick.

Just before I closed the door, I distinctly heard Katie whisper to Matthew, 'I reckon that was a coded message of some sort, don't you?'

'Now *you're* being silly,' her brother countered scornfully.

Twenty

The night was cool, windless, and there was no moon. I left the Range Rover in the car park behind the one-time council offices currently being used by the Avon and Somerset force. It was about a ten-minute walk from there to Abbey Street if one cut through old and narrow lanes, a horse-drawn vehicle wide, between the buildings. Determined not to resemble Jethro's current lay under any circumstances, I had donned a blonde wig bought at a Hinton Littlemore jumble sale, right now hidden under the hood of my jacket, black jeans and very comfortable sheepskin boots that enabled me to walk quietly and run like blazes if necessary.

Some fifty yards from the gallery in Abbey Street, at the end nearest the city centre, there was a little square surrounded by iron railings. As I approached it, a church clock struck one. I stifled a yawn. From the gate, which was open, no one was in sight – I hadn't expected to see anyone. It was dark within under several ilex trees as it only possessed a few dim lamps that illuminated the paths across the grass. But as I went in I saw a couple sitting on one of the seats. They ignored me. I turned to go out again and almost went full tilt into a man behind me.

'You're too close and supposed to be inconspicuous!' I snapped.

'I'm a police officer. May I have your name, madam?' he replied woodenly, not appearing to have realized my knowing exactly what he was by the cut of his jib, as my grandad used to say.

'Ingrid Langley. NCA,' I told him. When he said nothing in response, I produced my ID, which he examined tediously closely using a small torch.

'OK,' he grudgingly acknowledged, returning it. 'Seen anyone suspicious?'

'No one.'

I left the square, turned left and, walking quickly, went right past the gallery and took the next turning on the right. From this road one could access the gallery's car park, which was signposted for deliveries at the junction. Nothing moved but a scurrying cat. Shortly afterwards, just inside the entrance to the car park, I paused while my eyes got used to the dark, the only thing visible from where I was standing the weak light over the gallery's rear and emergency exit.

Right now, it seemed stupid to go further and creep about as I would only trigger nerves, or something a lot more drastic, among the watching police. I could just about make out the outlines of what looked like three parked cars about two thirds of the way down the car park, which had probably once been a garden. There even appeared to be climbing plants still growing up the walls.

Matt Dorney was cutting it fine if he wanted to outmanoeuvre Kenneth Mackie. This was an interesting point, as the previous evening Carrick had told me that the Avon and Somerset force had received an anonymous tip-off that

Dorney was indeed planning to steal the Pyx, intending to snatch it right out of Mackie's hands before shooting him dead, together with as many of his gang as possible. The DCI had said he would take close heed of this but did not regard it as 'gospel' as the message had come from an unknown source.

Not wishing to be in sight of any arrivals, I went back to the roadway and walked for about thirty yards until I was in the vicinity of a bus shelter. Almost immediately, I heard a vehicle approaching and a car turned into the road, its headlights sweeping around towards me. I had already ducked into the shelter, which had large advertisements on the ends. The car went right by.

Three quarters of an hour later, I was still there and nothing had happened. I was thinking what a crushing disappointment it would be for Patrick if his plan failed when two cars appeared. One turned into the car park and carried on going, the other turned round and parked just beyond the entrance, its headlights switched off. Three men got out and hurried into the car park. I couldn't see them very clearly in the gloom but they appeared to be wearing hoods. This was the getaway car, then, and the driver was probably still sitting behind the wheel. I would have to risk whoever it was seeing me if I went any closer.

Unless . . . A thought went through my mind. Were these actually undercover cops?

I made like a drunk, lurched along to the car and tapped on the window. It was wound down and a black face stared at me that I recognized from

The Dog and Duck. This was on account of a scar that partially closed his left eye.

'Are you a taxi?' I slurred, having already made sure that my blonde tresses were almost obscuring my face.

'No. Fuck off.'

'But you look like one,' I went on in a whining voice. 'I want to go home.'

He repeated the instruction, only louder.

I staggered away, then turned before he could close the window and said, 'Did you know you have a flat tyre?'

He swore again and came rocketing out of the car. Giggling, I pointed towards the rear wheel and, as he bent down to have a look, whacked him on the back of the neck with the butt of the Smith & Wesson. He went over, hitting himself again on the bodywork of the car. Finding all kinds of strength from muscles I didn't know I had, I handcuffed his arms behind him, this useful bit of kit having been appropriated from a locker I probably wasn't supposed to know about in a beat manager's office.

He was too heavy for me to lift into the car, so I dragged him, groaning, across the road to the other side, where there was a wide pavement, and left him at the base of a wall. No one seemed to be around.

Just then a howling alarm went off, shouts and sounds of frantic confusion audible above it coming from the direction of the gallery. Lights came on. Then a shot was fired, muffled as though within the building. I cautiously stood to one side of the car park entrance and saw a man hurrying towards me, silhouetted against the sudden brightness. He paused fractionally to fire behind him and I saw that someone to the rear of him had fallen.

'Armed police!' I yelled, running out. 'Drop—'

I got no further. He fired at me, missed and kept on coming.

I took a shot at him and then had to jump back as he stumbled, ran forward for a few yards and then pitched forward on to the ground, almost knocking me over. Seconds later an armed support officer panted up.

'Who are you?' he demanded to know.

I told him.

'He was hiding behind one of the cars and ran off when I challenged him. Then I tripped on something and went flying at the same time someone took a shot at me. Was it you?'

I assured him that it wasn't me, found the small flash lamp I had brought with me in my pocket and switched it on.

He carefully turned the man over, who clutched at his right leg and then literally snarled at us.

'God, it looks as though you've shot some old tramp.'

'No, this is Kenneth Mackie,' I said.

Among the mêlée of the arresting and arrested, most of the latter on their feet but flattened against the walls of the corridor by the sheer weight of cops, and the rest on the floor, Patrick, who didn't look surprised to see me, was patiently waiting for someone in charge to arrive and formally identify him. That is, he was standing with his back to the inner door that led into the gallery with his hands in the air while two officers of the law meaningfully trained their guns on him. Carrick didn't seem to be present so it was left to me to produce both our NCA IDs, pulling off my blonde wig after being given puzzled looks. The alarm seemingly right above our heads thankfully having been switched off, Patrick then asked to have his Glock returned to him and it was handed over. I suddenly remembered the man I had left on the other side of the road and reported his whereabouts.

'Where's the DCI?' Patrick then asked.

No one seemed to know but there was then a diversion as various vehicles could be heard drawing up at the rear. This proved to be more police in vans and cars plus an ambulance. Those arrested were hefted outside and suddenly there was room to move.

'Someone fired a shot in here,' I said to Patrick.

'One of that lot. It hit the ceiling.' He pointed upwards. 'What about the other shots I heard somewhere out the back?'

A quizzical gaze having heavily landed on me, I related what had happened.

'Is he dead?'

'No. I got him in the leg.'

'Shooting just to wound armed mobsters is going to get you killed one day,' he remonstrated, not for the first time.

'I didn't exactly have time to take aim!'

We were on the point of leaving when there was a massive bang somewhere at the front of the premises, the inner security door bouncing in its frame. Different alarms went off and, then once more, were silenced.

'Where's Carrick?' Patrick bellowed, the pair of us having rushed outside. He still didn't seem to be around.

'Any idea what he planned to do?' Patrick asked me.

'I think that was still being worked out when I last saw him.'

'Who's senior here?' he then demanded to know of the others.

'There's a sarge dealing with the suspects by one of the vans,' someone in the armed contingent answered.

'OK, he's busy. Follow me.'

They did.

I already knew that the inner door we had been standing by was, when locked, virtually impregnable. This meant there was no choice but to go round on foot – no time to manoeuvre vehicles – in order to reach the front.

Just before the junction with Abbey Street, Patrick halted and waved the six men behind him to a standstill. Then, going forward slowly and carefully, Glock drawn, he looked around the stone wall on the corner. I stayed where I was, at the back. I don't get involved in situations like this if I can help it.

Patrick came back and spoke softly. 'This has to be Dorney's lot. There are a couple of vehicles parked just this side of the gallery entrance and what appears to be cops standing by them. But I can't be sure it isn't people in fake uniforms and I'm not taking any chances, so I want three of you to cross the road, fan out and, using all care, lie flat, keep the vehicles in your sights but concentrate on people coming out of the building. Take care as they might be undercover police. If challenged, issue warnings and be prepared to fire. The other three, come with me. Ingrid, please stay right back.'

They all disappeared from sight around the corner, bent low.

I counted up to twenty slowly and then, keeping well to the side, also went to the corner, took a quick peep and then had a longer look. The three who had crossed the road were taking up position to lie flat on their stomachs, the others seemingly having come to a halt on the pavement. The drivers' and passengers' doors of the two cars appeared to be open. Were some of those present police? There were no vehicles with flashing blue lights. Then I saw Patrick beckoning the first three forward, positioning them as they had been before, only closer. He went on alone, leaving the others to his rear.

Step by cautious step, I approached. Yes, I would stay right back but reckoned it did not mean that I should refrain from going any closer at all. I, too, was wondering what had happened to the police who were supposed to be watching out here. And where the hell was Carrick?

The three over the road had seen me and one raised a hand in recognition. Two shots were then fired in rapid succession somewhere inside the building and, fearing that a firefight would boil over into the open air, I ducked down behind a low wall fronting the property next door to the gallery and stayed there for half a minute or so. Anxiety really can feel like being torn apart.

When I stood up again, Patrick, the three who had been with him and some of the others by the vehicles had disappeared, presumably having gone inside. Not taking my eyes off the entrance, I saw a man emerge. Moving stealthily, he descended the steps and understandably did not notice the presence of the police, who immediately rose and challenged him, shouting at him to lie face down. With an air of resignation, he did so.

Close by now, I hurried forward and said, 'It's all right; I know this man. He's not a criminal.'

'Are you sure?' I was incredulously asked. Well, he *was* unshaven, haggard and filthy.

'Positive,' I replied.

After permission was granted, Piers Ashley got to his feet, gave me a rueful smile when he recognized me and said, 'I was hoping to slip away.'

'But where's Dorney and the rest of his gang?'

'I think they've all been arrested but I didn't see Dorney. The police were right behind them as they rushed in after they'd blasted open the door. I dived into the manager's office. I apologized for frightening her but she didn't seem to take it in.'

'What the hell was she doing here?' I exclaimed. 'But look, you must make a statement – you'll have to give evidence against this lot.'

Ashley sank down on the steps. 'Yes, sorry. My brain's addled. I haven't really slept for a week.'

I held out a hand to him. He took it but didn't need any help to rise.

We went in and, as we did so, more police followed us, presumably having run round from the rear of the building. I couldn't see anyone I recognized for a moment, and then noticed Patrick, who was calmly seated on one of the squashy black leather sofas. He looked extremely tired but content. Moments later, there was a commotion behind us and the man we had known as John Fielding appeared, being firmly propelled forward by a rather out-of-breath James Carrick, who had a hand firmly grasping Fielding's jacket collar. Despite Fielding's, or rather, Dorney's struggles, he was steered across the gallery and delivered to members of Carrick's team. We discovered a little later that the DCI had run him down and tackled him in the little park nearby when he had tried to escape.

Dorney noticed Piers Ashley and yelled, 'That's the man you want! That's who organized all this! He's the one you want, not me!'

Despite being practically surrounded by police, on the point of being handcuffed and Carrick in the process of cautioning and arresting him, the man suddenly lunged forward to escape. He was grabbed from behind but fought free and succeeded in getting another few feet before he was again seized but by his leather jacket, bringing him to a standstill. But he shook himself out of it and, for the second time that night, I had a mobster coming at me like a train.

But he was really aiming for Ashley, who stood his ground and, in a swift movement that I tried, and failed, to analyse for hours afterwards, as good as folded him into four, bent him over with his head near his feet, hands gripped behind his back. A quick tweak of his arms wrung a cry of pain from him.

That was for Rolt, then.

The DCI took over and Dorney was probably relieved to be taken back into custody. Any shot, or shots, from the police contingent would have been out of the question – there were too many people in the line of fire.

As the suspects were removed from the room, I noticed that the glass in a couple of the exhibition cases had been shattered, but if any shots had been fired at the one containing the Chantbury Pyx it had remained unscathed. It was the only thing visible from where I was standing that could described as beautiful, the remaining scowling 'suspects' somehow incongruous. No, odious.

'Where did you find Ashley?' Patrick whispered when I went over to him, gazing to where he now stood to one side, looking a little out of things.

'Outside. I think he was hoping to escape any publicity at home.'

'That man frightened the living daylights out of me, bursting into my office like that,' said a woman, I guessed the manager, Sarah, stomping up from the direction of the entrance lobby. '*That* man there, the scruffy one that looks like a real criminal,' she went on in case there was any doubt in our minds.

Ashley gave her a huge, charming smile.

'You shouldn't have been anywhere near here, madam,' said Carrick severely.

'I felt I it was my responsibility to be here but honestly didn't think any of this business of raids

293

would happen,' she huffed. 'Anyway, who on earth do you think turned the alarms off? I'm the only one with the codes.'

'Who *is* this?' Carrick asked Patrick, jerking a thumb in the one-time F9 man's direction.

Patrick introduced him, adding a short explanation.

'I ought to arrest him,' Carrick said, his Scottish accent very crisp.

'Bliss. A plank and a blanket for the night,' Ashley said. 'But I did give you a tip-off – *and* I've just apprehended the bastard after you let him go.'

Carrick wagged an irate forefinger under his nose. 'You. My office. Nine o'clock. Sharp.'

We took Ashley home with us and, after a shower and something to eat, he slept on a sofa until late afternoon.

'Thanks for the back-up,' Carrick said exactly twenty-four hours after the time stipulated to Ashley. That individual, in borrowed clothes, was in the room with us but the DCI had been addressing Patrick. The detective had not expressed any desire to speak with Ashley in private and, in my view, there was no good reason why he should.

'A little liaising between the two policing groups prior to the fun starting would have been helpful,' Patrick said, voicing something that I had resolved not to air myself.

The DCI glanced at Ashley, who affected looking out of the window and said, 'I had to play it by ear – no one knew what would happen.'

'And no one of real seniority was in overall charge of the armed contingent at the rear.'

'Yes, I know. That was supposed to be Lynn. She was involved in a traffic accident on her way to the nick beforehand and was slightly hurt and shaken. I told her to go to A and E for a check-up and then home. A man's been arrested for driving under the influence of drink and drugs.'

'I'm content, though,' Ashley said. 'Matt Dorney's under arrest just as I got his old man.'

We all looked at him and Carrick said, 'I'm bending the rules by not charging you but you'll have to make an extremely detailed statement. Be warned, though, that I may change my mind when I've read it.'

'I've written it already on Ingrid's computer and it should be in your inbox. It's professionally done,' he finished by adding.

'Look, we have to regard you as a civilian now.'

Ashley shook his head. 'No. I'm still a part-time cop – one of Rolt's ghosts.'

We subsequently discovered that Piers Ashley had not known about the attack on Rolt before I'd told him, the commander having had a very good idea what would happen if he had. For his one-time personal assistant to be involved in any subsequent investigation was the last thing he had wanted as, correctly, he had deemed him too emotionally involved and was concerned about his physical fitness after his close brush with death. In Patrick's and my view, this had been the right decision but, of course, things hadn't turned out like that. When Ashley had visited

Rolt in hospital, the 'ghost' had declared that he would go after Matt Dorney, whatever anyone said. Rolt had had no choice but to give him his full support.

'In view of the fact that Matt Dorney might have seen him in the past, he took an appalling risk,' Patrick said that same afternoon when we were at home, having had a long conversation with Rolt over the phone. 'And, as we know, Dorney only took on people who came recommended or that he knew personally. But I understand that Ashley brazenly said he had worked for Len, which was perfectly true, of course, and even had newspaper cuttings in his possession with accounts of the court cases, his name – not his real one – listed among those convicted of crimes. Matt took him on. He liked the references, as he called them.'

'And the fires at the pub and the club?'

'Rolt was a bit cagey about it, so I came to the conclusion that Ashley had acted under orders. Let's be quite clear about this – F9 is a police department apart but I do wonder if the extent to which they are off-piste is understood by those in higher authority.'

'What are you going to tell Greenway?'

'The bare bones. It's not my business and Rolt did tell me all this in confidence.'

'Will Piers' mother and Thea have to find out, d'you reckon?'

'Only if he tells them – and why should he?'

When all the family were together on Saturday evening and I had cooked for five adults, four children and a baby who had just started eating solid food, we had a little ceremony. Patrick gave Katie back her silver pony mascot together with another, only this one was eighteen-carat gold. The other young people were not forgotten – there were presents for them too and it was a bit like Christmas Day.

This was fortunate, as it would be the last time we were all together.